LUCKY
STRIKES

LUCKY STRIKES

Louis Bayard

Henry Holt and Company

NEW YORK

Henry Holt and Company, LLC
Publishers since 1866
175 Fifth Avenue
New York, New York 10010
mackids.com

Library of Congress Cataloging-in-Publication Data
Names: Bayard, Louis, author.
Title: Lucky strikes / Louis Bayard.
Description: First Edition. | New York : Henry Holt and Company, 2016. | Summary:
    "Set in Depression Era Virginia, this is the story of orphaned
    Amelia and her struggle to keep her siblings together"—Provided by
    publisher.
Identifiers: LCCN 2015023829 | ISBN 9781627793902 (hardback) |
    ISBN 9781627793919 (e-book)
Subjects: | CYAC: Orphans—Fiction. | Poverty—Fiction. | Brothers and
    sisters—Fiction. | Depressions—1929—Fiction. | Virginia—History—20th
    century—Fiction. | BISAC: JUVENILE FICTION / Family / Orphans & Foster
    Homes. | JUVENILE FICTION / Girls & Women. | JUVENILE FICTION / Social
    Issues / Homelessness & Poverty.
Classification: LCC PZ7.1.B379 Lu 2016 | DDC [Fic]—dc23
LC record available at http://lccn.loc.gov/2015023829

Our books may be purchased in bulk for promotional, educational, or
business use. Please contact your local bookseller or the Macmillan Corporate
and Premium Sales Department at (800) 221-7945 ext. 5442 or by e-mail at
MacmillanSpecialMarkets@macmillan.com.

Book design by Anna Booth
First Edition—2016

Printed in the United States of America by R. R. Donnelley & Sons Company,
Harrisonburg, Virginia

10 9 8 7 6 5 4 3 2 1

In memory of Marjorie Braman

Chapter
ONE

Mama died hard, you should know that.

Nearly died alone, too. Now, most nights, she'd so much as groan, I'd come running, but this was late March, ten days shy of Easter and spring barely a thought, and a dream come and snatched me. I was the princess of a mountain people, and they come right into my bedchamber and asked if I could tame the dragon that was cleaning its teeth with people's bones, and I said sure. The dragon was living at the bottom of a cavern, half in water, and when it looked up with its yellow-purple eyes, I said, *You got some nerve.* That was all it took! The thing slunk away, its spiky tail dragging after. And the mountain people, they started cheering for me, calling for me by name, and that was the rub 'cause it took me a long time to hear the voice on the other side of theirs. Calling my name, too, only drawing it out as far as it could be drawn.

"Melia . . . Meeeelia . . ."

I scrambled out of bed, threw open the curtain. Mama was rolled over on her side, staring at me.

"What's wrong?" I said.

"I'm so sorry."

I set down next to her, ran my hand on her brow. It was cold like a pumpkin.

"Sorry for what?" I said.

"Your daddy," she said.

Her eyes were white and sweaty.

"What about him?" I said.

"He's . . ." Her fingers were bent like talons. "Your daddy, he's . . ."

She never finished, but I set there just in case she did. Then I felt something. I felt the bed settle.

You know how a mattress sinks under you when someone climbs in? Only there was no one else there climbing in. Just us two.

I don't know why, but my hand went straight to her hair. And I could feel, beneath the hair, her whole scalp crackling. I think now maybe that was her soul flying off. I'm nearly sure of it because when I looked at the rest of her—her face, her hands—her bare white legs—her eyes—she was empty.

Gone. That's what they always say about dead folks when they don't want to say *dead.* But that's how it was with Mama. Whatever'd been there a second ago, making her eyelids twitch and her breath hitch . . . well, somehow or other it'd slipped away when I wasn't looking. *Gone.*

I rolled her onto her back. Settled her head on her pillow. Combed her hair one last time. Then I left the room.

Janey and Earle was still asleep when I slipped back into bed. I laid there all night, not an ounce of sleep in me now, trying to figure out how to tell them. At dawn, I shook them awake, same as usual. I said, "Guess what? No school today."

Which, looking back, was about the worst way I could've gone about it. 'Cause they got crazy excited. *Is it a holiday? Is tomorrow a holiday? Are we going to miss school all the way clear to Easter?*

I didn't say anything, but there must have been something in my face because Janey spoke up.

"It's Mama, isn't it?"

She's funny that way. Such an odd, dreamy thing you think she's not even part of the world, only she's more in it than anyone.

Well, Earle's face started to crumple, and then the rest of him crumpled, too. Janey set by the stove, wailing and clawing at her head. I tried to think of all the things a grown-up'd say. *She's with God now. . . . She's gone to a better place. . . . We'll meet her on the other side.* They just sounded sour on my tongue. I couldn't even say "She's at peace," 'cause when I thought back on how she'd looked—in that very, very last moment—there weren't a lick of peace in her.

"You got five more minutes to cry," I said. "Ten minutes to eat your oatmeal. Then we got work to do."

I wrapped Mama in her two bedsheets, and me and Earle carried her to the truck. Considering how thin she was, she weighed quite a bit. We laid her in the flatbed, and Earle and Janey climbed in the front with me, and we drove out to the hill overlooking Jenkins Orchard. This was Mama's favorite spot. Back when she was healthy, we'd come here every Sunday afternoon, rain or shine, with a basket of chicken and corn bread and dried-apple stack cake, and we'd sit and watch the sun set over Mr. Jenkins's silo.

This time, I drove the truck right up to the edge, so close I could hear Earle suck in his breath. We got out, and we were staring down at a hole. Six feet long, three wide, another three or four deep.

"It's magic," said Earle.

"Ain't nothing magic about it," I said. "I dug it myself."

Next to the hole was a pile of dirt, neat as I could make it. Janey tapped it with her shoe. "Must've taken you a month of Sundays, Melia."

"Took me five."

I never told them, but when Mama took sick, I kept coming out here every week. On account of it was just easier to think. After a time, I started bringing a shovel. If you'd asked me what I was going to do with it, I couldn't have told you. Even when I was digging, I never stopped and thought, *This is where we'll put Mama.*

On that fifth Sunday, I looked down, and sure enough, there was a big old hole and but one thing to do with it.

"Here, Earle. Give me a hand."

The boy give a little shudder, but he tucked his head down and set to work. Together we lifted Mama out of the flatbed and laid her in the ground. I pulled the top sheet off her face, and the three of us, we stood there on the lip of the grave, just looking. I don't know for how long. Ten minutes, an hour. All the time, I was thinking it was a mistake. She was taking a breather. Any second, she'd jump up and swear about ten thousand oaths (Mama was gifted that way) and ask us what the hell we were doing.

4

But she didn't do none of that. She didn't move a grain.

I knelt down by the hole and reached in until I could touch her forehead. Damn, but it was cold.

"She needs a coffin," said Earle.

"We can't afford one."

"Then we ought to say something."

"Like what?"

"I don't know, something holy."

"Well, don't look at me," I said. "When was the last time you saw me in church?"

"I been to Sunday school," said Janey.

"Then give it your best crack," I said.

She tugged on her collar and cast her eyes off.

"The Lord is my shepherd, I shall not want. He makes me lie down. I will fear no evil. Blessed are the poor. Do unto others as you would have them do. He who is without sin. For thine is the kingdom. Now I lay me down to sleep, I pray the Lord my soul to keep. The Lord is my shepherd. . . ."

She kept going for a good spell, circling, circling. I didn't care. I was looking down into the valley, past the Jenkinses' silo, past the Hammonds' horse farm, all the way to the mountains at the other side. The dogwoods weren't out yet, but the tulip magnolias were just starting. I could hear bees and mockingbirds. A handsaw pushing through green wood. I could see Mrs. Jenkins carrying eggs in her apron and someone way out in the distance cutting hay. And a Studebaker crawling down the mountain road, with a little puff of smoke following. Stupid me, thinking the world would stop just 'cause of us.

I took one last look, then bent down and pulled the sheet over Mama's face.

"Reckon we better fill it up," I said.

Well, they didn't have the heart for it, so I took up the shovel myself. It was a queer business. I couldn't stop thinking she was *feeling* every little clod and pebble. It got so I'd have to stop every couple of minutes and wait. Listen for some faint little cry. *Wait, stop.* But there was nothing.

Sweat was coming off every part of me. I threw down the shovel and set there at the edge of the grave. From out of the woods came Janey, carrying a mess of wildflowers. Bedstraw and golden ragwort and wild phlox.

"They look nice," I allowed.

Earle come right after. He'd gone and whittled a couple of sticks and tied them into a cross with a strip of bark.

"Most fitting," I said.

We took some time arranging everything. We never did get it perfect. The dirt was loose, so the cross couldn't help but tilt a little, and the wind took a good share of the phlox blossoms.

"Well, now," I said. "Time to say good-bye."

Janey spoke first. Her voice was clenched like a fist. "Bye, Mama."

Earle, he spoke straight to the ground. "Bye."

I didn't say a thing.

Driving back home, I kept glancing at the other two. Janey was quiet and still. Earle's big jaw was working away, like he was chewing on turkey gristle, and his hands made fists and then unmade them.

"What?" I said.

"We done it all wrong, that's what."

"How do you figure?"

"She should've been buried at church."

"She wouldn't have wanted that. You know that."

"There should've been a preacher," he said. "And hymn singing. That's how God likes it."

"God don't care."

"He does, too. He's going to be pissed off. He ain't gonna let Mama in."

"Then the hell with him," I said. "After all he put her through." Earle didn't answer.

"Listen now," I said. "Whatever we done wrong with the burying, that ain't on Mama's account."

He looked out the window. "What the hell do *you* know?"

By then we were pulling into the station. I saw a Cadillac V-16 two-door coupe parked by the pump. The driver was standing alongside it, his foot on the running board, a cigarette hanging off his lip.

"Closed!" I called out.

He straightened up, tossed his butt on the ground. Give me a dumbass smile.

"Can't you read?" I said. "We're closed."

"So you are," he said, squinting at the sign in the window. "But now you're not."

"We're closed all day."

"Listen, honey, you think you can make an exception? I just need a gallon to get me to Front Royal."

"Mister, we're closed. If you need gas"—Lord, how it pained me to say it—"you can try Blevins's Standard Oil, eight miles down the road."

"That's out of my way."

"Best I can do."

He looked at me awhile. Then, out of nowhere, give me a wink. "Listen, sweetie, is your daddy around somewhere? Maybe you can run get him for me."

Now, here's the deal. Any other day, I'd have told him how I felt about being called "sweetie" and how, if he wanted me to fetch my dad, he'd have to tell me who my dad was, and if he wanted to talk to my mom, I'd be glad to take him there, only she wasn't talking so much. I had it all lined up inside me, but it got stuck in my throat somehow, and my eyes was stinging so hard all I could do was go into the station house and lock the door after me.

I waited till I heard him drive away, and then I tried to stand up again, but the tiredness pulled me back down. So I set there, on the damn floor. Dozed off for a spell. Next thing I knew, Janey was standing over me.

"You hungry?" I said.

She nodded.

"Earle, too?"

She nodded.

"Okay, then," I said.

The real poser was what to do with Mama's eating chair. Didn't seem right throwing it away, but it looked awful creepy setting idle by the table. So we just kinda turned it around, and we picked at our Ralston wheat cereal (no milk) and Royal gelatin desserts, and every so often, we'd raise our heads like we was about to say something, only we forgot what it was.

At last Earle pushed his plate away. "Don't seem right," he said. "Eating when she can't."

"She'd *want* you to," I said. "So you can grow into a big strong feller."

"She won't be around to see," said Earle, lowering his chin to the table.

"Melia," said Janey, "you reckon you miss her more than me?"

"Well, it ain't no pie-eating contest. I reckon we can each miss her our own way. You don't quit loving somebody just on account of they're dead."

Janey stared at the back of that chair for a long while. Then she drew her arms round her.

"Melia," she said, "what're we gonna do?"

"Get to bed, that's what."

"Nooo." She always gives you the kindliest look when she thinks you're being a dumbass. "Without Mama."

"Carry on. What choice we got?"

"We gonna starve?" Earle asked in a dull, flat voice.

"What're you talking about? You don't think the station is clearing money? You think—what, we fix people's cars and pump their gas for free?" I give them a nod just to show I meant business. "God didn't make no petroleum trees that I know of. Long as folks got automobiles, they're going to need us, ain't they? And in case you were wondering, there's a plan. Me and Mama worked it all out."

"What?" said Earle.

"Well, I'm gonna run the business 'cause it's what I been doing anyways."

"You can fill a radiator faster than anyone this side of the Blue Ridge," said Janey.

"I suspect you're right. Now, Janey here's gonna learn how to cook and sew and garden, and then, when the time's ready, we're going to get her a husband."

"He can't be more than thirty," said Janey. "And he's got to have his teeth."

"Fine. As for Earle, he's going to college."

"What if I don't want to?"

"What if I don't care? I'm telling you it's been planned. You just got to do your part, that's all."

"When we gonna tell folks?" Janey asked.

"It ain't none of their business."

"But we need to tell 'em. They need to know."

I leaned across the table and glared at her. "You think this here town had any use for Mama when she was alive? How's it going to be any different now?"

"But Mama had friends," said Earle. "Minnie-Cora Harper and Mrs. Bean. And what about Mr. Gallagher?"

"He's gonna be *all* broke up," said Janey.

"When the time's right," I said, "we'll tell them all. I got stuff to take care of first."

Janey made a little tower of gelatin cubes on her plate. Then knocked it down, then built it up again.

"I know why you don't want to tell," she said. "'Cause if they find out, they'll split us up."

See what I mean? She's a silly child, but she'll surprise you.

"I never heard such foolishness," I said.

But Earle was looking mighty ashy. "Is that so, Melia?"

"'Course not."

"Hannah Smartt," said Janey.

"Who's Hannah Smartt?" said Earle.

"She was in fourth grade, same as me, and she set in the back, and her hair weren't never combed, 'cause she didn't have no ma. Then she lost her pa, and she didn't have no kin left, so Hannah and her two brothers, they got sent to Lynchburg, and what I heard?" Janey lowered her voice. "They didn't even get sent to the same family. They got split up. *Fos. Ter. Care.*"

I could see Earle's lips forming the words.

"Listen, missy," I said. "You think I'd let 'em try such a thing? Anybody with eyes can see I'm the nearest thing to a mama as you brats is likely to get. Who's feeding and dressing you? Putting you to bed every night?"

"That don't count," said Earle. "You're not a grown-up."

"Oh, yeah?"

And to prove my point, I sent them right to bed. Oh, they made me tell them a story about Abdullah the Merman, but when they asked for more, I told them what I always told them.

"Show's over, folks. Come back tomorrow."

I tapped down their eyelids, and I set there until I heard their breathing. Then I walked over to the window.

The moon was fierce that night. I could see the shape of the leaves on the elm tree and the tire swings moving in the breeze.

Go home, why don't you?

That's what Doc Whitworth'd told Mama after he'd sprung the news on her. *Go home, Brenda. Get things squared away. Make your peace.*

Well, whatever she made, it weren't peace.

Fos. Ter. Care.

I closed my eyes and listened to the crickets. Then I felt a tug on my trousers. It was Janey. Skinny as a goddamned muskrat in her newly mended gray shift and half asleep in the moonlight.

"Come to bed," she said.

"I ain't tired," I said. (Though I was, I purely was.)

"You need your sleep," she said. "Ain't no man going to marry you with them nasty ol' coon rings under your eyes."

"Maybe I don't want no man to marry me."

Janey didn't answer right off. But when she was pulling the sheets back over her, she said, "Wanting's got nothing to do with nothing."

Chapter
TWO

I woke up when the sun did. Eyes blazing, hair heavy on my head. Janey was breathing into my neck, Earle's knee was gouging my hip. I laid there, waiting for the dark to peel away.

"Let's get this carnival on the road," I said to myself.

I fried up the last of the eggs, and then I rolled the kids out of bed. They each dragged a blanket to the table. Earle just stared at his plate.

"So help me," I said, "you make me throw that out, I'm gonna kill you."

"What'd you pack for lunch?" he asked.

"Apple butter sandwiches." And when he give me that scowl, I said, "Excuse *me*, Daddy Warbucks. Filet mignon'll be here tomorrow. You don't like my lunches, why don't you trade 'em?"

"He already does," said Janey.

It was a hair past seven when I shooed them out of the house.

There was a hard wind coming down the mountain, right in their faces. They stood rocking in it.

"Listen now. Not a word. It's a day like any other."

"Then why aren't you open yet?" Earle asked.

"'Cause I got business in town, and that's the last nosy-ass question you get."

I give them each a light little kick in the butt. It's what I do every morning, and when they were littler, that kick would send him laughing up the hill—halfway to school. Today, they was like a pair of jennies in harness. I watched them just to the point where they disappeared around the bend, and then I called after them.

"Watch out for cars!"

It's a queer town, Walnut Ridge. Some half a century back, the citizens got a little cash in their pockets and a couple stars in their eyes and figured they was going to be the next big deal in Warren County—bigger than Front Royal, even. So they went and built themselves a main street. 'Course they couldn't run it but the two blocks before it reached the nearest cliff, but they was so keen on their prospects they decided to call it *First* Street. As in first of many to come.

Well, fate had other plans for Walnut Ridge, and it turned into one of those places that just straggles along. Most of the townsfolk just bled back into the mountains till about ten years ago, when they was coaxed back down with the promise of digging soapstone. Company made a bunch of ugly houses for 'em—raw clapboard with tin roofs, each looking like the next. But the Depression took care of the soapstone company, and today the quarry's closed, and folks are back to straggling.

14

Carpentry, masonry, Civilian Conservation Corps, whatever'll answer. There's some work to be had building Skyline Drive, and there's talk of a rayon plant in a couple years, but that's talk.

First Street, though, is still there in all its glory. Walkways on both sides. A five-and-ten-cent store. A drugstore. A Primitive Baptist church. There's an empty tobacco warehouse that some rich old lady was trying to turn into a temple for the arts, but that never took, and right there at the end of the street, before it drops off the cliff, is a white farmhouse with green shutters.

It's an old house, built before the War Between the States, and it don't look like it's been painted since. The planters are rotting in the window boxes, and the grass in the front yard is losing ground to the weeds, but it's mostly clean and well tended, and it has the best view of the valley. I used to think if a pot of gold was to drop from the sky (it wouldn't have to be a big pot), maybe this was the house I'd want for myself.

Only I would've had to live there all alone. Wake up that way, go to bed that way. And before I moved in, I'd have had to get rid of the birdbath 'cause if a bird can't find itself some water, it's got no business being a bird. But the part that *really* would've had to go was the tiny slat bench in the front yard under the elm tree.

It wasn't the bench I minded, it was the two white plaster kids sitting on it. From a distance, they looked close enough to the real thing to make you wonder who'd been keeping 'em out of the sun. It was only closer you saw the lie of it, and that was when the heebie-jeebies kicked in. 'Cause it was like some terrible enchantment held them on that bench.

So the stone children, they would've had to go.

To speak true, I hadn't come down yet on the door knocker. It was a little fancy for my tastes, but I liked the way it rested in your hand, and on that particular morning, I made sure to hold it a space before I let it drop.

The door swung open, and there was Mina Gallagher, looking like she was already bracing for me. Thin and pinched, with a mouth always folding in and brown eyes always pushing out. Her fingers ran to the collar of her dress.

"Morning," she said.

"Is Mr. Gallagher there?"

"It's not even eight."

"Yeah, I know."

She give me a good look-over.

"Chester," she said. He didn't answer. "Chester!"

"Yes?"

"Visitor." She looked at me a spell longer. "Won't you come inside?"

Chester was already jogging down the staircase in an old wool bathrobe. I could see patches of electrical tape on the soles of his slippers.

"Everything all right?" he asked.

"I was just going to ask Melia if she cared for some coffee."

"No, thank you."

"Well, then," said Mina Gallagher, "I'll leave you to it."

She followed the straightest line to the kitchen.

"This is a surprise," said Chester.

"Reckon so."

He looked down at his hand, found a lit pipe in it. "Do you mind if I . . ."

"Nope."

He took a drag. Jammed his free hand into the pocket of his robe.

"Here you are," he said.

"Yep."

"Like you said you'd be."

After a day's practice, I weren't no better at telling the news. All I could do was stand there like a fool on the cracked parquet tile.

"She's gone," he said.

He sat on the bottommost stair. "Sorry. I should have . . . do you want any—"

"Coffee? Your wife already asked."

"She did, didn't she?"

He stared for a while at his pipe, not really seeing it.

"When did it happen?" he asked.

"Night before last."

"Ah. Okay. So you—I mean, I'm guessing there'll be a funeral."

"Already done. No offense, Chester, it was a private affair. Family only."

"Of course."

I give his knee a little nudge with mine. He slid over on the stair till there was room for the two of us.

"Thank you for telling me," he said.

"Well. You being her lawyer and all."

His mouth turned up at the corners.

"Last time I saw her, she fired me."

"She weren't in her right head."

"Oh, I think she was. It was me who wasn't." He stared at his pipe. "The will. You'll want to see the will."

"Seen it."

"Well, you know how it goes then. The—the service station, that's held in trust with the bank. Me being the trustee. Till such time as you gain your maturity."

"Yep."

"Of course, there are sundry possessions. The pie safe. The ring. There's a—there's a wedding dress, I think."

He took off his glasses. Pressed a thumb against each eye. "Sorry, Melia."

"It's okay. I got a day's start on you."

He put his glasses back on. "The first time I ever saw your mama, she was in these bib overalls. Covered head-to-I-don't-know-what, jamming her face in some carburetor. I wasn't even sure she was a woman till she says *'Scuse me* in that—that *voice* of hers. She comes back, oh, twenty-four seconds later, and there wasn't a speck on her. She looked like Venus in her half shell."

"It was a gift," I said.

"And I'm standing there, all at sea, and she says—you know what she says?"

I knew, but I let him go.

"She says, 'You any good at this lawyering business?' And I say, 'Well, if I'm not, we'll find something else.'"

His chuckle come out like a sigh.

"Melia," he said. "I want you to know there wasn't—"

"I know."

"I mean, I'm a married—"

"Chester, I *know*. She knew, too."

"That she did."

"So you're in the clear."

"Is that what I am?"

From the kitchen came the sound of something having its life cleaned out of it. A counter, probably.

"Listen," I said. "I gotta get back. There's one thing I need to ask you."

"Certainly."

"Did you ever ask Mama who was going to look after us? Once she was gone?"

"Did I *ask*? Only about a million times. I said, 'This isn't just you, Brenda, you've got to think about your kids. They're going to need a guardian.' And you know what she said?"

"'Keep your pants on. I'll figure it out.'"

"Exactly."

"Only she didn't."

He looked at me.

"You mustn't think badly of her, Melia. I just think it came on faster than she was expecting. Folks like her—so *alive*—I think it's hard for them to think the living can end."

It was so quiet in that damned house. Nothing to listen to but the ticking of the grandfather clock and the squeak of Mina Gallagher's dishrags.

"I can't lose Janey and Earle," I said.

"You won't."

"Oh? You gonna tell me Virginia law says something different than I think it says? Last I heard, orphaned kids become wards of the state. Did I get that wrong?"

His eyes went sidling off.

"Chester, I can live on the bum if I have to. I can dig ditches, I can lay trestles, but I won't see those kids turned over to some thin-lipped Christians with birch rods. I won't."

"Y'all must have kin," he said weakly.

"Mama's people are all gone."

"Janey and Earle? They've got a father somewhere."

"If you call the Moundsville prison somewhere, then yes, they do."

Through the cloud of pipe smoke, he squinted at me. "What about you, Melia? Someone had to be the father of you, right?"

"You tell me who," I said, "and we'll both know."

Your daddy. He's . . .

Chester tapped the stem of his pipe against his chest. "What if someone were to adopt you? All three of you."

I folded my arms across my chest, give him a hard stare.

"And just who's gonna do that?"

There come another squeak from the kitchen.

"Jesus, Chester. You know folks in this town ain't got the time of day for us. You really see any of 'em fighting over who gets to keep us?"

"Then what do you want me to do, Melia? I mean, I could try to roust up some money."

"You ain't got much more than us, Chester."

"Then what?"

"Don't do nothing, don't say nothing. Not till I got everything worked out."

And when his face started to trouble, I said, "Chester, this is probably the easiest thing anyone'll ask you to do all day."

"You're asking me to help perpetrate a fraud."

"Oh, yeah?"

"I mean, as a friend of the family, it's one thing. As a lawyer— as a bank director—I'm sworn on oath to—"

He stopped. Rocked his face back toward the ceiling. "Jesus, will you listen to me? No wonder she fired me."

"All I need's a few days," I said.

"One condition," he said.

"What?"

"Hire me back."

"Don't be dumb. I can't do no hiring."

"Sure you can. Just repeat after me. *I, Melia Hoyle.* Well, go on."

"I, Melia Hoyle . . ."

"Hereby name Chester Gallagher . . ."

"Hereby name Chester Gallagher . . ."

"To be my attorney."

"To be my attorney."

"I will pay him what you would pay a dog."

"I will . . ." I couldn't help it, I started laughing. "We can't even pay a dog," I said. "But you're welcome to our scraps."

"Wouldn't have it any other way."

He put out his hand, and we shook on it.

21

"*Well,*" he said. "Being that I am now bound by attorney-client privilege, I cannot possibly divulge any information without your express consent. So help me God and the state of Virginia."

Just the barest trace of a smile on him, and then it was gone.

"Doesn't seem right," he said. "Girl like you taking on all this."

"I ain't no girl, Chester. Oh, and hey, there's one other thing. I need you to get us a death certificate."

"Out of thin air, you mean."

I shrugged. "It's what I hire you for, ain't it?"

Chapter
THREE

It was near eight in the morning by the time I got back to the station. Just in time for the trucks to start piling off Highway 55. Regular as the sun, these fellers. All through the night, they ride the mountains, living on tobacco and coffee and maybe chasing it with a little whiskey. Then they crowd in a few hours past dawn. Eyes sagging, faces mashed in. Legs dragging after. The only dream they got left is to make Pittsburgh or Philly or Baltimore before the light goes. So you give 'em a little coffee, and they flop in one of the Adirondack chairs under the general-store awning, doze for a bit. Then they spring up, good as new.

But even as they tear east, they remember those ten minutes they spent at Brenda's Oasis. All those whiskery men with their big sunburned arms—I couldn't tell 'em apart at first, but then I started remembering things about them. Dutch was the one singed off his eyebrows when his rig caught fire near Altoona. Elmer lost half his ear in a bar fight in Kansas City. Glenmont had the anaconda tattoo on his neck. Joe Bob was the feller with the moon face who set in his truck and sobbed on the steering wheel. (His wife left him for an encyclopedia salesman from Wheeling.)

Then there was the fearsomest one of all. Six foot four, three hundred pounds. Big ol' white scar down the left side of his face. Arms the size of my body, feet like manhole covers, black hair running from his neck to the tips of his fingers. A mouthful of rotten teeth. He came barreling down the hill one morning—all the way from Oak Ridge without a rest—and, before he even stopped his rig, he leaned out the window and roared (at nobody to speak of), "Fix the goddamn rattle!"

Then he staggered off to grab a coffee and take a piss, and when he came back, I was slamming down the hood.

"The choke in your carburetor is stuck," I said.

"So unstick it."

"I did."

He glared at me. Then he jumped in the cab, turned on the engine, and set there, listening.

"What's your name?"

"Melia."

"Where'd you learn about engines?"

"My mama. She's in the back if you want me to—"

"I don't wanna. You're the one who works on this truck from here on in. Got it?"

As he was pulling away, he leaned out his window one more time and said, "Name's Warner."

Now, I'd never call Warner my angel, but when some trucker's telling me to run get my daddy, Warner's been known to grab the guy by the nap of his shirt—one hand is all it takes—and hoist him straight to the sky. And when that poor sap is seven feet off the ground, Warner says, in the sweetest voice he's got, "You let this little lady do what she needs to do, all right?"

Mama used to worry I didn't have me enough friends, but I always told her I had the morning shift.

And they were there that morning in late March, when I most needed them. Merle. Trevor. Joe Bob. Oh, they knew Mama hadn't been round for a coon's age, but they never asked me what was going on. They just asked me to fill their tank or check their oil or figure out where that trail of black smoke was coming from.

The hours rolled by, and then it was cold, hard noon. Everyone gone. A good three or four hours before the late-afternoon shift would start pouring in from the east. I used to welcome the peace, but today, Mama was swirling round in my brain. Her duck boots. The little mole just under her lip. That smell of hers, like blackberries.

If you'd have held a gun to my head, I'd have said what I missed most was Mama's laugh. Which was crazy 'cause it was the most embarrassing laugh a mother could have. It was a whole crazy parade—snorts, grunts, screeches. It could go on for minutes, and every soul from a mile round would be staring, wondering how a body could make such sounds.

I set behind the counter, chewing on beef jerky, sipping ginger beer, flipping through Photoplays. Somewhere toward three in the afternoon, I heard a squeal. A truck was rolling past me—a flatbed, loaded with coal—making that hard right on Totten. Its rear tires slipped a little on the gravel, the truck give a shudder, the back gate popped open, and a man come rolling out.

He landed hard, in a puff of dust, and started rolling toward me, but me, I was running the other way—chasing that truck down the hill.

"Hey, wait!" I called. "Hey, mister! You left something!"

But the truck kept going. And such was my state of mind that, by the time I give up the chase, I plumb forgot about the feller who'd fallen out. It wasn't till I got back to the station that I found a heap of mud and hair, a cotton shirt, and a pair of torn-up trousers planted squarely in the path to pump number two.

With a growl of frustration, I jogged over to him. Somewhere in the tangle, I found a mouth. I put my ear to it and waited till a little tickle of air straggled out.

Alive. Which didn't make him any less of a pain in my ass. Or any easier to drag. Every pound of his was pulling against every one of mine. I stood up to catch my breath. Just as I was reaching down again, another pair of hands come out of nowhere.

"Jesus," I muttered.

"Just trying to help, Melia."

"I *got* it."

To speak true, I was glad for the help. But once we'd curled the fella round the pump, I looked up and saw a Dudley I never seen before. Some kinda bullshit aviator's hat on his head. Shiny leather shoes. More leather on his shins. Fancy balloon pants—I don't know what you call 'em—the kind rich people ride horses in. And a jacket, military-like, cut to the waist.

"Holy God," I said.

A creek of red was washing out his cheeks as another voice come bellowing after us.

"Don't he look smart!"

I turned my head real slow. Harley Blevins lay due west of me. Leaning against his butternut Chevrolet Eagle. Tipping his straw boater.

"What you're *looking* at, Miss Melia? Why, that there's the future."

"He looks like the top of a cake."

"You ain't seeing it. Dudley there, he's an aeroplane pilot or Buck Rogers or something. It's how I got all my attendants gussied up."

"They pump gas in that?"

"Sure they do! You know, Melia, public servants like us, we can't just expect to totter out no more in big ol' greasy overalls. Nasty *rag* hangin' out our pockets. Standard Oil wants its employees to take their work serious. Ain't that right, Dudley?"

"Yes, sir."

"Aw, but listen to me. I ain't come to lecture you, girl. I only stopped 'cause my little chariot here is famished. Gimme a buck's worth, will you?"

I swear I could hear Mama whispering in my ear. *Smile, honey. Smile them all the way to hell.*

So I did. And when I cleaned the windshield, I did it extra hard, and the only thing that ruined it was Dudley hanging back a few feet.

"You ain't much of a spy," I muttered.

"I ain't spying."

"Your uncle is."

"Melia!" called Harley Blevins. "Get me a Coke, too, will you?"

I walked back into the store and pulled a bottle from the icebox, uncapped it, and brought it out. Harley Blevins made a big show of taking out his money, peeling each bill from its neighbor.

"Word to the wise, Melia. Next big wind, that sign of yours gonna come right down."

"I'll keep that in mind."

"Funny old thing. Looks like a tombstone."

In fact, it was. Mama got it cheap off a Harpers Ferry stonemason, painted it herself.

"I can order you a new one," said Harley Blevins.

"We'll get by."

"Makes an old feller sad, thinking how many challenges you and your mama got on your horizon. Now, don't mistake me, independent operators has got their place, but here's what I've always said, Melia. When a person's driving down the road for a spell, he wants to see a station looks just like what he left. Makes him feel like he ain't gone so far after all. Like he's still in the same by-God country. Yes, *sir*, you drive down State Fifty-Five, you see *one* brand, *one* sign, *one* uniform every step of the way. Till you get here." His eyes give a little swell. "Say, you got a match, Melia?"

"Sure."

"I been meaning to ask how your mama's doing."

"Still a little poorly."

"That's too bad."

"She'll come round."

"'Course she will. Only I gotta tell you, Melia, seeing as

nobody's laid eyes on her since I don't know when, everybody's fearing the worst. *Hoping* the best, of course."

Smile them all to hell.

"She's okay, Mr. Blevins. I'll tell her you asked, though."

"But seeing you struggle like this. Goddamn if it don't make an old feller's heart crack a little."

"We're A-okay, Mr. Blevins."

"Well, you tell your mama anytime she wants to come and talk business with ol' Harley, she just has to say the word, you hear?"

"I'll tell her."

"Say now, Dudley, what do you say we—hang on a minute! I near forgot what I come here to tell you. We're cutting prices again."

This time, I couldn't even smile.

"Times being how they are. So many of our fellow Americans out of work. Nine cents a gallon, that's the least we can do, huh?"

He tipped his hat.

"Now listen, Melia, you gotta promise me you'll take care of that sign. Being an old man, I worry."

He give me one last wave as the Chevrolet Eagle pulled away, but I weren't even seeing him no more. No, sir, I was running the figures. Brenda's Oasis was already running five dollars behind every week, and that was with me pumping the gas and running the store and doing near everything there was to do. We wasn't just in debt to Standard Oil, we was in debt to the egg man and the milkman and the iceman. Most Mondays, there weren't nothing on the dinner table but what was left on the store shelves. If we was to drop our gas price another cent a gallon—and what the hell choice did we have—we'd lose forty more dollars every week.

Which would mean an end to living. And Harley Blevins knew that as well as he knew his own name.

Here's something else you'll learn about me. I don't cry, mostly. Instead, I rolled myself a cigarette, and I went and stood on the edge of the road, watching the cars go by. I took a harder drag, then a harder.

From behind me I heard a moan. I looked back and saw that old bum, curled up against pump number two.

I went to the well. Filled a bucket and carried it over. I had an idea of drenching him in one fast pour, but there was a meanness in me just then, so I did it bit by bit. A squirt in the eye, a squirt in the nose. When I was done pouring, I dropped the pail in his middle. He jerked straight up.

"Sleep well?" I said.

He give his head a mongrel shake. Run his tongue round his lips. Then he dropped his head between his legs and threw up.

Chapter
FOUR

He got up real slow, the puke still hanging in strands from his chin.

"Your ride went thataway," I said. "They got a few miles on you by now."

He didn't seem to hear me.

"Look, mister. Either buy something or move along."

"Would you . . ." He paused to slap some life back in his legs. "Would you have a cigarette by any chance?"

It was deep and dark, his voice, like something calling from the bottom of a well.

"Five cents a pack," I said.

"Ah . . . I know I've . . . got a few coins here. . . ."

He shoved his hands into his dungarees, but there weren't no pockets left, so his hands ended up at his knees.

"Jesus, don't clean out your bank, mister. Here."

I pried the cigarette off my lip and offered it to him.

"Very kind of you," he said.

He took a puff. Watched me roll myself another.

"Delicate fingers," he said.

Well, here we come to the greatest mystery of them all. Why didn't I just send that feller on his way?

In the two years we'd been in Walnut Ridge, I'd seen dozens of hoboes stagger on by, looking for a bite or a nickel or a smoke. Fellas as bad off as this one or worse, and they was gone from my thoughts as soon as I saw the back of 'em. So you'll ask me—one day you'll ask me—what was it about this one?

And I'm not even sure I can tell you. Maybe it was his eyes. They was blue like the veins on the underside of your arm, but one was lazy and dawdled away while you was looking at it, so you didn't know whether to follow that one or stick with the eye that weren't going nowheres. It was almost like two different fellers watching you.

"You don't sound like you're from around these parts," I said.

"My people were from Maryland. Cumberland."

"That's where my mama's people were from."

"That so?" he said, politely.

We smoked in quiet.

"So that where you're coming from?" I asked. "Cumberland?"

He shook his head.

"That where you're bound?" I asked.

He shook his head.

"Where *are* you bound?"

"Oh." He give the cig a twirl between his fingers. "I hear the

Shenandoah Valley's lovely this time of year. Had it in mind to do some apple picking in the fall. Come winter, I'll make for Tennessee or Florida. World's my oyster."

"So you ain't going nowhere."

"I beg to differ."

It so happened I was looking over his shoulder just then. Looking at our sign. Which, if you was to believe Harley Blevins, was ready to come down in the next gale.

"You got a trade, mister?"

He shrugged. "I suppose I can hammer things together well enough. Woodwork. Tinsmithing. Threshing. Tobacco planting. Cotton picking."

"What else you got?"

"Uh, cow and goat milking. Whitewashing. Tutoring. Shoe repair. Trout fishing. Harmonica and recorder. Beginning Latin. Elocution. Deportment. Shakespearean soliloquies. Waltz instruction . . ."

"Wait. Shakespeare."

"Never mind that."

"Like, you read his plays? Out loud?"

"Sure I do."

"From memory?"

"Naturally."

"Why would you go and do that?"

"You raise a good point. I was an actor once." He spread out his arms in their ragged cotton sleeves. "'Look on my works, ye mighty, and despair.'"

"That ain't Shakespeare."

"No, ma'am." A crinkle of surprise around his eyes. "It is not."

From down the road came a two-door Chevy roadster, black like a hearse, front fender dangling to one side. I watched it slow down when our station come into view, go through all those little stops and starts that cars do—*the courtship,* Mama used to call it. It kept going.

"An actor," I said. "Like on the stage?"

"For a time."

"Did folks, like, pay to see you?"

"Sometimes. I played Casca to Charles Coburn's Brutus."

"Who's Charles Coburn?"

"It was in Chicago. At the Athenaeum. Would you mind not doing that?"

"What?"

"Staring. I'm not so accustomed to it as I was."

"I was just thinking you're not as old as I thought."

"Thank you."

"I mean, your beard's all gray, but on top, you're mostly black. No more 'n fifty, I'd guess. Fifty-two?"

He didn't answer. I dropped my cig on the ground, mashed it under my boot.

"That acting stuff," I said. "Is it something you can pick up again?"

"Pick *up?*"

"I mean, if you ain't done it in a while, does it come right back?"

"The old lines, you mean?"

"No. The *doing* of it."

He give me the saddest smile then. Flicked a hunk of ash on the ground. "Child," he said, "I never stopped doing it. What's your name?"

"Melia."

"It's been a pleasure meeting you, *Meel*-ya. However, you don't appear to be in the business of theatrical booking, so"—he stubbed his butt on the pier—"I'd best be on my way. I do thank you for your kindness."

"You ain't got nowhere to be."

"I have many places to be. I only said no one was expecting me at any of them."

"In my book, that's the same thing. Now listen up, mister."

I fastened my two eyes on his one good one.

"For now, you can stay in the room over the store. We can feed you three squares a day. You don't need to pump gas or nothing, but I wouldn't be put out if you helped around the place. We got a sight of fixing needs to be done."

"I don't understand. Are you—"

"And there'll be no funny business, you hear? None of the handsy stuff you old fellers go for. I won't stand it. And there's one thing I'm real particular about. You can't be drinking."

"I don't recall ever—"

"Don't pull that act, I can smell it on your clothes. Now, I don't know what troubles you got—I got 'em, too—but I can't be dragging you out of ditches in the middle of the night. I can't have Earle doing it, neither."

"Earle? Who the hell is—"

"Now just *stand* there, will you, and let me get a look at you."

He didn't lift a finger when I started tugging on him.

"You can keep the shoes," I said. "The rest of the clothes has got to go."

"Go," he said.

"Well, not right off. We'll have to find you some new ones first. You're an inch or two taller than Chester, but he might have something that'll fit. Till then, we'll just give your duds a good scrub. Janey's a whiz with the washboard."

"Janey . . ."

"You'll need a bath before another day's out. We got a tub out back with soap. And Jesus *Christ*, have we got to shave off that beard! Shouldn't take me but a couple minutes. When I'm done, you won't be an old man no more."

He was standing just where I left him when I come back with the comb.

"Maybe you remember this," I said.

He winced as the teeth dug into his roots. "Goddamn it, girl. . . ."

"Look, I know you just fell off a coal truck, but you don't got to *look* that way. Lord only knows what critters and cooties you got living up here. Well, never mind, that's a little better. Now let's wash you up."

The still eye was calm. "What in heaven's name are you talking about?"

"Janey and Earle gonna be here any minute, that's what I'm talking about."

"What's that got to do with—"

"Oh, hush up, will you? The well's over there. Get going."

I found a clean rag propping up a corner of the cash register.

Every swipe I took at his face, he got a year younger. I'd about scrubbed the dirt from under his fingers when I saw Earle and Janey, tumbling down the hill like a pair of old barrels. Earle had a bruise on his brow, and Janey had some kind of dandelion chain around her neck—weeds was gems to her. Any other day, they'd have dropped their satchels at my feet and started right in with the whole newsreel 'bout Miss Hyde and her willow branch and Johnny Sack smoking ginseng over by the quarry and what a frog looks like after it's been cut open and is it true warts come from the devil. But not today.

"Who's that?" Janey asked.

"He stinks like a polecat," Earle whispered.

I give the boy a smack. "Show some respect now."

"How come?"

"How *come*?"

I reached my hand over and rested it on the man's shoulder.

"This here's our daddy," I said.

Chapter
FIVE

You'll know it soon enough. That feeling you get after you send some words into the world and there's no taking 'em back, so they kinda *spin* there in front of you. That's how it was now. Me and Janey and Earle—and that stranger, gray as fieldstone—all just watching the words spin.

Earle's satchel dropped straight off his shoulder.

"That ain't funny, Melia."

"Do I look like I'm funning?"

"Then you gotta be crazy," said Janey. "Our daddy's in jail."

"No, this here's *my* daddy. Which means he belongs to *all* of us."

Earle's eyes got real small. "You never told us you had a daddy."

"Never come up."

"Sure it did."

"Either one of you ask me straight out?"

Earle thought on that.

"Mama always said you was dropped on her front porch one morning. Along with a pint of buttermilk."

"She told me you come right out of her forehead," said Janey. "Like a wart."

"Jesus, she was pulling your leg, that's all. I got a daddy just like you, only he ain't a felon."

"Well, if he's our daddy," said Earle, "what in Sam Hill's he doing here?"

"Why, soon as he heard the bad news, he come a-running, didn't he?"

"And who told him 'bout it?"

"Me, that's who. Wrote him a letter."

Janey got quiet, thinking about that letter and all the distance it must have traveled. But Earle come up to that stranger like he was ready to crawl right up his shirt.

"He don't *look* like you," said Earle.

"Shows what you know."

"If he's kin, he should look like kin."

"That's just 'cause you ain't seen him smile yet."

I hadn't myself.

"Go on, mister," I said. "Go on, Mister Daddy. Give your babies a smile."

His lips shook a little, but they couldn't get a mind to leave each other, so I had to pull them apart myself. And there they stuck.

It wasn't what you'd rightly call a smile. When I tried to fix my own mouth the same way, it felt downright unnatural.

"See?" I said. "Don't we look like blood?"

"I'm pondering," said Earle.

"Neither one of you's much for smiling," allowed Janey.

"Well, there you go. Third degree's over. Now I believe y'all got some chores and homework to do, less you talked Benito Mussolini into doing it for you."

But now it was Janey's turn to dig in.

"If he's our daddy, where's he been all this time?"

"Traveling, that's where."

"How come he never come round to see us?"

"Business, that's how come. Keeps him on the road."

"How come you do all his talking for him?" said Earle. "Someone run off with his tongue?"

I was all set to hush both of them children but good, only—I can't explain it—the gumption went out of me. All I could do was stare at that poor varmint and wait for something to happen.

And now him and his good eye and his crazy eye and every other part of him had gone someplace where *nobody* could follow. Then, from the deep dark cave of his mouth, a little peep of tongue come crawling out.

"I'll be," whispered Janey.

"Happy?" I said.

"He still don't look glad to see us," said Earle.

"Sakes, he just got here! Traveling day and night, all weathers. Lord *knows* how many buses and whatnot."

"He ever been on a train?" Earle asked.

"Prob'ly a good dozen in the last day, ain't that right, Daddy? And now he's all wrung out, poor thing, so if you don't mind, Mister and Miss Nosybird, I'm gonna take him to his room and get him settled."

"Get him washed," mumbled Earle.

Before I could say a thing, Janey caught him in the ribs. The very next second, she was dragging her big brother toward the house, and I was hauling the stranger into the store. It's on account of we're women, I guess, we didn't need to plan it.

"That's some grip you got," the stranger said.

My fingers had left white marks around his wrist.

"I'll go without a fight," he said.

Sure enough, he followed me past the counter and all the way to the back of the store to where the steps were, and when I started climbing, I could hear his feet, soft behind. His breath, too. I waited on the landing till he caught up. Then I pushed open the door.

Mama used to call the place our guest suite but only when she was putting it over on somebody. Do not be fooled! It was merely a bare room—sixteen by twelve, maybe—with a single sash window that never opened but a crack and a tick mattress full of straw and corn shucks.

As I remember, on that particular day, there was an apple box in the corner. This box was empty except for some bottles of liniment, a Spanish-language dictionary, and the 1912 Spotsylvania County criminal code.

This was the one room that could break Mama's will. Anywhere else, she'd have gone in with a broom and a rag and some vinegar and a burlap sack, and she'd have made it bend. But every time she come up here, she'd take one look and say, "Next week."

The stranger took a few totters around the room—polite-like. Then he bent to read the cross-stitched sampler hanging by the window.

Cheer up. It might be worse.

He stood up and give his jaw a scratch.

"I'll take their word for it."

He spun in a slow half circle and, before I knew it, started tipping back. The wall caught him, but it was a near thing.

"You want some water, mister?"

"Just need a moment."

I closed the door after me.

"Listen," I said, "I ain't gonna sugar it for you. Room's hotter than damnation in the summer. Colder than an Eskimo's ass in the winter. Tolerable nice in spring, but you can't keep the window open too long or you'll get all fumey from the gas."

He didn't say nothing.

"That bucket over yonder," I said. "You can use it for your business. Saves going to the privy. The other bucket is where you can burn your charcoal. Being as there ain't no fireplace."

His mouth was forming words now, but I couldn't make 'em out.

"Listen now," I said. "This ain't nothing you can't walk away from. Ain't no one here holding you captive."

He walked toward the little rhododendron-root table in the corner. Which was the one thing in that room that seemed made for something better. In a nice house, it would've had a family Bible sitting on it or a couple of old tintypes in a silver frame. Would've been waxed once a week. Here it was all on its lonesome, thick with grease and soot.

"Maybe you can tell me," he said, "what kind of mess I've gotten into."

"It ain't no mess. Least it don't have to be."

He set himself on the mattress. A puff of dust flew up.

"Go on," he said.

"My mama's name was Brenda Hoyle, and she got belly trouble in January, and one thing led to another, and she went *over*."

Weird how it all came flooding back. Mama clawing herself so fierce she'd have blood on her hands. Or laying back in her sheets (wet with piss because we never could get her the bucket in time) and staring the bejesus out of the ceiling.

"Point *is*," I said, "I ain't old enough to be in charge of them two children. Which is the goddamnedest stupidest thing I ever heard, but that's the state of Virginia for you. So what I'm proposing is— well, it's a *business* arrangement, that's all. Say some folks from the county come out here and they say, *Whoa, now, where be the father to these here children?* Why, all you got to do is step up and say, *That's me. I am the feller in question.* Then these selfsame folks, they go away and leave us alone. It's a romp in the clover when you come right down to it."

"Oh, sure," he said.

"Well, it ain't hard."

"It's against the law."

"Yeah?" I hocked a fleck of tobacco spit onto the floor. "Then I ain't got time for your damned law. 'Cause that *law's* what's going to split the three of us up. So if you're feared of a pack of old spinsters—"

"Could be a hell of a lot more than spinsters. Could be a sheriff."

"If you're so feared, then why don't you just catch the next coal truck heading west?"

He looked down at his fingers. Long spindly things.

"I'm not your father," he said. "I'm not anybody's father."

"That don't matter. You just gotta *be* here when the spinsters come a-knockin'. Like, just pretend I'm, what's his face, Coburn? And we're in this play together, and I got lines, and you got lines, and we fool 'em into thinking it's all true."

"What about your brother and sister? Are we going to fool them, too?"

"They'll think what I tell 'em to think."

Though just then I was recalling the look on Janey's face as she hustled Earle into the house. An *old* look.

"Like I said before, mister. If you got someplace else to be . . .'"

He was quiet.

"Hell," I said. "You ain't got a bindle on you. Bet you ain't even got a toothbrush. Less it's in one of them holes you call pockets. Here I am offering you food and a bed and a roof over your head. I call that a square deal."

Quieter still. I could've busted a head on that quiet.

"Well, goddamn it, mister, what's it gonna be? You in or out?"

His eyes went straggling around the room again till they found that little rhododendron table.

"It won't work," he said.

"Well, if it don't, it's on me. And you don't need to bother yourself about the sheriff or nothing. If things go south, I'll tell 'em it was my idea."

"Not sure they'll believe you."

"Sure they will. I got witnesses to my bad character."

He come very near to smiling.

"So we got us a deal?" I said.

"We got us something, all right."

44

I tossed him a packet of Lucky Strikes as I was walking to the door. And a book of matches.

"We don't got no ashtray," I said. "But you can use the bucket."

"I thank you."

"Listen, mister." I give my forehead a scratch. "Maybe you should tell me what your name is."

"Name?"

"Seeing as I should know it, probably."

"It's Hiram. Hiram Watts."

I let the sound of it settle in my ears.

"Well," I said, "reckon you can hold on to that. I mean, it ain't like you and Mama got hitched or nothing."

"In fact, no."

"Keeping it simple is all."

"Of course."

"So make yourself at home, Hiram Watts. There's food down in the store if you're hungry. If you're just fixing to sleep, that's okey, too."

He ran his fingers round the rim of that root table. Once, twice.

"All right," he whispered.

I closed the door after me.

Now I was all set to go back downstairs, but instead I sat down on the floor and leaned my head against the door. A minute or two later, I heard his voice on the other side.

"Thanks for the smokes."

Even then I stayed. Till I heard his snoring. Which was 'bout as high as his speaking voice was deep.

Hiram, I said to myself. *Hiram Watts.*

Chapter
SIX

I can't say why, but I remember exactly what we had for breakfast the next morning. A jar of French's mustard and a can of Del Monte country gentleman corn.

In those days, it was just easier to take our meals straight from the store shelves—whatever hadn't been bought or gone rotten. Mama used to say it was like eating your own profits, but when she took sick, there weren't nothing else for it. And Janey and Earle, they was all in at first, but as time went on, I could see the sag in their souls every time the food come squooshing out, still holding the can's shape. And on that particular Saturday morning, they was specially gray in the face.

"Melia," said Janey, "don't you wish you could cook?"

"Ain't got the time to learn."

"Reckon you could learn to heat something up," muttered Earle.

"There's the stove," I said. "Be my guest."

Janey poured out another glob of mustard. Studied it with one eye, then the other.

"Thing is, Melia, if you cooked, you could make biscuits like Mama's."

"Ain't nobody can do that," I said.

And this was the truth. Mama's biscuits tasted fresh no matter how long they set out on the counter.

"Could be she's making biscuits right now," said Janey.

"I suspicion they're letting her put up her feet awhile."

"You reckon she still smells like blackberries?"

"Yes, ma'am. That's how they knew who it was. *Brenda Hoyle, we smelled you a-coming.* Saint Peter's very words."

"He didn't say no such thing," said Earle.

"How you gonna know what Saint Peter says?" said Janey.

"I know as much as you two. Which is nothing at all."

I had a certain speech in mind, but then Hiram Watts opened our front door and walked in.

And now that I look back on it, I can see this was the turning.

'Cause up to that point, I do believe I could've swerved back. Could've sent Hiram Watts and his thundercloud beard back to where they come from and schemed my way clear to some whole new future. All that could've happened—but then he walked through our door.

Like a man coming home to his family, I can see that now—only shocked to find a family there, and the family no less shocked to find him, and the future speeding toward them all.

"Morning," I said.

"Morning," he said.

The voice was even deeper with a little sleep in it. The color of oil out of the crankcase.

He stood there a second, like he was steadying himself against a wind. Then he closed the door behind him.

"Oh, look," said Janey. "Somebody gone and dressed him."

It was true, the rags from yesterday were gone. (I never saw them again.) He was wearing a gray cotton jumpsuit, which stopped about halfway down his shins but helped some. He'd also given his hair a rinse, which helped some as well.

"Found 'em in a corner," he said.

"They was bought for someone," I said. "Mechanic Mama hired last fall. He lasted 'bout three seconds."

"'Cause he was a crook," said Janey. "And a drunk and a lech."

"Still, he left the clothes behind, and they ain't too far off your size."

"How come you don't have no clothes your own?" asked Earle.

Hiram thought a bit.

"They must be in transit," he said. "I expect you're Earle."

With great care, like it was the last time he was gonna see it, Hiram put out his hand. Earle's didn't budge.

"Shake it," I said.

"I ain't," said Earle.

"Shake it or I'll—"

"I ain't gonna shake it, and nobody can make me."

Hiram was just looking for an empty chair to fall in.

"Why the hell is he here?" said Earle.

"'Cause he's kin, that's why."

"I don't care who he is. We don't need him. We was doing just fine on our lonesome."

"Hush up now."

"I won't. I'm the damn man of the family."

"That so?"

"Mama told me, and that makes it so."

"She meant till a real one come along. You ain't but eleven years old."

"You shut up! I'm twelve next February, and I can hunt and fish and . . . and I know what a man and woman do when they love on each other, and I can . . . I can climb that hickory tree by Squabble Creek . . . ain't nobody in the whole fifth *grade* can do that . . . so don't you *even* . . ."

He jolted up from the table and run out the door. From somewhere in the vicinity of the front porch, he was heard to wish me dead.

"Earle's strung tight," Janey explained.

Hiram give a nod. "Coffee," he whispered.

"Right here, Daddy Hiram." I pushed the pot toward him, slid a tin mug his way. "Go ahead now."

His hands trembled as they poured, and very little of that coffee made it into the cup.

"Apologies," he said.

I ran to the kitchen for a rag, but when I got back, he was wiping up the spill with his hands.

"I'll clean it, Daddy Hiram. Pour you another one, too, how would that be?"

He watched the brew rise up in the mug. Then he bowed his face over it and give it a good loud sniff. Then another sniff and another.

"He right in the head?" Janey whispered.

"Hey, Daddy Hiram, maybe you'd like a smoke, huh? I rolled one just for you."

I lit the cig myself, with one of the Zippos from the store. He took a deep drag, then let out a single skull-rattling cough.

"Much appreciated," he said.

"We got mustard left," said Janey.

He give his head a shake.

"Sure is nice to see a man smokin' at the table," she said. "You ever been to California?"

Hiram said nothing.

"You seen an elephant?"

Nothing.

"What's wrong with your eye?"

"It's a little lazy," he said.

Janey looked at him for a space. Then she carried her plate to the slop bucket.

"These dishes ain't gonna wash themselves," she said.

Hiram stayed in his room the rest of the day. That night, when I knocked on his door, he was setting on the edge of the tick mattress. Looking out the window, I guess, though there weren't much of a view on that side. Just an old storage shed, falling over on itself, and the lean-to where Earle kept his Great Heap o' Treasure till the junkman come around every month.

"Evening," I said.

I laid out a pair of scissors, a Gem razor, and a can of Colgate's Rapid-Shave Cream on the root table. A mirror and a washbasin.

"The beard's gotta go, Hiram. It's enough to scare a pack of horses."

He rested the razor in his palm. "Can't remember the last time I shaved."

"I reckon it'll come right back." Though I had no idea if this was so. "After you're done, you should feel free to come on downstairs. I got some Aunt Sally rolled oats, right out of the box. Reckon you're mighty hungry by now."

His hand curled round the razor handle. Shook a little.

"Listen here," I said. "You ain't gonna try something dumb, are you?"

"No, ma'am."

"'Cause if that's what you got in mind, I'll take you to yonder railroad tracks. I got too much on my mind to be cleaning up some fool's blood."

"Yes, ma'am."

"Don't forget about the oats," I said, and shut the door.

If I'd been the kind, I'd have sent up a prayer that Hiram Watts not take that razor straight across his neck, but all I could do was what I done the last time. Set against his door, listening. Till I heard the squeak of scissors.

He never did come for dinner, but next morning, he showed up at breakfast again, and it was near as shocking. From out that ratty old beard, a face had clawed its way. Half-dark from the elements, half-white from where the whiskers had been. The biggest surprise was his mouth. Not the long full line I expected, but a small crimped thing, loath to unpinch.

"Morning," growled Hiram.

He tucked into the stewed tomatoes, never mind they'd gone cold. Drank 'em down with Nehi and then went after a pair of old dinner rolls that were so hard, even Earle had given up on 'em.

"I believe it's Sunday," said Hiram.

"All day," I said.

"I suppose you'll be going to church."

Earle and me, we shut up about it, but Janey said, "That's 'bout the funniest thing I ever heard."

"What's so funny?" muttered Hiram Watts.

Now, Mama got each of her babies baptized—just in case—but from there, she figured, we was on our own. *I got a business to run,* she'd say. *You think I got three hours to listen to some fool tell me I'm going to hell? Hell's gonna be a lot more fun than church.*

Which is when she'd start into her dance. A little Lindy, a little Charleston, dash of hoochie coochie. She did it only for us, but that didn't matter, 'cause the folk of Walnut Ridge had long ago cottoned on that the Hoyle clan was not to be found in the pews of Free Will Baptist nor of Happy Creek Methodist. There was some thought we might be Catholic or Jewish, but since nobody ever saw us observe a single holiday, they drew the conclusion we were not much at all.

One afternoon, Mama was picking up some turnips and potatoes at M&L Produce when she caught sight of two ladies talking in the next aisle. Now, she'd never laid eyes on these ladies in all her life, but as soon as she heard the words "flame-haired hussy," she knew who they was talking about. So she ducked behind the cucumber barrel and give a listen.

"Three children by *two* different fathers."

"More like *three* fathers."

"Weren't married to a one of 'em, probably."

"Spends her days in men's clothes. Flirts with truck drivers."

"Uses language'd make a miner blush."

"I've even seen her working on the Sabbath."

On and on it went, Mama grinning like a mule eating briars and just about ready to slip out the store when one of them ladies said, "Grace, as a Christian, you just gotta steer clear of them gas station pagans."

Now there weren't no help for it. Mama come tumbling out from behind the cucumber barrel, a-roaring with laughter. And when she caught a look at those two ladies' faces, she roared even louder. Still laughing an hour on, telling us about it. But later that night— after her and me'd settled into the hickory split chair by the stove—she said, "Know what? Gas Station Pagans is 'bout the best name they could've given us."

She was scooping her hand through my hair, even though I'd been telling her I was too old.

"We're gonna put that name on a banner," she said. "Fly it every Thanksgiving and Christmas and Fourth of July."

We never made us a banner—Mama weren't much for sewing— but the name stuck. Say we'd had a good week at the station. Well, then, Mama would set down the ledger and declare, "Sun shines bright on the Gas Station Pagans." Or when Janey and Earle took too long getting on their clothes of a winter morning, she'd holler, "Get it in gear, you Gas Station Pagans!"

I started using the name myself before long, then Earle. I knew it had settled in for good when I heard Janey telling one of her schoolmates, "We ain't allowed in church no more on account of we're pagans. The gas station kind." To my ear, Gas Station Pagan sounded just as good as Pentecostal or Baptist, and we could sleep in of a Sunday.

'Course ours was not a denomination recognized in Walnut Ridge, and that's why the idea of us heading to church—any church—struck Janey as a great amusement. But sitting there at the breakfast table with Hiram Watts, I didn't see the point in going into it.

"We ain't much for churchgoing," I said.

"Thank Christ," he said. "Ten hours of hellfire is more than I could stomach."

Janey and Earle stared at him without a word. Then Earle said, "There's another can of nectar syrup on the shelf."

Here's where I should say that Mama did for a time consider attending Calvary Episcopal. *'Cause they're done in an hour and a half, Melia, and they don't look all beaten about the head and neck. They look like they went for a nice stroll.*

Which is just how Chester Gallagher looked later that morning when he come walking back down Main Street in his one blue blazer. Like he'd met his maker, and it'd all gone down nice. But my eyes kept snagging on the two freakish stone children who sat in the Gallaghers' front yard.

"You reckon them kids is gonna come alive some night, Chester? Kill you in your sleep?"

"I've had worse clients," he said.

"Don't see Mina nowhere. She must not be feeling holy."

"Guess it's never occurred to you to call her Mrs. Gallagher. As it happens, she's got a headache."

"Mrs. Gallagher has got it rough."

"Let's go round back," he said.

It was the first time I'd been in his office. I was expecting lots of diplomas on the walls, but he had only the two—both from the University of Virginia—and you barely noticed them between the moth-eaten deer heads. I set on his cane-bottom chair and twisted the gooseneck lamp till it was pointing at the ceiling.

"This father of yours," said Chester. "Just dropped from the sky, did he?"

"Something like that."

"That's mighty convenient."

"The Lord is able."

"Melia . . ."

"It happens all the time, don't it? Families coming together again."

Chester leaned back on his chair casters. Used his hands to make a fort around his nose.

"I don't even know where to begin, Melia. This fella could have a criminal record. He could cut your throats while you're sleeping. I mean, what do you even *know* about him?"

"All I know is he can't pour hisself a damn cup of coffee."

"Then how're you going to pass him off as your father?"

"Oh." I flapped my hands at him. "He's just gotta stand and be counted."

Chester shook his head. "Sometimes you really are a child."

"Then show me what I'm missing here."

"How about this? When they come calling—and they *will*—they're going to need proof that he's who you say he is. At the very least, they're going to demand a birth certificate."

"I don't even know where my birth certificate is. Truly."

"It's in my safe."

I confess this caught me unawares.

"Your mama left it in my safekeeping, Melia. And you should know that, under the category of *Father*, it very clearly says *Un. Known*."

"Well, there you are."

"No, not there you are. If he's unknown, he could be anybody. Which means you'll need some *other* proof that this particular fellow—what's his name again?"

"Hiram Watts."

"That he's your real daddy. Absent said proof, you've got no legal case."

"And they got nothing to say he ain't."

Chester made a noose of his tie.

"Listen," I said, "we just gotta come up with some story is all. Tell 'em the birth certificate got lost."

"It won't *stay* lost. If they don't find it in my safe, they'll find one someplace else. All it takes is someone making inquiries."

"And who's gonna care enough?" Then I thought of Harley

Blevins. "Know what, Chester? I ain't got time for speculation. I got affairs to run. Talkin' *of*. We'd be most tickled if you'd come out to the house tonight. We're holding a wake for Mama."

His throat give a swallow. "I'll be there."

"Wake starts at six, you be there at five."

"Why so early?"

"We need clothes."

Chapter
SEVEN

That very afternoon, I sent Janey into town to spread word.

"You only gotta knock at the three houses," I said. "Mrs. Hicks. Mrs. Buckner. Minnie-Cora Harper."

"Why them?"

"'Cause they're the three noisiest jays this town has got. Give 'em ten minutes, and they'll spread it to the hills."

"What should I say, Melia?"

"*Our mama has passed on.*"

"Passed on."

"*Our family—*now be sure you say *family . . .*"

"Family."

"*. . . would be most pleased to have you at her wake.*"

"Wake."

"*Tonight at six. Don't be late.*"

"Tonight at six don't be late."

"Now, remember, they're gonna try and hug you and cry and slobber on you. You don't let 'em, you keep movin'.'"

"I should wear black," said Janey.

"Well, you ain't got but the one dress, and it's dove gray, or was."

But Janey's got a bear trap of a mind, so she kept looking for something black—rooting, rooting—till in the back of Service Bay B, behind a stack of secondhand Lee tires, she found an old tarp that was not so far off of black, owing to the things it had soaked up. She wrapped that thing round her, and when I let her off at the north end of First Street, she went forth like Queen Eleanor of Aquitaine, tarp trailing after. Wasn't a soul didn't turn and watch that girl pass by.

She still had it on when she come walking back.

"They was weeping in my hair, Melia. Nearly took the curl out."

By then I'd already swept the house as clean as I was able. Earle, he'd gone to his Great Heap o' Treasure and found some beaten-up brass candlesticks, and I dug up some candles from the root cellar, and we covered our dining table with a bedsheet of Mama's. It had roses of Sharon on it and no obvious stains.

"Don't it look nice," I said.

"Says you," said Earle.

Chester came at five prompt, carrying in his arms a white shirt and duck trousers and a green herringbone tweed vest. "Can't promise any of it will match," he said. "Or even fit. Now where is the gentleman in question?"

Well, if you're looking for a sign, here's one. *In that same instant,* Hiram Watts come through the front door. Looking like it was his own wake.

"My." Chester give a low whistle. "He's a skinny one. Good thing I brought a belt."

"Take him back to his room," I said. "And don't hurry dressing him."

"Meaning?"

"Meaning don't come back till I tell you."

"What am I supposed to do in the meantime?"

"Converse."

"That's going to cost you extra," he muttered. Next second, a professional smile pushed through his lips. "Well, hey now, Mr. Watts! What a pleasure meeting you. Name's Gallagher, put 'er there. . . ."

To my vast surprise, Mina Gallagher come walking through the door a minute later. Blinking in her black wool.

"Very sorry," she said, thrusting out a mess of hothouse lilies.

I didn't know what to do with them—there weren't a vase in the whole damned house—and things was deeply awkward till Mina said, "Maybe I could arrange them."

She grabbed an old iron pot off the kitchen rack and threw the lilies in it, then threw in some of the cowslips Janey had picked the day before. By the time she was done, it was like flower stew. She set it down in the middle of the dining table, then went and set in the rocker by the hearth.

"Are folks bringing pie?" asked Janey.

"Certainly," I said.

But the first to show up was Maggie McGuilkin, and all she brought was her crucifix. It pulsed in her hand like a vole's heart. Lizbeth Shafer held her crucifix straight out in front of her,

Gwendolyn Davenport let hers dangle to her waist from a chain of dried berries. Frances Bean forgot her crucifix, so she said "Lord have mercy" three times under her breath.

They brought fear in their hearts, these Christian ladies. Probably expecting to find Old Scratch himself dozing by the fireplace, his cloven hoof a-twitching. Failing to find said devil, they grew no easier in mind. Cast trembling looks, mouthed questions at one another. Finally Mrs. Buckner, who was the boldest of 'em, said, "Melia, honey, where is she?"

"Who?"

"Your mama. Is she . . . I mean . . ." She cut her chin toward Mama's bedroom.

"Hell, no," I said. "She's in the ground."

Well, you'll learn this. If you're gonna throw a wake, make sure you got a body on the premises. Someone they can sit and stare at and weep over and shoo the flies away from and say, "My, don't she look natural?" 'Cause if you don't give 'em a body, they wander round your drafty old shotgun shack, telling you how homey it is and saying things like "She's gone to her reward" and "She's in His loving care" and not believing a word of it and wondering why no one brought pie.

After a time, I went to Mama's room and closed the curtain after me and laid on her mattress.

"Melia?" Janey was peering round the curtain. "Mrs. Goolsby brought applesauce cake."

The cake brought with it Pastor Goolsby.

"Lord," he said, standing in our doorway. "Whither thou goest I shall go."

He didn't pull out no crucifix, but I could see those smoky eyes of his hunting for a Bible or a hymnal or one of those old magazine cutouts of Jesus with the beauty-parlor hair.

"Now, see here, Melia. Between you and me and the Lord, was your mama properly funeralized?"

"'Course she was."

"I mean with a man of God in attendance."

"God was there, Preacher."

I reckon I didn't put him at peace, 'cause, before another minute was out, he'd laid hands on Janey's head and attempted to do the same with Earle, who suggested he reconsider.

Minnie-Cora's current beau brought a mandolin, and now that folks were realizing no hymns was in the offing, Minnie-Cora told him to play "Barbara Allen," and she sang along in her quavery voice. Jesus, but that song has a lot of verses. I never knew. The rose was just growing up from Sweet William's grave when the door to the house opened and in walked Dudley Blevins, wearing knickers darned at the knees.

"Here," he said, pushing some bearded irises at me.

"Throw 'em in the pot," I said.

But Mina Gallagher—like a servant answering a bell only she could hear—rose from her rocker and snatched those irises before he could take another step.

"Terrible thing," said Dudley.

"Much obliged."

"I mean I'm sorry."

"Well, okay, then."

We stood there awhile, listening to Minnie-Cora sing "Mid the Green Fields of Virginny."

"Ain't never seen you in a dress before," said Dudley.

"Why in hell would you?"

Even to my ear, that sounded harsh. So I said, "Glad you don't got to wear that stupid uniform."

"You and me both," he said.

"Where's your uncle got to?"

"He's coming."

"Planning a big entrance, is he?"

"Something like that."

Sure enough, Minnie-Cora had just finished off "Black Jack Davis" when the door breathed open and Harley Blevins's silver hair flashed out of the night. Was the only part of him that could've flashed. He was wearing a black serge coat and pants. Black leather gloves. He took off his black hat and bowed his head, then swung his way right into the room. Went to each Walnut Ridge lady in turn and squeezed her one hand between his two. He knew their husbands' names, their kids' names, the names of their dogs and mules, and if there'd been a baby, he'd have kissed it.

"Now who made this here applesauce cake? 'Cause I do not believe I have tasted such opulence in my life. Mrs. Goolsby, this your doing? That's what comes of being married to a man of God. No, I ain't jesting. But don't you go telling my wife what I said, 'cause bless her, she does consider herself a baker, but this here cake. Say now, Preacher Goolsby, I don't like to step on a man's toes, but I was wondering if I might offer a brief word on behalf of the departed."

"Go right ahead, Brother Harley."

"Why, thank you." He placed his hat against his chest. "Brothers and sisters. I mean to tell you. The late Brenda Hoyle—why, she was something else."

"Amen," whispered Janey.

"First time I ever met her, I said, 'How's a little bitty thing like you gonna run this service station all by yourself?' And she said, 'With my little bitty hands, that's how.' Yes, sir, she had gumption. How many times did I query myself why such a radiant thing should be spending down her days in hardship and toil? Smearing herself with dirt and lubricant when she could be casting her beauteous face upon some deserving husband?

"Well, she went her own way, God bless her. Cut her own switchbacks up the mountainside of life. And while she and I may have had our disagreements about the direction of the petroleum industry and the vis-à-vis relationships of Standard Oil and the independent proprietor, never once did our disagreements hamper my deep esteem for her. Nor did I waste a second wishing her anything but the best in her pursuits.

"And now, my dear friends, the Lord has seen fit to bring our sister Brenda home. And I hereby call unto Him—that's right, Sister Doris, let's us hold *hands* and pray that our Gracious Creator will take pity on these here lambs that Brenda done left behind. Lord, shine Your loving eye upon Melia and Earle and Janey. Let them not be tossed to the pit of lions after all the grievous suffering that has been laid upon them, and grant that, in these lean times, they may find the family and home they got comin' to 'em. Grant that when they look back upon this

64

benighted place, with its sign near ready to come off and its substandard pumps, they may feel no bitterness nor gnashing of teeth. Only joy in the light of your eternal goodness. In Jesus's name, amen."

"Amen," whispered Janey.

For the first time that night, the women of Walnut Ridge were beaming.

And who was I to ply my tongue against that of Harley Blevins? I'm the sort that'd sooner die than speak in public, but through a crack in the front door, I saw Chester's face. And then his thumb, pointing up. So I swallowed once, twice, and I climbed on the dining table and cleared my throat loud as I could.

"Evening, folks. . . ."

But they kept buzzing amongst themselves.

"Evening!"

A slow swivel of heads my way.

"I was just—well, first of all, hey there. Y'all know who I am, so—so I wanted to—to thank Mr. Blevins there for his kind words. They was right kind. I also wanted—I wanted y'all to know that God is great."

"'Course He is," said Preacher Goolsby.

"I repeat, God is great. 'Cause He has answered our prayers."

Harley Blevins's eyes widened a grain.

"Yes, indeed," I said. "The Lord has seen fit to bless us with a miracle."

I waited.

"A miracle!" I said louder.

Through the door shuffled Hiram Watts. If he'd've been

Herbert Hoover, he could not have terrified those Walnut Ridge women more. They fell back, clutching each other.

As for Hiram, he looked nearly as feared. I took him by the sleeve, led him to the center of the gathering.

"Y'all, I want you to meet Mr. Hiram Watts. Our daddy."

Had I to do it again, I'd have made sure his clothes fit. The stuff Chester brought was too big in some places, too small in others. He looked like he was being stretched and shrunk right before our eyes.

"Pleased to meet you," he whispered.

A deep silence fell across the room. Then, from out the quiet, came the tinkling voice of Frances Bean.

"Likewise."

(I will always think kindly on Frances Bean.)

"Reckon you can imagine how joyous it is to be reunited," I said. "A family once more, under the same roof. Carrying on Mama's wishes and dreams."

More quiet.

"What I mean is I hope you'll find it in your hearts to be glad for us."

"'Course we are," said Mrs. McGuilkin, rallying.

"It's a little sudden is all," said Mrs. Davenport. "We didn't know nothin' about no daddy."

"He's been on the road a lot," said Janey. "And he's been on trains."

"Lordy," said Harley Blevins. "Let me be the first to shake this feller's hand. Give Uncle Harley a shake, will you? There you go, that's the—oh, Jesus, I didn't hurt your hand, did I? Folks tell me

I got a strong grip. Hiram, you an outlander? From the three or four words I heard so far, I figured you for an outlander."

"His people are from Cumberland," I said. "Just like Mama's."

"He don't sound like he's from Cumberland. He sounds like he's from, I don't know, Ohio. Maine. Maybe nowhere. Where you *from*, Mr. Watts? You can hear me in there, can't you?"

Hiram nodded.

"We was just wondering where you're from."

"All over," said Hiram.

"That so? Why, that's a very general place to be from. You fixin' to stick around awhile?"

Hiram said nothing.

"I mean, it's awful fortuitous," said Harley Blevins. "You floating in here like this."

"It's the Lord's doing," I said.

"It's *some* doing."

Bit by bit, he peeled his eyes off Hiram. "Know what, Melia? Me and you need to talk."

The house was still swarming with folk, so Harley Blevins pointed his elbow toward the door. Opened it easy and slow and motioned me outside.

I caught a glance of Dudley on the other side of the coffee urn. His mouth swung open a little, but the door was already closing after us.

Lord, it was chilly. And not 'cause of the weather but on account of I was wearing a dress for the first time in I don't know how long.

"Melia," he said. The chaw in his mouth kept pushing against his cheek, like a hornet fighting to get out. "We known each other a good long while, ain't we?"

"Couple years."

"That's a lifetime in business, darlin'. Point I'm making is, we can be straight up."

"Sure thing."

"Now, this daddy of yours. He didn't land here by no accident, did he?"

"There I must differ, Mr. Blevins. It was every bit an accident."

The weirdest smile took hold of his mouth. "I can't hardly believe it," he said. "You're holding on to this shit heap."

"It's what she would've wanted."

"What do *you* want, Melia?"

Standing there in what passed for a front yard, I could see pretty much the store, the gas pumps, the air pump, the service bays. That damned sign, creaking with every breeze. It all looked like the world's saddest carnival.

"I don't recall my wants having much to do with anything," I said.

"Well, there ain't nothing keeping you here now. I mean, assuming we could arrange for your comfort and all, why, you and yours could be on your way tomorrow."

"We could," I said. "But we won't."

"And why's that?" he said.

"'Cause I think Brenda's Oasis should stay as is."

He smiled.

"'Course you do. Say now, how 'bout I keep the name? In memoriam, like."

I shook my head, turned away.

"Ain't just the name, Mr. Blevins. Them truckers come down the hills every morning, and they're looking for a *place*. Not just any place, neither, but somewhere they can shake out their legs and, I don't know, whatever they got coiled inside. Oh, I know this ain't a *real* oasis—like they got in the Sahara—believe me, I know *all* the things it ain't. But for them fellers, for a few minutes every other morning, it's real. Kinda. And that's something. At least it ain't nothing. With all respect, Mr. Blevins, if you get your hands on this here station, it'll die."

"Ain't no business ever died on me."

"Oh," I said, "it'll make you some money, but it'll be good as dead."

I stared off to the road, where a couple beards of fog had crept down from the mountains.

"Seems to me," I said, "if we let you take this here station from us, the way you done all those other stations, from Winchester to Strasburg to Marshall, then the taking'll never stop. We'll get something taken the next day and the day after and the rest of our natural days 'cause once you get in the habit of rolling over, there's always someone to roll you. And that's another reason to hold on. And maybe the best."

Harley Blevins said nothing for a long while. Then he spit out a line of tobacco juice, and he turned on me, and everything else burned away.

"You really think you got the *sand*, girl? To take me on?"

If you'd've put a gun to my head just then, I suppose there's a chance I'd have said no. But what I said was . . .

"I mean to try."

He smiled. He nodded.

"Then it's been nice knowing you," he said.

I stumbled back inside. The room seemed crazy bright all of a sudden. I stood for a bit, getting my balance. Then I climbed back onto the dining table.

By now, folks was getting merry—Minnie-Cora's beau had brought along a banjo, too, and some old gal I'd never seen was cutting the pigeon wing—so I had to clap my hands three times.

"Listen now," I said. "Being as Mama's buried and all, we won't need folks to watch all night, so—so don't stay on our account is all I'm sayin'. Oh, but I nearly forgot to tell y'all! Brenda's Oasis is still open for business. Six days a week. And will remain so for *all* your petroleum and general-store needs."

The front door opened. Harley Blevins edged back in.

"And guess what?" I said. "In honor of our mama, we're gonna be cutting our price to nine cents a gallon. Starting tomorrow. Least we can do for the working man, ain't that right? *So come on by, why don't you!*"

When next I looked, Harley Blevins was leaning his head against the door. Eyes all the way shut, like he'd gone to sleep.

Chapter
EIGHT

Word travels fast in the Blue Ridge. If you need proof, consider this. The morning after the wake, every trucker that come down from the hills already knew about Mama.

Not that they said a word on the subject or breathed her name. Mostly they just brung me stuff.

"Hey now, Melia, here's a piece of quartz. From down by Staunton."

"Found this here oilskin hat at the Wheeling bus depot. Thought it might fit."

"My wife, she wanted you to have this handkerchief. She made it herself. Got a blue border, see?"

Joe Bob brought an old pinochle deck. Glenmont brought canned cabbage. Dutch give me a sample bottle of Gilbey's Spey Royal, and Trevor, he had a back issue of *Photoplay* with Jean Harlow on the cover, looking half-asleep.

Warner didn't bring a damn thing, he just barreled in like always, shouting, "Fix the goddamned radiator!"

Didn't take me long to figure out the coolant was leaking, so I went and fetched some pepper—it was a trick Mama taught me—and sprinkled it in, and by the time I slammed down the hood, Warner was standing there with his third cup of Sanka, stirring it with his pointer finger.

"Your mama was plenty all right," he said.

He downed his coffee in one gulp. Crumpled the paper cup in his mitt, tossed it into the cab of his rig.

"You run into any trouble," he said.

Then he was off.

I can guess what you're thinking. Couldn't just a one of 'em have said "Sorry to hear"? But if you was to twist my arm, I wouldn't trade that quartz or that hankie—or Elmer's brand-new toothbrush or Merle's cracked compass—for a week's worth of sorrys.

I was sorry to see 'em drive off, though. The midday lull was gray, for all that the sun was needle-bright. I set at the store counter, flipping through the *Photoplay*, but all I could think was, *How the hell we gonna get by charging nine cents a gallon?*

That missing penny kept multiplying in my head. Twelve cents less every truck. Fifteen dollars less every day. A hundred dollars less each passing week. Coins and dollars flying out the door, and me and Earle and Janey down to our last can of stewed tomatoes, and a crazy ol' ghost of a man rattling over our heads.

A rattling in the air around me, too. Just loud enough to crawl in my brain. I looked up and found a redbird pecking away at the store window.

No, pecking don't cover it. That bird was *throwing* himself at the danged glass—beak and claw and body—like he was fixing to bust right through. At first I took it personal, thinking he was picking a scrap with me, but when I crossed to the far side of the store, he just kept hammering at the one square of glass.

That's when it hit me. Fool bird was attacking his own reflection.

Not just once, I'm telling you—a dozen times, three dozen times. *Take that, you son of a bitch!*

Don't recall how long he stayed that first time, but he was back next day, a hair past noon, madder than ever. The day after, too. *Take that!* In my head, I began sorta waiting for him—not exactly pining—just curious to know what was on his mind.

"Why you hating on this other bird so much?" I'd say. "He ain't done nothing. He's got just as good a right to be there as you do."

He never listened.

On Saturdays, Earle and Janey minded the store, and when I asked 'em if some redbird had come a-peckin', they looked at me like I was touched. Sundays we was closed, and then come Monday, and if I'd been a betting type, I'd have put money on that bird being dead, but seven minutes after noon, he was back, slamming his fool self against the glass.

"He's got some temper on him," said Hiram Watts.

He'd gone and crept down the stairs without a sound.

"It's kinda crazy," I said. "He thinks he's fighting some other bird. I can't seem to explain his mistake to him."

Hiram frowned. "Have you got something we could stick on the window?"

The only thing I could find was a decal for Quaker State Oil. I put it on my side of the glass, right where the bird was pecking, and he flew straight off. Didn't see him for the rest of the afternoon. But sure enough, he was back the next day, pecking at a new stretch of window.

"I think that's about the most cussed bird I've ever seen," said Hiram.

In those days, it was strange to see Hiram anywhere but his room. Oh, he'd come down every so often for a snack or a smoke or to empty out his pot, then steal back upstairs. I asked him once or twice if he wanted a magazine or paper, but he shook his head. To this day, I'm not sure what he was doing up there, hour upon blessed hour, but with each passing day, he started coming down a little more. Mostly to check on that damn redbird.

It was a late Friday afternoon—in May, I believe, 'cause I have a memory of dogwoods—I looked up from filling a Studebaker to see Hiram over by the tulip-tree swing. You'll learn this. If there's one thing that Brenda's Oasis has got plenty of, it's tire swings. Hanging from every oak, poplar, and butternut. But Janey, she'd only ever swing on the tulip tree. Maybe it give her a view of the hills.

So there she was, swinging, and there was Hiram just back of her. Close enough to give her a push if he'd had a mind to, only his arms never left his sides.

My point is that's where they was, the both of them, when the police car drove up. Slow and tickly, like a caterpillar. In the front seat, Sheriff Claude Motherwell, with his white-blond hair and his pimple-scarred face.

"You need a new muffler," I told him.

"That ain't why I'm here."

I waved Janey over, leaned into her ear.

"Go to the phone in the store and give Chester a call. Can you do that?"

"What's his number?"

"Melody one-oh-five-one."

"What'm I supposed to say?"

"Tell him I need him here lickety-split."

She was disappearing round the corner when I said, "Hey, Sheriff, let me wash up a little."

I went to the well, poured some cold water over my hands, and then pressed my hands against my face. After a minute or so, I heard a light tap from the sheriff's car horn.

"Guessing this ain't no social call," I said.

"No, it ain't."

"Then what you got to say?"

"I've received word that a fraud is being perpetrated in these here precincts."

"And who told you that? Does it start with a Harley? End with a Blevins?"

"Now, Melia. If there's a crime being committed, I'm obliged to look into it."

"You see any crimes going on?"

"That ain't for me to decide."

"Who, then?"

He reached over, give a rap on the car window. The rear door opened with a groan, and out climbed a woman I never seen before. Holding a sheaf of papers that didn't want to be held.

"This is Miss Wand from the Warren County Juvenile Court."
Sure enough. A spinster.

Though this one was younger than I was expecting and had the kind of hair you couldn't put in a bun if you tried. She reached behind her ear for a pencil, give the point a quick gnaw, and said, "Are you Amelia Hoyle?"

"Yes, ma'am."

"Is that . . ." She squinted at the tulip tree. "Is that Mr. Watts?"

"Yes."

"Would you mind calling him over, please?"

He come at us like he was on stilts.

"Good afternoon," said Miss Wand. "Is your name Hiram Watts?"

"Yes, ma'am."

"Do you hereby swear that you are the father of Amelia Hoyle?"

Hiram's lips give a little swell.

"I'm wondering if you heard me, Mr. Watts. I need to know if you are this girl's father."

His steady eye cut toward the ground. The wobbly one followed.

"Sure," he said.

"He don't sound persuaded," said the sheriff.

"That's just his way," I said. "Ain't that your way, Daddy?"

"Suppose it is," said Hiram.

"Guess that answers y'all's question," I said. "Don't want to take up any more of—"

"In point of *fact*"—Miss Wand give her ear a fierce tug—"the Virginia code—Section 3, Clause 23—stipulates that an individual's word may not be considered dispositive evidence of paternity."

"Which means?"

76

"We can't take Mr. Watts's word on whether or not he's your father. Nor can we take yours, Miss Hoyle. We require some kind of documentation."

"That right?"

"A birth certificate would be a good starting point."

"Mine's lost."

"Lost how?"

"In a fire."

"Then you mean it was destroyed, not lost."

"How 'bout we just call it gone?"

"We'll need to find a duplicate."

"We sure will. I will get right on that."

The social worker drove her pencil into the thicket of her hair. "Miss Hoyle, can you tell me where you were born?"

"West Virginia."

"Which county?"

"Garrett."

"Home birth or hospital?"

"Hell if I know."

"Melia," said the sheriff, "you ain't helping yourself none."

"Maybe you can tell me where *you* was born."

"In my granddaddy's barn, that's where."

"As it happens," said Miss Wand, "I'm personally acquainted with the Garrett County clerk. I'll be glad to contact him myself."

You do that, I was about to say, only another car was easing itself behind the sheriff's. A Buick sedan with dual taillights. From the driver's seat jumped Chester, in a seersucker suit, tightening his bow tie.

"Sheriff," he said, "you didn't invite me to your party."

The sheriff hocked a loogie at the ground. "It ain't like we gone and handcuffed her, Chester."

"You're asking questions of her and her kinfolk, and I believe her lawyer should be on hand for that."

"We got wind that Melia made herself up a daddy," said the sheriff.

"Now why on Earth would she do that?" asked Chester.

"So as not to face consequences."

"And what would those consequences be?"

"Absent a surviving parent," said Miss Wand, "Amelia and her brother and sister would become wards of the state. In that event, the Warren County Juvenile Court would be legally required to find them a suitable home."

"*One* home? For all three?"

"We work with what's available."

"I fail to see why you're in such a rush to move these children. After what they've been through."

"Mister—I'm sorry . . ."

"Gallagher."

". . . *Gallagher*, we have *three* minors who meet the legal definition of orphans. In such cases, the county is obliged to act in loco parentis."

"You haven't even established that they're orphans."

"They are unless I can verify Mr. Watts's paternity claims."

Chester leaned back against the grille of his Buick. "So what you're saying is, you need a birth certificate."

"Indeed we do. Now, tomorrow, I intend to phone the clerk's office in Garrett County."

"Oh, I'd hate you to go to all that trouble."

"No trouble at all."

"What I mean is, there doesn't seem to be much point when I already have the document in question."

Miss Wand blinked. "We were told it had been lost."

"Oh, well, Melia wasn't to know. Her mother left it in my care."

He reached into his seersucker coat.

"Janey," I said, "why don't you go help Earle with the wood chopping?"

"I ain't going nowhere."

"You sure as hell are, missy."

Then Hiram spoke. Which was a wonder 'cause I'd gone and forgotten he was even there.

"She's all right where she is."

I swung my eyes toward the road. Told myself to watch the Chevy delivery truck that was crawling up the hill to Mr. Tompkin's horse farm.

"Well, I'll be," said Sheriff Motherwell.

My birth certificate was sitting in his hands. There, under the heading of *FATHER*, sat the name . . .

HIRAM WATTS

"I think you'll see everything's in order," Chester said. "Official Maryland seal. I can certainly see about getting copies made."

"That won't be necessary," said Miss Wand.

She got in the car without another word. The sheriff stood there a spell. Then he climbed in and drove away.

Nobody let out a cheer. Hiram went inside. Janey got back on her swing. Chester, he went and collapsed in one of the Adirondack chairs in front of the store.

"You got a light?" he asked.

He sucked on a Chesterfield for a good five minutes.

"Lester Mashburn," he said.

"Who's that?"

"Unfortunate soul with a troubled childhood and what they call a checkered history."

"What's he got to do with anything?"

"Last January, I helped him beat a class-one burglary charge. He didn't have any cash to pay me with—at least none he could lay hands on—but he was grateful all the same. Turns out, he has a particular gift for forgery."

"Good for Lester Mashburn."

I set in the chair next to Chester. We watched the sun drop over Spring Mountain. Gold, then red, then purple.

"I could lose my license," said Chester.

"Naw. The devil will just make you run one more lap round Fire Lake."

"That was your mama's line," he said.

"So it was."

"Thing is," he said, "they can still locate the original birth certificate. And when they do, they'll be back. I'd guess we've bought ourselves maybe a week or two of grace."

"Well, now," I said, dropping my head against the chair. "That's more than I'm used to."

Chapter
NINE

That Saturday, a real gully washer swept in from the west. Lightning zippering cross the sky and thunder gunning like a race car and rain hammering all night long on the tin roof. It was the kind of noise that made any other noise impossible. Earle, he wanted to listen to *Death Valley Days*, but all we could find on the radio was some Charlottesville preacher going on about 2 Corinthians, so we turned off the set and played pinochle. Then I put Earle and Janey to bed. I told 'em the "Tale of the Lover Who Feigned Himself a Thief," and they went right off, and I had a mind to clean dishes, but I went off, too.

The rain pushed through sometime in the night, but it give the air a good scrubbing. The next morning, I put on a sweater and set on the front porch with a mug of coffee, watching the fog yawn off the mountains. It's a good time of year in Walnut Ridge. Forsythia blooming by the fence. Pink azaleas budding out of the forests.

Robins and bluebirds. I set watching a spell. Then, out of habit, I give the station a once-over.

Something was wrong.

Only I didn't know what. I checked the pumps first, then the service bays. The truck. Nothing. Then my eyes, with nothing else to do, drifted skyward.

The sign.

The sign was gone. From the iron scroll atop the signpost dangled a length of chain . . . and nothing more.

In a daze, I walked over to the patch of ground just beneath where the sign had been. I stared down at a heap of broken granite.

From somewhere in the mess, a few letters peeped through. *B . . . A . . . O . . .* all that was left of BRENDA'S OASIS.

I went down on both knees. Scooped my hand through the clumps of stone.

"A little early to be praying, isn't it?"

I whipped my head round. Hiram Watts had come up behind me. Wearing a pair of long johns, two sizes too large, and sucking hard on a Lucky. He started to say something, but then he got a load of my face.

"What is it?" he said.

Next second, he was standing alongside me, looking at what was left of our sign. "Jesus," he whispered.

I stood up, angled my face toward the road. "Reckon that's what we get," I said, "making a sign out of a tombstone."

It come flying back then. The day we first loaded that granite slab in the truck. Mama grinning as she give it a coat of plaster and painted on the letters, slow and steady.

Gotta spell it right, she'd said. *'Cause this ain't never coming down.*

Just one more thing she was wrong about.

Hiram bent down, grabbed the length of chain that had once held the sign in place. "Holy cow," he said, with a soft whistle. "It's cut clean through."

And now it was someone else's words that come swirling up. *Next big wind, that sign of yours gonna come right down. . . .*

"Harley Blevins," I said.

Hiram's face creased. "That fellow from the wake? With the black clothes and the silver hair?"

"Same one."

His eyes ran up the signpost, all the way to the top. "Scampered up there all by himself, did he?"

"He don't do nothing by hisself."

I confess I thought of Dudley in that moment. In those stupid knickers, holding his irises like they was rattlers.

"What's this Blevins fellow got against you?" said Hiram.

"It ain't me, it's Brenda's Oasis." I took a step back. "Can you believe it? This dump? He wants it more 'n mother's milk."

"Why?"

I watched a logger truck come down the hill, gears gargling.

"He's got all the rest," I said. "Every Standard Oil station from Winchester to Strasburg to Marshall. If he gets Brenda's Oasis, he gets the last one."

"Little kingdom of petroleum."

"And him the king. Emperor, too."

Hiram flicked the end off his cig butt. "And he doesn't mind knocking down a sign or two to get it."

"Oh, this here's what you call a warning shot. Not the first one, neither. Who you think brought the sheriff here the other day?"

"That's a tough thing to prove."

"I don't need to. Least of all to you."

Hiram dropped the cig on the ground, mashed it under his boot. "What did *I* go and do?"

"Nothing. That's what you went and done. When that sign was being cut down last night, where were *you?*"

"In bed. Just like you."

"And how much closer was your bed? Hell of a lot nearer than mine. If anybody could've heard what was going on, it'd have been you."

"Through all that rain and thunder, I suppose."

"You set up there in that damn room. Day in, day out. Staring out the window or up at the ceiling or whatever the hell you do. You never lift a finger to help. We could be starving to death for all you care." I snatched the dead butt from the ground. "You don't even pick up after your damn self!"

He stared at the butt, then looked away. "All you ever asked me to do was to *be* here, Melia. Stand and be counted. That was the deal."

"Yeah, well, I might just give that deal a look-over. 'Cause you keep coming out ahead."

"I'm risking jail—isn't that enough?"

"Bet you've risked worse. Bet you've done worse."

I could see the grooves carving in around his eyes.

"Guess you'll never know," he said.

"Guess not."

84

"Guess I won't be sticking around long enough for you to know."

"Fine by me."

He started to walk away, then turned back. "You know what? The next time you hire someone to be your father, don't expect an actual father. You get what you pay for."

"Yeah, well, my real daddy would be a damned sight more use than you are."

"Then where is he?"

And now it was me walking.

"Melia," I heard him say.

• • •

I think I told you, I don't make a habit of crying. So when I get in a rage, I walk. Mama used to call it Melia's stomp, and I suspect I *was* stomping, just a little bit, as I crossed Sheep Creek Road and turned up Mountain Vale Lane. I'd walked near half a mile before I knew where I was going.

The grave looked pretty much like we'd left it. Janey's wild-flowers had long since blown away, but the cross Earle had whittled, that was still there, poking out on a slant. I tried to straighten it, but it wouldn't.

"Hey," I said.

That's as far as I got.

It's a thing no fool has ever been able to explain to me. What do you say when you're standing over somebody's grave? Whatever's in the ground is all bones and rot, and if it's the person's soul you're after, well, for all you know, it could've flown clear to the other side of the world. Nothing to stop it. So I didn't say another word to

Mama, because I couldn't be hundred percent certain anybody was listening.

She come back all the same. The end days, mostly. Those minutes—hours, sometimes—when she could pry herself clear from the pain. Her eyes'd get buttery, and she'd look around like she was seeing everything for the first time. It was then I could come and sit with her. Even touch her.

'Course her skin was like paper, you could tear it just by looking, and if you come near a bone, you'd be sorry, but her hair never caused her no pain, so I just combed it. Over and over. Waiting for her to say whatever come to mind.

"Melia, we should start selling road maps."

"Melia, we should get us a windmill."

"Uniforms, Melia! With our names all stitched over the pockets."

It was kind of like her Christmas list, I guess. Santa, get me a new furnace. Plate-glass windows. Another underground tank. She'd talk awhile, then fall asleep for a stretch, then wake up and start in again.

It's funny, when she was healthy, Mama was always so by-God happy with her lot. You could shake her all day long, and not a single beef would fall out. So it threw me, I confess, hearing how much *wishing* she had hoarded up in that heart of hers. Wish upon wish. Curtains in the parlor. A gramophone. Encyclopedias. A pianola!

Late into the evening, though, she'd get scary quiet, like a pot that's about to fall from a shelf. I think those were the times it come home. There wouldn't be no pianola nor windmill. No Santa. Not for her. That's when she'd turn and find me. Yes, *find* me, even though I'd been in that room for hours, and her face'd kind of fall open, and she'd say, in a high, thin mountain voice, "My baby girl."

Jesus, I hated that.

Baby girls don't hold a house together. They don't keep a business running while the gal who *bought* the goddamned place is busy dying. Ain't nothing baby about that. I'd get so mad, I'd have to leave the room. Covering my ears because I didn't want to hear her calling after me.

Maybe she wasn't calling.

I don't know how long I stood by her grave that Sunday. At some point, I stopped thinking and started in to listening. There was a robin in a crab-apple tree, some field mice in the sagebrush.

By the time I got back to the station, the sun was high in the sky. I could see Janey on the front porch, stepping through an old iron hoop. For the millionth time that day, probably. Stepping through, lifting it back over her head, starting over.

"You missed all the hubbub," she said.

"Tell me about it."

"Daddy Hiram took the truck."

"Say again?"

"He took the truck."

I did a quick pivot. Scanned the house, the road, the station, everything in between.

"You having me on?" I said.

"No, ma'am."

My heart shrunk to the size of a taw.

"Why in *hell* didn't you come find me?" I shouted.

"I didn't know where you was."

A spike of shame.

"Listen to me, Janey. Listen real careful, okay? Did Hiram say where he was going?"

"Don't know as he did."

"Well . . . God al*mighty*, when did he leave?"

"Hour ago. Maybe two."

In a daze, I ran the mileage. Two hours at forty an hour. Eighty miles. If he was heading north, that'd take him nearly to the state line.

"Don't know why you're carrying on," said Janey. "He's our daddy."

"I don't care who he is! He can't just go running off with our truck like that. Goddamn! I'm gonna . . ."

Call the police, but the thought struck itself down. *Call 'em and what, Melia? Ask 'em to arrest your own father? For taking a truck that, by rights, belongs to him?*

"Now, don't go making a stink," said Janey. "You'll just get Earle in trouble."

I looked at her. "How'd Earle get into this?"

"Well, who do you think was driving?"

"Earle?"

"Why, sure," said Janey. "Daddy Hiram said he don't know the local byways too good, and Earle, he's tall enough now to see over the wheel."

"He ain't never drove before."

"That ain't so. He said he drove with you."

"Once or twice! When there was no one else on the road!"

88

"Well, it must've took 'cause Earle climbed in there like a champ. Never looked back. They went yonder."

I followed her finger down the road to where it curved east.

"Oh, dear God," I said. "Lord help us all."

"They said they'd be back 'fore nightfall," said Janey.

You'll learn this about me. I ain't no good at waiting. First thing I did was go to Hiram's room. I found his comb, his razor, his Colgate's Rapid-Shave Cream. Half a pack of Luckys. A bar of Octagon soap. A mangled-up back issue of *Time*.

He wouldn't have left these behind, would he? Not if he was fixing to leave for good. He would've at least taken his cigs?

Question on question, and behind 'em, the question Chester had posed.

What do you even know about this fella?

So that afternoon was about the longest I've passed on this bitter Earth. Couldn't sit, couldn't move. Couldn't stand to be talked to, neither, as Janey learned to her regret. Best I could do was break open a can of succotash round about seven and heat it up on the stove and then leave a plate of it by the mulberry bush where she was hiding. I was too stirred up to have a bite myself.

The night come down slow, and I was giving some thought to Emmett Tolliver's medicine.

Emmett had gifted us a jug of it two years before—when Prohibition was still on—'cause he didn't have cash for a new carburetor. Mama had a way of letting folks pay how they could, so when Emmett brought over the medicine, she took one look and bust out laughing. She'd given up hooch a while back, and me, I took one sniff and nearly lost my supper. "It's safe with us," Mama said, laughing. She put it in the root cellar, and there it had stayed, mostly, but if there was ever a time I was tempted to sample, it was that night, waiting on Hiram and Earle.

A little past nine, I heard a swell of gravel . . . the little squeal song our Ford makes shifting into second. Next thing, I was out the door running, with Janey following after.

The truck was just pulling up in front of the house. I didn't even wait for the engine to shut off, I drug Earle right out of the cab and sent him sprawling on the gravel. Give him a kick for good measure.

"What the hell?" he said.

"Don't you *never* do that again!"

"Do what?"

"Drive off in that truck without telling me is what."

"You wasn't here to tell."

"I don't give a shit!"

Earle picked himself off the gravel. "We was on a mission, Melia."

"What kind of fool talk is that?"

Like an answer to my query, Hiram Watts climbed out the passenger's side.

"Reckon you're mighty pleased with yourself," I said.

"Partly," he allowed.

"Reckon you thought it was a good idea putting a child behind the wheel of a pickup."

"He was the nearest to hand."

"And it never crossed your mind he might kill hisself?"

"It's Sunday. Roads were empty."

"Plus I'm a natural," said Earle. "Ask Daddy Hiram."

"It's true, the boy's a prodigy."

Now, I've never seen a rhinoceros in real life, but I imagine he'd charge just the way I charged Hiram Watts in that moment. Snorting. Head lowered.

"Know what?" I said. "It was one thing having you up in that room all day doing nothing. That was just irksome. But now you've gone and *done* something, and it's worse. It's the most—the most stupid goddamned . . ."

Problem was I didn't have a word in mind, so I flailed.

"*Irresponsible!*"

Earle laughed first. Then Janey.

"I swear I'm gonna smack you both," I said.

"It's because you sound like a mama," said Hiram.

"Not *our* mama," said Earle. "But somebody's."

"Excuse me, am I the only one here—on this whole goddamned planet—who cottons to how crazy this was? You could've got pulled over or thrown in jail. You could've got driven off the road and left to die."

"We're here," said Hiram.

"Well, congratulations. Congratulations on both of you."

"Geez," said Earle. "Don't you even want to see it?"

"See what?"

Hiram had already walked round to the back of the truck, and he was pulling down the flatbed gate.

"Earle," he said. "Keep those headlights on."

With a wheeze, Hiram hoisted up a burlap bag. Set it in front of the truck, then pulled the burlap down.

The first thing I saw was a desert.

Maybe the finest desert I'd ever seen. The sand the color of a deer's flank, and in the center of the sand a blue pond, and from this pond a camel, drinking. Above the camel was a blue sky, a different blue from the pond. In this sky was a string of clouds, and the clouds spelled . . .

BRENDA'S OASIS

I knelt down. Ran my finger through the sand, waiting for some of it to lift off.

"It's made of porcelain enamel," said Hiram. "Lasts forever. Easy to clean."

"They told us you wash it like a car," said Earle. "Hose it down, and it's brand-new. I'll clean it, Melia, I swear."

For the first time, I saw the pyramid. Tiny little thing, not much more than a blond shadow in the far corner, but you couldn't mistake it for nothing else.

"This is ours?" I said.

"Free and clear," said Hiram.

"But we can't afford it."

"We already have."

I looked up at him. "Just how'd you manage that?"

"From my Great Heap o' Treasure," said Earle. "We found a junk dealer out by Flint Hill, and he paid out two dollars and sixty-seven cents. That old loom alone, the one you said was ugly as sin, that fetched us a buck ten. And it was the dealer told us where we could find a sign maker."

"Who wouldn't mind working on the Sabbath," said Hiram. "An enterprising artist by the name of Roscoe Barnes. Knocked it out in record time."

"For two dollars and sixty-seven cents?" I said.

"Well, very near. I'm making up the rest."

"How?"

"A month's worth of elocution lessons."

"Elocution?" said Janey.

"It's the art of speaking. Mr. Roscoe Barnes has ambitions for his firstborn son. Wants him to go into law."

Next thing I knew, Hiram was kneeling next to me. His head even with mine. Both of us studying that sign in the headlights.

"It's yours, Melia. If you want it."

Don't know why I held back. I suppose it was just that, if the sign stayed, *I'd* have to stay, and all of us. We'd have to stay and live up to that sign, and fight Harley Blevins with all we had in us, and who was to say that was enough?

It was a cool night, I recall—the rhododendron leaves seemed to be curling up at the edges—and I hadn't thought to put on a coat. But when the shiver took me, I shook it out again.

"What you waiting for?" I said. "Let's put her up."

Chapter
TEN

The next day, Hiram showed up for breakfast. Ate a bowl of Wheaties with no milk and washed it down with two cups of black coffee, then went straight back to his room. I didn't see him again till later that morning when I headed back to the store. There he was, setting on the stool behind the counter. Quiet and fixed, like he'd been there all his days.

"What the hell you doing here?" I said.

"What's it look like?"

"Like you're minding the store."

"So it would seem."

"Maybe you can explain why."

"Somebody has to do it."

"Yeah," I said. "Me."

"Melia, you can't do that *and* pump gas *and* work on the cars."

"Watch me."

He leaned back on his stool, propped a heel on the counter. "Melia, can I ask you something?"

"No."

"When you're out there tending to people's cars, what's to keep them from coming in here and robbing you blind?"

"Our system, that's what."

In the old days, Mama and me, we'd get so busy out front we didn't always have time to police the store. So we left a Union Carbide mining can on the counter and a plate of small change and a sign that said DO WHAT'S RIGHT. Mama had another sign that read GOD IS WATCHING, but that didn't sit right with Gas Station Paganism, so she switched it out for a pair of eyes, drawn in charcoal on a piece of cardboard. "Let 'em *think* it's God," she said. "Or their grandma, I don't care."

But Hiram Watts was not to be swayed. "How do you know this little system of yours works?"

"'Cause there's always money end of the day."

"How much?"

"I dunno. Six, seven bucks."

"Maybe you've got more coming."

"Or maybe not."

"Do you track the money against your inventory?"

"Ain't got time."

"So you're busting your ass day in and day out, and you don't even know what's coming in and going out? What's your biggest-selling item?"

"Coffee."

"After that."

"I don't know, cigs."

"Which brand?"

"Luckys. Camels, maybe."

"If you knew which brand sold the most, you could stock more."

Oh, I knew he was talking sense, but it was the kind of sense a Harley Blevins would talk. *Business* sense.

"I don't know as I can trust you," I allowed.

"What do you think's going to happen?"

"Maybe some of my profit'll walk away."

He come near to smiling.

"Melia, have I stolen a dime from you in all the time I've been here?"

"Not that I know of."

"Then why would I start now?"

"Why does any fool start?"

He give the counter a slow sweep with his hand. "You said it yourself, Melia. Sitting up in that room all day, I'm not doing anyone any good. Tell you what," he said. "You let me mind the store today, then when you're done, you come back and check the till. I guarantee you will find at least *eight* dollars, if not more. Deal?"

He put out a hand, but still I couldn't bring myself to take it.

"Melia," he said, "when a man's ready to step up, you ought to let him."

So after that, I pretty much had to shake on it, but my mind weren't no more at ease. I hung round the store long as I could, and even when the late-afternoon rush come, I kept swinging by to see what I could see. Every time I glanced in, though, Hiram was just where I'd look for him to be, doing what I'd look for him to be doing.

Come quitting time, I went strolling into the store. Wiping the grease off my brow.

"My," I said. "Starting to get warm out there."

"That so?" said Hiram.

"Reckon summer's not too far off."

"I expect you're right," said Hiram.

We watched each other a spell. Then he opened the register, pulled out the tray, and set it on the counter.

"Count it," he said.

So I did. Counted it twice, just to be sure. It was the same both times.

Ten dollars and thirty-three cents.

Somehow or other, Hiram Watts had figured how to squeeze four more bucks out of a single afternoon. Dear Lord, I thought, what couldn't we buy with that two bucks? A sack of sugar or a spring chicken or a can of paint. Five pounds of bacon, eight pounds of cheese. A new doorknob, a new grease trap. A month of eggs.

And what if tomorrow brought two *more* bucks? Another twelve by week's end? Another six hundred by year's end? It was more than my poor brain could even twine itself round.

"Well, now," I said. "I guess this'll do."

I took the money and stuffed it in the pay pouch. Put the pouch in the safe just beneath the counter.

"We got lima beans for supper," I said.

"You go on," he said. "I'll lock up."

• • •

He was up early the next morning, and when the first truck blew in, Hiram was already at his post behind the counter. I don't mind saying I was uneasy. Even as I was pumping the gas, my eyes kept ticking over to the store, watching as each of my truckers traipsed inside . . . and then stopped stone dead.

By now, I should say, we'd got Hiram looking very close to human. Earle had biked over to Old Man Purdy's estate sale and brung back an old linen suit and a pair of denim trousers and a couple of gray denim shirts. And Hiram was doing his bit for the cause—shaving every morning, brushing his teeth every night, bathing at least twice a week. What I'm saying is, he didn't look like the feller who'd just rolled off a load of coal.

So I reckon what pulled those truckers up short was they'd never seen a face quite like Hiram's. So grave, I mean, and craggy and beaten on, with that one eye wandering wheresoever it listeth.

Now, truckers don't scare easy, but they are fools for habit, so if you throw a wrench at 'em, they need time to make it right in their heads. I recall Joe Bob staggering out like the Last Days had come.

"Who's that feller?" he gasped.

"My daddy."

"Huh." Joe Bob swung his head back toward the store. "He don't take after you."

Merle, he was thrown all out of whack. "It don't seem right, Melia. It's very near to wrong, I'm telling you."

As for Warner . . . well, he strode straight to the counter,

98

grabbed himself some coffee, and stormed out again. It weren't till he was driving off that he leaned out the window and said, "You sure about this one?"

"I reckon," I said.

"See you next week."

I guess that's when I knew it'd be okay.

It helped that Hiram met them halfway. Took time to learn all their names, their ways. He knew Warner liked his coffee bitter and hot and Joe Bob liked it cool enough to do the backstroke in. Elmer loved a sprinkle of cinnamon, Billy Ray wanted shredded-wheat biscuits for dunking. Merle took tea—two bags of Lipton, steeped for three minutes. And Frank? He didn't care what was in the cup so long as there was a couple inches left over for Johnnie Walker.

Hiram got it down so tight, he was filling their orders soon as they drove up. "Why, it's waiting for me every dang time," said Joe Bob. "Now that's what I call *service*."

So each day got a little easier, and before too long, I'd be hearing, "Oh, man, Hiram better have my coffee waiting" or "Where's that Hiram with my joe?" or "Hey, Melia, tell Hiram I like his new blend. That ol' chicory takes me back."

One morning—it was a Friday in mid-May, I think—I was pumping diesel into a Chevy Confederate when I heard a shout and a crash. Now, Elmer and Dutch was already hustling into the store, and me, I weren't but three steps behind. The first thing I seen was Hiram flat against the icebox and a pair of hands pressed hard—*hard*—against his chest.

Didn't take long to see the hands belonged to Glenmont, one of the biggest, baddest mothers on the road. The kind of feller showed up every Monday with a black eye and half a tooth missing and dried-up blood on his knuckles.

"Hey, now!" I said. "Quit that!"

Truth be told, I was less fearful for Hiram than the icebox, which had customized glass panels.

Well, it took two fellers to pry Glenmont off, and even so he kept coming at Hiram like a drunk reaching for his last whiskey.

"What the hell's gotten into you two?" I said.

"This bastard just 'cused me of stealing," said Glenmont.

"I didn't accuse him," said Hiram, panting. "I saw him."

"Like hell you did."

"He took three quarters right out of that drawer."

The anaconda tattoo on Glenmont's neck was pulsing like a fist. "You're a goddamn liar, old man. You didn't see nothing."

"I can even tell you the years on those coins. They're 1929, 1932, 1933. The thirty-three's got some kind of green oxidation on it, and the twenty-nine's black around the rim, like someone rolled it in coal dust."

Even in the midst of the ruckus, I had to wonder how a body could make such a study of a quarter.

"That so?" shouted Glenmont. "You wanna look for them there quarters?" With a slow smile, he turned out all his overall pockets, front and back. "See?" he said. "Nothin'." Then he rolled up both of his shirtsleeves far as they would go. "Ain't nothin' up there, neither."

By now, the driver of the Confederate had followed us into the store, and a whole knot of truckers come hard after. Jake and Colton, Rance and Elwood. All tense in the jaw, squared off in the shoulders.

The sight of 'em seemed to give Glenmont a head of steam. He started strutting round the store, yanking on his overalls.

"I tell you what, boys! I tell you what! That old coot is touched in the head!"

"Well, now," I said, clearing my throat. "I can see how there might've been a mistake."

"No mistake," Hiram said, soft and low.

"What I mean is if there's been, like—I mean, like, a misunderstanding—I'm sure we're all real sorry about it."

Glenmont's lip curled up. "Sorry don't cut it, Miss Melia. You want to keep my business, this old man here's gotta go."

"Come on, now. Ain't no need for that."

"Pointing a finger at honest folk. I ought to punch his lights out."

And boy, did he try. Come back swinging free and hard. It was all Elmer and Dutch could do to pull him off again.

"Say, now," I heard Elmer whisper. "You can't ask her to can her own daddy, Glenmont."

"Don't care who it is! She don't toss him out, I ain't never coming back. And I'll tell all my buddies to do the same."

I could see Hiram leaning back against that wall, studying his fingernails. I could see Glenmont, clawing his tattoo like a bull pawing at a patch of grass. Each second was a drum pounding in my head. Then, from the back of the store, come a voice even deeper than Hiram's.

"Hold on, now."

The other truckers parted like hair before a comb, and out stepped Warner. Without a word, he grabbed Glenmont—all two hundred pounds of him—took him by the collar, lifted him straight up in the air, and then flipped him like he was an egg timer.

"What the hell?" gasped Glenmont.

There came a ping, bright as a song. It was a quarter, falling from some deep, secret well of Glenmont's overalls and twanging on the oak flooring.

Warner give Glenmont a little shake, and out come another quarter. One more shake, one more quarter.

With a measure of gentleness, Warner set Glenmont back on the floor, then scooped up the coins. Lifted 'em, one by one, to the light.

"The year is 1932, check . . . oxidized green, check . . . coal dust round the rim. Check." Nodding, he handed the quarters back to Hiram.

Well, by now, every single eye in the store was boring down on Glenmont.

"Come on now, boys," he said. "Don't be that way. Old man, he probably planted 'em on me. He's sly that way. Got that funny eye, don't he?"

A few more seconds, he might've left on his own, but Warner decided to move things along. Grabbed Glenmont by the stitches on his overalls and flung him out the door.

The morning rush was done by eleven, but I took another hour or so to sweep away the elm pods and stack some tires. Finally, there weren't nothing for it but to take myself into the store, where Hiram was back on his stool.

"At it again," he said.

I swung my head toward the window. There was that crazy red-bird, pounding his idiot self against the glass.

"I used to think he'd kill himself doing that," said Hiram. "Now I think it's the thing that keeps him going."

For a good while, I studied that bird. Then I give the floor a good once-over.

"Listen," I said. "I want you to know—well, I just wanted to say I *believed* you. Back there with Glenmont."

"You did, huh?"

"It's just—I don't know how to—how to handle a *scrap*. I mean, I can change your oil, put in new brake pads, but a ruckus—I mean the kind menfolk get into—I don't know my way around that."

"Is this your way of saying sorry, Melia?"

"Close as I get."

He set for a spell, watching the redbird.

"You don't need to apologize," he said. "Girl like you shouldn't have to adjudicate squabbles amongst grown men."

"Adjudicate?"

"Means *judge*."

"Oh." I stuffed my hands in my pocket. "Guess you'd know a word like that. Seeing you was once an actor."

"Actors only know what you tell 'em."

I stood there awhile, rocking on my heels.

"Can I ask you something?" I said.

"Sure."

"You're bringing in two, three bucks more every day, and it makes me kinda sad."

His head tilted. "Why is that?"

"'Cause it means Mama and me was wrong about trusting people. Folks like Glenmont, they must've been stealing from us all along."

"Not necessarily. If you ask me, ninety-nine percent of your customers are honest folk."

"Then how come we're getting more money with you in the store?"

"Because I'm suggesting things they didn't know they wanted."

"How's that work?" I said.

"Well, now," he said, giving his knuckles a crack. "Imagine some lady comes in here of a Saturday afternoon. One of those tourist ladies with the beaver coat and the Leica camera."

"Sure."

"She walks through that door there, and all she wants is a pack of Wrigley's Spearmint. So she can freshen up her breath for her fella, who's back in the car. 'Course you get her the gum, but before you hand it over, you say, 'Hey, now, are you sure you've got enough film for that camera?' 'Well,' she says, 'I think so.' And you say, 'Oh, my maiden aunt, I'd hate to have you run out of film when you're standing on top of Signal Knob and nowhere to buy more.' And she says, 'Maybe you're right.' And you say, 'Now, you sure you got an up-to-the-minute map?' And she says, 'I don't know.' And you say, 'Well, they're changing the roads every day in these parts, so you'd best take care. Now this map here is the most up-to-date map there is. Can't go wrong with H.M. Gousha.' And she says, 'Okay, I'll take it.' And then I say, 'Now, are you ready to get nibbled on? 'Cause the bugs are getting awful bitey right around now.'"

"Not so much in May . . ."

"'Excuse me, miss, but in the Blue Ridge, bugs are a year-round menace. How about I fix you up with some Flit? You can take it back to DC, too, use it when the skeeters come calling. And I'll tell you what, since you're such a valued customer, I'm gonna throw in a couple postcards free of charge. For your sweet mama and papa back home.'" He shrugged. "That's how ten cents becomes two dollars."

"How'd you learn that?"

"Used to sell ladies' hats."

"Where?"

"I. Magnin and Company. San Francisco."

If he'd told me he'd sold flying carpets to Aladdin, it couldn't have sounded any stranger. What sort of lady would've bought a hat off of Hiram Watts?

"I wonder if I could take a nap now," he said.

"Don't see why not."

He put his feet on the counter and tipped himself back until his head rested against the wall. It was about the scariest position a man could find to sleep in—one tip in the wrong direction, the stool would've gone right out from under—but Hiram, he kept his balance, and when I checked back a half hour later, he was sleeping in the exact same position. Soon as he heard the bell over the door, though, his eyes sparked open and the stool come back down, and the words was out of his mouth before he'd even quite woke up.

"How may I help you?"

Chapter
ELEVEN

The letter from First Bank of Virginia came in the next day's mail. It was addressed to a dead woman.

Dear Miss Brenda Hoyle,

It has come to this bank's attention that you are three months in arrears on payments relating to Account #3231A.

Previous communications have met with no response. We ask therefore that you consider this your final notice. Please be advised that, should you fail to remit one hundred and thirty dollars by June the first, your account shall be considered in default, and repossession proceedings shall be undertaken.

Most sincerely yours,
Mr. Wallace Paxton
Commercial Loans

So here's the thing that I haven't made crystal clear yet. For all the green Hiram was bringing in through the store, we was drowning in debt.

It started from the day Mama bought the place. She had to take out one loan for the station, another for the house. We owed the bank, we owed the jobber. We owed the Pillsbury supplier, the Coca-Cola supplier. We owed the cheese man, the iceman, the Kelvinator man. We owed Ma Bell, we owed Standard Oil. We was okay on taxes, but we didn't have a scrap of insurance. We couldn't even afford to pay ourselves wages.

The only thing we owned free and clear was the truck, and that was about nine months away from being a piece of junk—it was held together by chewing gum and pagan prayer—and if I'd gone and sold it that very day, I'd have got maybe forty bucks. Ninety bucks less than what I needed to find in two weeks.

And I wouldn't have had no truck.

Well, first thing I did was call Chester. He got there toward sundown, looking damp and wilted in his blue blazer.

"Let's walk," I said.

We couldn't walk very far, 'cause I had to keep an eye on the station. So we'd travel 'bout a hundred feet down the road's shoulder, then cross and walk back the other side. We did that a couple times, then I handed him the letter.

"It's a pickle," he said after reading it.

"That's one word."

He folded the letter back up. Tapped it against his temple.

"We could go to court," he said. "Buy you a little time."

"How much?"

"Depends on the judge. A month, maybe two. Worse comes to worse, we declare bankruptcy."

"Shit."

"That's not the end of the world, Melia. It just gives you a little breathing room, keeps your creditors at bay."

"For how long? How long you think before Harley Blevins comes swooping in? You don't think he's got half this county's judges in his pocket?"

We angled our heads toward the road. Watched a mare drag an old hay wagon up the hill.

"I can help," said Chester.

"Yeah? You're telling me you got a hundred and thirty dollars right there in your trousers."

"Well, not in my trousers . . ."

"Come on, Chester, you can't even afford to paint your house. You spend your days keeping poor crackers out of jail. You telling me they're paying in *cash* now? I thought it was quilts and moonshine, mostly."

"I could call people."

"Listen. It means a lot you trying, but you don't even know what we're up against here. I mean, we're deep in it."

"Then let me do something."

I kept walking.

"At least give me credit for trying," he said, following after.

A crow landed on a split-rail fence, give us the eye.

"I'm at my wit's end," I said. "I mean, how long do we keep trying? Mama used to say if you can't make a go of a thing, it weren't never meant to be."

"You think she honestly believed that?"

"Hell if I know." I swung my head back toward the station. Hocked a gob of spit on the ground. "I could never be sure what was goin' on in that head of hers. Brenda's Oasis—this is just another one of her damned dreams. And I'm the one who gets to clean up after."

Once Chester had gone, I headed back to the house to make sure Earle was on top of his homework. (Boy's all right with sums but will do anything to get out of reading.) From the edge of my sight, I caught a little figure out there between the tire swings. It was Janey, her hands full of linen bandages and an old tangerine peel cupped like a stethoscope to her ear.

If there's one thing you'll learn about that child, it's that she loves playing nurse. She likes to think she's at the Battle of Manassas, tending to soldiers. (Blue, gray, she don't care.) She takes their pulse, listens to their hearts, checks their joints, but mostly she bandages. Limb by limb till each of those soldier boys is a by-God mummy.

In the old days, she'd make Earle play soldier, but she'd want him to lay there for *hours*, dying slow, till he couldn't stand it no more. Then she started doing it with logs and branches and fallen tree trunks, and that's what I thought she was doing now till I saw the trunk move. A flesh-and-blood arm, answering to Janey's call, and another arm doing the same, and soon as I drew near, I could see the arms belonged to Hiram. Flat on the ground, quiet as church, half-smothered in bandages.

"Janey!" I called. "You oughtn't be wrappin' up Daddy Hiram."

"It's all right," he called back. "She's fine."

So on they went, Hiram laying there and Janey whispering in

his ear—*You shall live, brave soldier.* I stood for a stretch watching. Wondering, I guess, how it all might look through the eyes of Mr. Wallace Paxton of the commercial-loans division.

Then I remembered.

I had met Mr. Wallace Paxton!

The last time we'd fallen behind on payments, Mama had asked him to come over for supper. He was thin and pink and easy to bruise, with a bow tie that drooped almost to his chest and a mustache that looked like it was ready to crawl off his face. Mama fed him some of her ham and biscuits and sun tea, and just to seal the deal, she worn a green cotton housedress that showed off her assets. For near an hour, she shined on him, and when he staggered on out of there, she said, "What do you think, Mr. Paxton? Another couple months?"

"Well, all right," he said.

I took his letter out of my pocket, read it through one more time. Asked myself how I could possibly sway Mr. Wallace Paxton without Mama's dress or Mama's figure. Hell, I didn't even know how to smile. Seemed to me all the advantages of being a girl was lost on me.

I heard a whisper of tire on the gravel behind me. Rolling up to the pump was Harley Blevins's butternut Chevrolet Eagle. The door opened, and out stepped Dudley, in that damn Buck Rogers suit, rumpling his hair and staring round.

"You cut it right close," I said. "Five minutes more, we woulda been closed."

"I know what time it is."

"Yeah? And where's His Highness?"

"Back home."

"Plotting his next devilment, I guess."

"I don't know nothing about that."

"Like fun you don't. Social workers and sheriffs. Loan officers. Before long, I reckon the U.S. Army'll come down on us."

He left some spit on the ground. Smeared it into the gravel with his shoe.

"Y'all sell Bit-O-Honeys?"

"Sure we do."

I watched him walking toward the store, all arms and legs, his head bobbing like it wasn't quite screwed on, his ears sticking out like gourd shells. How many times had I seen him walkin' that self-same way and never given it a thought? What was so different 'bout this time? All I know is one second, I was reaching for the nozzle, and the next, I was following him.

"Hey!" I called. "Got something you should see."

He followed me round to the back of the store. The noise from the road fell away, and the sun dropped from sight, and it felt like the world dropped from sight, too. There he was, looking at me, wondering what the hell was going on, and I was wondering the same thing till something lit up in my head, and I shoved him against the wall and mashed my lips against his. So hard I could feel his front teeth banging against mine.

Now, I had always had definite notions about how my first kiss should go. It was gonna happen in a glade. Bees drowsing, birds humming. It was gonna be soft and tender, and the boy was gonna lead, and I was gonna *yield*, the way ladies do in the movies, all rustling silk.

But my first kiss happened against the back wall of a general store, with gas fumes in my nostrils, gravel crunching under my feet. It weren't tender, and it was the boy who yielded. Looked kinda like he'd been stabbed. (I found out later I'd knocked the wind out of him.) Whole thing didn't last more 'n a second or two.

"Sorry," I mumbled.

Which, now that I think on it, was the first time I'd ever said sorry to Dudley Blevins.

I jerked my head away and took a step back, but then he wrapped his hands round my shoulders and pulled me toward him and kissed me right back. I could feel his tongue folding round mine. I could taste the peppermint inside his cheeks, feel his breath on my skin.

When we pulled apart again, there wasn't a smile on neither of our faces.

"I don't know," he said. "Maybe we should take a walk sometime."

"Okay."

"How 'bout Sunday?"

"Sure."

"Only it can't be during church. My aunt'd kill me."

"How about after?" I said.

"After," he said.

"Four, maybe?"

"Four," he said.

"Okay, then."

So I went and filled the Chevy Eagle, and he went in the store and bought his Bit-O-Honey and left some money on the counter and got in his car without a look my way. I started to wonder if maybe I'd dreamed the whole thing, but as he pulled out, he lowered the side window and poked his hand out. Let it wiggle a second in the breeze. Like an aspen leaf.

Chapter
TWELVE

"**M**elia!" said Janey.

It was Sunday afternoon, and Hiram was dozing in his armchair, and Janey and Earle was sitting under the dining table—their den of thieves, they liked to call it—playing their ten millionth game of old maid, and I thought my way to the door was clear, but then Janey poked her head out.

"Where you going?" she asked.

"No place."

"How come you put on a dress?"

Now it was Earle's head poking out.

"Would you look at that? For crying out loud!"

"Reckon I'm allowed to wear a dress," I said. "Don't have to be just for funerals."

But Janey was crawling toward me now like a bluetick on a coon. "It's more 'n that. You combed your hair and washed your face."

"Sweet Jesus," said Earle.

"Something ain't right."

I was about to answer, but the heat went rolling up my throat. The next second, Janey sprang to her feet.

"Holy smokes! Melia's going out with a feller."

"No, she ain't," said Earle.

"She is, I tell you!"

"Melia, are you going out with a feller?"

"Well—Jesus, I'm—I'm goin' *out* is all."

"Who with?" Janey wanted to know.

It crossed my mind to lie.

"Dudley Blevins," I mumbled.

"Who?"

"*Dudley Blevins.* Now you leave it there or . . ."

But Janey was giving me her look. That I'm-so-sorry-you're-so-stupid look.

"What?" I said.

"You sure took your ever-sweet-lovin' time about it, that's all."

"I don't even know what you're talking 'bout."

"Dudley's been sweet on you since forever," she said. "What'd he have to do, hire a crop duster and scrawl it cross the sky?"

This was news, I confess.

I started running through all the things Dudley would do around me. Tip his head to one side. Shove his hands in his pockets and jangle the coins real loud. Sometimes I'd catch him leaning back against the car, like he owned it, only as soon as I caught him doing it, he'd straighten right back up and start itching round the back of his head. That's what being sweet was?

"Nuff of your fool talk," I said. "This ain't a date. It's a business meeting."

"Bet I know what business," said Janey.

"Hush up."

"Business!" she shouted.

Just loud enough to shake Hiram out of his nap. He come rolling up from his chair, eyes wild. "What? What is it?"

"Guess who's goin' walkin' with Dudley Blevins?"

The clouds on Hiram's face melted off. "Well, now," he said. "Mr. Sun Tzu would be most pleased."

We stared at him.

"*The Art of War*," he explained.

We stared some more.

"*If your enemy's forces are united, separate them*," he said.

"But Dudley ain't our enemy," said Earle.

"He let me bandage him all the way to the shoulder," said Janey.

"He may or may not be our enemy," said Hiram, "but he's most definitely related to our enemy. As such, he might be useful."

Well, if there's one word I'd never have thought to put alongside Dudley Blevins, it was *useful*. How exactly was I supposed to use him? I thought of Mama plying herself against Mr. Wallace Paxton from the First Bank of Virginia, and then I thought of me banging teeth with Dudley, and it was like two different games.

"Y'all make my head ache," I said.

I was nearly to the door when I heard Janey say, "You shoulda put on rouge."

Now, I was too shamed to admit it, but I'd spent a good half hour looking for Mama's rouge. Her clothes was all where we left 'em, still full of her smell, but those little female tricks she used to have at her call—the lipstick tube and the eye pencil and the face powder and the tortoiseshell hair clips—they was as good as gone.

Well, never mind, I thought, walking out to the road. I wouldn't have known what to do with 'em anyway. *He's gonna get the real me,* I thought. *God help him.*

Now, it so happens I also had particular notions about my first courting. The feller was supposed to get there on time, for starters. He was supposed to roll up in—well, not a Bugatti or nothing, but a Caddy or a Packard. He'd be wearing a shirt with peppermint stripes and suspenders and a nice boater and black patent-leather shoes. Maybe an alpaca scarf.

Well, Dudley wore a work shirt and scuffed work shoes, and he rolled up ten minutes late in an old DeSoto delivery sedan that looked like it'd been driven round the moon and back.

"Where's the Chevy Eagle?" I asked.

"Hell, my uncle'd kill me if I took that out on a Sunday. This here's my buddy Elmer's. Drives like a peach."

"I bet."

"Climb on in."

Also in the courtship of my dreams, the feller was gonna open the door for me.

"Where we going?" I asked.

"I dunno."

But he drove straight and true, like he had a place in mind. Sure enough, once we'd gotten off the Loop Road, he pulled over in a clearing and cut the engine.

"What about here?" he said in a casual kind of way.

I peered out the window. All I saw at first was a row of poplars, but from the late-afternoon shadows, a little notch peered back. A trailhead.

"Holy Christ," I said. "You want to go walking in the woods?"

"Sure."

"But I didn't wear no dress so I could get all nature-y."

To be honest, it wasn't even the dress I was thinking of, it was Mama's sandals. She'd seen Joan Crawford wearing them in a *Movie Mirror* feature, so she'd ordered knockoffs from J.C. Penney's, but they never did fit right, so after a couple of weeks, she'd tossed 'em to me.

"You're the one that's got the dainty feet," she'd said.

And what a wonder it was. To know I had something dainty about me and to be wearing Joan Crawford's shoes. Point is, I didn't want nothing happening to those sandals.

"Can't we just walk on a street somewhere?" I said. "Like normal folks?"

"It's cooler in the woods."

Well, here was something Mama and I had never got the chance to talk about. What exactly happened to gals who went walking in the woods with boys?

"I don't know, Dudley."

"What's to know?"

"It's just I ain't exactly acquainted with this here stretch of woods."

"I am."

"Besides, I gotta be back in an hour. Two hours tops. They're expecting me."

118

"We'll be back," he said. "I brung my pocket watch."

With a little smile, he drew it out of his dungarees. Old as time itself.

"Your uncle give that to you?" I asked.

"My granddaddy. He was with the railroad thirty years, and they let him keep it. Ain't it fine?"

Something in how he said that—proud and shy.

"All I care is if it keeps time," I said.

"It does."

"Well, okay, then."

I got out of the car slow. Watched Dudley hoist a rucksack over his shoulder and amble toward the forest. Long, easy strides.

"How 'bout I go first?" he said.

"Okay."

"Keep me in sight, now."

"Then don't go fast."

He slipped into those poplars like some kind of woodland critter, but me, I stopped right on the verge of that trailhead and made myself look back. There was the sky. There was the road. Dudley's cousin's sedan.

"You coming?" Dudley called.

The first step was the hardest. By the tenth, the sun had flown off, and the air was cool on my skin, and the sound of birds was tunneling into my ear. Robin, sparrow, yellowthroat.

The path was grown over at first, but it opened up soon enough, and before I even had my bearings, we was standing in front of a creek. A creek I'd never seen in all my days. Mighty and spring fed, frothing up on each side, clear all the way to the bottom.

"Does it have a name?" I asked.

Dudley shrugged.

"Well, which way do we go?" I asked.

"Up."

"I don't see no trail."

"Gotta follow the creek bed."

That water was rushing on down like judgment, and I weren't gonna go nowhere near, but then Dudley said, "Less snakes this way."

So there I was, stepping from one stone to the next in my Joan Crawford sandals, the moss making every rock slippery as a hog butcher's fingers. More than once, I thought I was fixing to tumble right in, dress and shoes and everything, but Dudley's hand found me each time—it seemed to know.

No denying he had a firm grip, and being as I was following him, I had time to study the rest of him, too. His waist, which was tinier than I'd have guessed. The ridge of his shoulders. Legs dancing from rock to rock, never missing a step. The place on his arms where now and then his sleeve would pull up to show a little rectangle of white skin against the red of his forearms. Seemed like that was the only way I could keep my balance sometimes, staring at that white band.

We saw but the one snake—a cottonmouth, wrapped round a fern. It didn't pay us no never mind.

By now it was hard to tell if the water soaking my dress was from the creek or my own sweat, but I felt freer with each step.

"Not much farther," said Dudley.

Farther to where? I wondered. How long had we even been gone? I saw berries shining out of arbutus bushes. Cedar creeping under a pine tree. Sun and shadow, shadow and sun. Off in the distance, Massanutten Mountain, changing from blue to gray and back again. And just up ahead, the biggest damn boulder I ever seen, splitting the creek in two.

"We're here," said Dudley.

He helped me up the side of the rock, and what do you know? Turned out there was a big ol' granite shelf on top, ten feet in every direction, with a view clear down to the valley.

There's folks would've paid ten thousand dollars for that view, but Dudley, he flung himself down on that rock like it was his birthright. Stretched himself flat on his back and gazed up at that sky. I was figuring to do the same, but I'd had so damned little practice wearing a dress I couldn't figure how to settle myself without showing too much leg. I ended up tipping onto my hip and tucking in my knees tight as I could.

"You hungry?" said Dudley.

He reached into that rucksack of his and brought out . . . peanut butter sandwiches . . . fried chicken . . . strawberries . . . fresh biscuits. Even a little jar of apple preserves. Now, I have heard a young lady is never supposed to be hungry in front of a young man, but I was ready to eat ten boars, so I piled in. And I will say it was tolerable nice, sitting there on top of that rock, eating chicken and licking the grease off my fingers.

"Dudley," I said, "can I ask you something?"

His mouth was full, so he nodded.

"Why you bothering with me?"

He give a shrug, kept chewing.

"No, I mean it," I said. "Best I can recall, I ain't never tossed you a kind word. Been nothing but a torment to you from the day we met."

"That's so," he allowed.

"Well, then, what is it? I would truly like to know."

He folded one arm over his head.

"My daddy," he said. "'Fore he died, he told me if a gal don't give you the time of day? Why, you pass right on by 'cause your chances ain't good. But if a gal takes a real pleasure in *devilin'* you, why, you stick around 'cause it probably means she likes you all right." He give me half of a smile. "I'm only telling you what Daddy said."

"Oh, yeah? What else he say?"

"Well." He set down his sandwich. "He said don't you never fix your sights on a gal till you see her for real. A lot o' girls, they can put on the pretty, but you make sure you're lookin' at 'em when they's *natural.* And hell, Melia, you ain't never been nothin' *but* natural. I can't even believe you wore a dress today. I mean, I'm not sayin' you don't look right nice in it. What I mean is, you look okay the way you are."

Made me right glad I hadn't bothered with the rouge. (Would've washed off anyway.)

"I reckon that's a compliment," I said.

"Yes, ma'am, it is."

Say something nice back. But all I could think to say was . . .

"How'd your daddy die?"

His eyes squeezed down a hair.

"I mean, I was just wondering," I said. "Did he take sick or something?"

"He was working a coal seam. Over in Mill Creek on the West Virginia side. They was down about two miles—my daddy and four others—and they hit a pocket of firedamp. Death was instant, that's what the company said."

I stared down at my sandals. "That when your uncle took you in?"

"It was more my aunt. She and Uncle Harley didn't have no kids of their own, so . . ."

"There you was."

"I guess."

"They treat you okay?"

"Good enough."

"You like driving him around all day?"

"Beats mining."

The boy had a point.

"What about your ma?" I said. "Did she—"

"She run off when I was two."

"You know where?"

"Nope." He jerked his head toward the water, but his voice was soft when it come back. "Used to think we had that in common, Melia. Me and you. Growing up without a parent and all. And then when your daddy come back . . ."

My face flushed hot.

"No, it's okay," said Dudley. "I was gonna say when he come back, I thought it'd piss me off 'cause we didn't have that in common no more. But I set and thought on it and turned out I was happy for you after all. 'Cause how often does it go like that? I mean, family comin' back to you."

"It's a rare thing," I allowed.

"Boy, you said it."

No longer was I thinking about my dress or if my knees was locked tight enough. I was thinking about kissing him. I tipped myself forward and brought my face right up to his. Wondering as I closed my eyes if we'd find each other, and we did.

His lips tasted of sun and chicken.

"That was the nicest one yet," he said.

"Well, there's only been the three, so . . ."

"So let's do another," he said.

And that was nice as well.

"Is this rock taken?" I said, pointing to the part alongside him.

"Why, no, it is not."

So I laid there, and he laid beside. Neither of us quite touching. The breeze was tickling on down from the hills, and the sun was mopping up the water from my skin. I should've been at ease, but something stole over me without my knowing.

Useful. He might be useful.

"Hey, now," I said. "What does your uncle say about me?"

His eyelids fluttered a little.

"Nothing much."

"Oh, come on."

"I'm serious. He don't bring up business with me."

My fingers crawled toward Dudley's hand. Did a little dance in his palm.

"I know he wants our station," I said.

"That's just business, Melia. It ain't personal."

His hands closed lightly round my fingers.

"You know what I was thinking?" I said. "We could come here every Sunday."

"Yeah? You think so?"

"Why, sure. We could bring food, and we could—you know, *talk* on things."

"What things?"

"Oh, you know, whatever folks talk about. I mean, if we're gonna be *friends* and all, friends share things, don't they?"

"I guess."

"Like things they *know*. I'd tell you stuff I know, and you'd tell me stuff you know. And that works out for both of us, see?"

That was when I felt his hand pry itself loose from mine. He sat up. He said, in a soft, lost voice, "You want me to spy on my uncle."

I confess I underestimated the boy.

"Whoa, now," I said. "Hold on there. That ain't what I—"

"That's what you meant."

"No. It ain't. I swear."

But he was already on his feet.

"Jesus. Is that why you come out here with me? To drag secrets out of me?"

"Don't talk crazy."

"You think *I'm* crazy?" Next second, he was on his knees, leaning his whole body at me. "How far was you planning to go, Melia?" He hooked his hand round the back of my neck. "How much was you thinking of sharing? For friendship's sake?" He pulled my head toward his. "How much?"

"Hey," I said. "Don't."

He stared at me a long time, then let go his hand. "That's what I figured."

He stood up, walked to the edge of the rock. "Write me down," he said. "Biggest fool ever lived."

"No."

"Thinking you was—"

"I am! I mean, I could be."

From where Dudley Blevins was came the saddest laugh.

"You *could* be."

"Listen," I said, rising to my feet. "You gotta understand. I don't know nothing 'bout—'bout *feeling*. All I know is fighting. And holding on. At the end of the day, I don't got much left for nothing else."

"Jesus, Melia. Everyone I know is holding on. They can still find a place for other folks."

"Yeah? Well, tell you what." I was walking at him now, slow hard steps. "Tell you what, Dudley. You get your uncle to back the hell off. You get him to call off his dogs at First Virginia Bank and the juvenile court and leave us the hell in peace and maybe then— maybe *then* I can be one of those lovesome lovebirds you're so hot on. Till then, I got a station to run and a family to hold together. So pardon me if I can't be your little chippie."

It was like the water itself went quiet. Dudley stood a long time, staring down the valley. Then he half turned round.

"There's still some strawberries," he said. "If you want any."

"You eat 'em."

"I ain't hungry."

"Me, neither."

"Then we'd best get back," he said.

• • •

Going downhill should've been faster, but it was about the slowest walk I ever took. I didn't slip once and wouldn't have cared if I did. When we come back out the trailhead, Dudley took out his granddaddy's pocket watch and, with a face grim as winter, said, "Look at that. Two hours on the dot."

Chapter
THIRTEEN

I asked him to let me off a few hundred yards shy of the station. He didn't question, just slammed on the brakes—never even cut the engine. I climbed on out, stood there a second, then slammed the door after me. He drove off without a look.

I don't mind telling you, I had cause to regret my pride 'cause I was bone weary. My dress weighing on me like tin, an evil itch throbbing at the back of my leg, my feet chaffy in their Joan Crawford sandals. In my head, I was already crawling into bed and pulling the sheets over me and sleeping straight till Wednesday. But then I turned the corner and saw Harley Blevins's butternut Chevy Eagle idling by the pumps.

The engine was still on, and the great man himself was sitting in the driver's seat, leaning one arm out the window. I had a notion I could slip by him, but he spotted me in his rearview mirror.

"Evening, Melia."

It was a different voice when there weren't nobody else around. 'Bout twenty degrees colder.

"'Fraid we're closed on Sundays," I said.

"Oh, I didn't come for no gas, child."

I kept walking. Stopped just as I come abreast of him.

"So you *can* drive yourself."

"Didn't have no choice, Melia. My driver took the day off. And do you know what he done on his day off? Why, he went and got hisself a date."

"That so?" I could feel his eyes on me.

"Reckon it was one of them local hussies," he said.

"You talking about the gal or Dudley?"

"I gotta hand it to you, Melia." He took a hankie out of his coat pocket and give the back of his neck a swipe. "Tempting a boy with forbidden fruit. That's a new one for you, ain't it? Why, you must've torn that page outta your mama's book."

Next second, I was leaning into the car. Grabbing him by his vulcanized-rubber bow tie and dragging his head half out the window.

"Listen, you sack of shit. You say another word about her—you so much as let her name drop off of those fat lips of yours—I will knock every single one of your goddamned teeth out your mouth and feed 'em to the squirrels."

He peeled my fingers off his throat, one by one.

"Truth is," he said, "my teeth's already out, mostly." He rearranged the lapels of his seersucker jacket. "But I do appreciate a gal with spirit, 'deed I do. Tell you what, Miss Melia, I'm gonna make you a proposition. How 'bout we keep our hands off each other's kin? Sound good to you? 'Cause the thing is I got plans for Dudley."

"Don't make me feel sorry for him now."

"Oh, well, if there's any feller needs pity, it's me." The tiniest shiver in the skin around his eyes. "Do you know I had to go and cut my prices again?"

Smile. Smile 'em all to hell.

"Down to eight cents a gallon. Sweet Jesus, it pains me, but there ain't nothing for it. We got to keep doing our bit for the working man, don't we? I reckon I'm lucky, having so many stations to spread the pain. Can't even imagine how the sole proprietor gets along."

I narrowed my eyes to get him in better focus.

"The sole proprietor will get along," I said.

"We'll just have to pray you're right." He reached for the gear shift. "Forgot to mention," he said. "I like your sign."

His stubby little hand was hanging out the window as he pulled out. Couldn't help but recollect Dudley's hand, hanging out the same window.

The second I walked in the house, Janey spun round in her chair.

"How was the *business*?" she cried.

I'll give the child this much credit, she needed but the one look at my face to know there weren't no point inquiring further. And Earle, he didn't even look up. He was writing down state capitals for school, and it was taking the usual forever, his hand crawling cross the page.

"Holy God," I said. "How long can it take you to write 'Tallahassee'?"

"I'm slow and steady," he said. "Like the tortoise. That's why I always win the race."

"Can't be much of a race," I said, "if you could win it."

Was out of my mouth before I could call it back.

"Don't listen," Janey whispered to him. "She's got her mean tongue on."

"Shut up," I said.

"We just gotta lay low till it wears itself out."

"Know what, missy? You'd get a mean tongue, too, you walked in my shoes."

"I ain't gonna walk in your shoes. I'm gonna get me a husband."

"Well, good luck with that. You can't even cook."

A little flush in her cheeks. "Ain't got nothing to cook *with*."

By now, I was getting so hot I didn't trust myself, so I stalked on out. Hiram found me ten minutes later, in one of the Adirondack chairs by the store, my knees pressed hard to my chest.

"Okay if I join you?" he said.

"Free country."

I don't know what made more cricks, Hiram setting down or the chair rising to meet him.

"Guess you and Dudley Blevins didn't exactly fly to the moon?"

"It was your goddamn fault," I said.

"That so?"

"You're the one told me to treat him like an enemy. The second I did, it got ruined."

Hiram frowned.

"So Sun Tzu wasn't exactly relevant to your situation?"

"Seems not."

He was quiet a stretch.

"I'm sorry, Melia. I didn't know you had actual feelings for the boy."

"I don't. I mean, I don't know."

He fished in his pockets for a cig. "Bet you wish you had your mama here right now."

"No more 'n usual," I said. (Though, truth be told, I was feeling it particular just then.) "It's just boys is too much work."

"I remember thinking the same about girls."

"Ain't got time for that nonsense nohow. Harley Blevins is lowering his price again."

Hiram tapped the cig, twice, against his wrist. "Trying to grind you down, I guess."

"Must be working 'cause I'm feeling mighty ground."

He struck a match against the chair, carried it to his cig. Held the first drag as long as he dared.

"You follow suit," he said, "you make this Blevins character a happy man."

"What other choice I got?"

"Stop playing in his yard. That bastard can keep slashing prices till the end of time 'cause he's got the pockets and the volume. You don't. So you figure out what *you've* got to sell."

I pressed my palms over my eyes. "Lord, Hiram. I sell gas."

"You're one of the best natural mechanics I've ever seen, Melia. No one else gets an engine up and running the way you do. What's more, you've got this *place*."

"Big deal."

"Why do you think those truckers come here every blessed day?"

"I dunno," I said, turning my hands skyward. "Location?"

"Harley Blevins's nearest station is eight miles down the road. They could blow by this place without another thought, but they don't. They get something here they don't get from the Blevinses of the world."

I set my hands in my lap. Give the station as hard a look as I could stomach. All I saw was the patched-up air hose and the gas pump that didn't ring no more when the gallons was ticked off and the outhouse door that wouldn't shut the whole way. And stains and pits and gouges that weren't never going away.

"Reckon they liked Mama," I said.

"But they're still coming, aren't they? By the dozens."

"If I got so many folks on my side, Hiram, then how come I ain't winning?"

"I'll answer that with another question. Would Harley Blevins go to this much trouble if you were losing?"

I set for a time, studying on that. I said, "We owe the First Bank of Virginia one hundred and thirty bucks by June the first."

"That so?"

"I don't have a hundred and thirty bucks. And lest you got some rich relation you never told us about, you don't neither."

"Not at present."

"So maybe it don't even matter what the price of gas is tomorrow. Maybe nothing matters."

"Do you know?" he said. "Now might just be the right time for Madame Ouspenskaya."

Chapter
FOURTEEN

He didn't say another word about it, but next morning, he asked me where the Western Union office was, and Thursday afternoon, he took the truck over to Front Royal, and come back that evening with a stack of handbills.

"Janey and Earle, you two done your homework? All right, I want you to walk these into town. Stick 'em wherever they won't blow away. Best place is on the windshield of a parked car, right under the wiper, but if you can squeeze 'em under a doorway or against a window, that works, too. Oh, and anyone passes you by, you be sure to give 'em one. Along with your best smile, Janey. Yep, *that's* the one I mean. . . ."

"Hold on, now," I said. "What exactly you planning to hand out here?"

"Oh," he said, and handed me the bill right on top.

SATURDAY ONLY!

NOON TO FIVE

at

Brenda's Oasis

meet

MADAME OUSPENSKAYA*!!!*

READS PALMS, TAROT, CRYSTAL BALL
OFFERS LOVE SPELLS, MONEY SPELLS, PROTECTION SPELLS
CARRIES MESSAGES FROM THE GREAT BEYOND!

5 CENTS PER VISION

Just below was a drawing of a gypsy lady. She had dangly earrings and a pair of heavy ol' lips and something on her chin that was either a beauty mark or a bullet hole. But mostly she had eyes, black as new tires, rising right off the paper.

"Who the hell is this?"

"That's the good madame herself."

"You're telling me this old hag is coming to our station?"

"Sure she is."

"She can't be for real."

"Close enough."

Those eyes was hard enough to cut through bone.

"Is this even what she looks like?"

"Close enough."

"Well . . . where is she?"

"I've still got to fetch her. Say, can I have the truck Friday night?"

"Friday . . ."

"I'll have her back here by Saturday morning."

It come flashing over me then. The image of that evil-looking lady sitting in my truck.

"I don't know, Hiram."

"I'm telling you, the townsfolk will love it. The worse the economy gets, the more people seek guidance from above."

"Ain't that what Pastor Goolsby's for?"

"Pastor Goolsby won't tell them how long they're going to live. Or carry messages from dead Aunt Sadie. Oh, but you missed the most important part of the deal."

"Where?"

"Right there, at the bottom of the bill."

Lubrication Special
Any car 98 cents

"Ouspenskaya's just the hook," said Hiram. "You're the one who's gonna pull 'em in. Once they get a load of what you can do, they're ours."

Was the peppiest I'd ever heard him talk.

"But this is just two cents less than we normally charge," I said.

"Which is what makes it a special. Keep reading."

"FREE! Inspect tires. Inflate tires. Check wheel alignment. Test brakes . . . Hiram, we already do that stuff for free."

"So what? People are always looking for a break. Oh, and I came up with a slogan, too. What do you think?"

If Your Car's PARCHED . . .
Bring It on by Brenda's Oasis!

"See, I chose the word *parched* because it makes a person think *desert*, doesn't it? Imagine now. You're dragging your sorry carcass over sand dunes. Sun beating down, no water in sight. Camels all dead. Lo and behold, out of nowhere comes an oasis. Not a mirage, either—the real thing. Praise the Lord."

"They'll get all that from a single word?"

"Sure."

I set the bill down on the dining table.

"Where'd you learn to think like that?"

"Oh." He shrugged. "I used to write copy for J. Walter Thompson. Back in the day."

Name could've been J. Venus Mars for all it meant to me.

"Listen, Hiram, our people ain't lawyers or bankers or Rotary wives. Our people is truckers and tourists."

"God bless the truckers *and* the tourists, but they won't keep you afloat. You've got hours and hours every day where nobody's stopping by. This afternoon, I drove by three of Harley Blevins's stations. Pumps working around the clock. You wouldn't think it in the middle of a depression, but they're there, *everybody's* there. Farmers

137

and coal men and schoolteachers. Bank clerks, stationmasters. They're going to Harley because they don't know about you."

"And Madame Whatsherhoozit is gonna bring 'em?"

"She's going to start. The rest is up to us."

I stared into those bottomless oil-black eyes. Then I glanced up at Janey and Earle.

"Well, what you waiting for?" I said. "Get moving!"

The bills all got put somewhere, and not another word was said on the subject of fortune-telling till after supper Friday when Hiram was climbing into the truck.

"Wait," I said. "You haven't even told me where this crazy lady lives."

"Washington," he said.

"As in DC?"

He nodded.

"That's a far piece," I said.

"Oh, it's not so bad. I've got a full tank."

"It's dark out, though."

"Fewer cars that way."

"You sure you don't want Earle to go with you?"

"No, I'm good."

"Well, okay." I closed the door after him. "Just don't—drive in a ditch or get yourself killed."

"I will do neither of those things. Tell me something," he said.

"What?"

"When did you stop being an *uh*-melia?"

"Sorry . . ."

"On your birth certificate, it says Amelia Hoyle."

"Oh. Yeah. Got shortened."

"Why?"

"I dunno. Mama always said I was in too much of a dang hurry to be dragging all those letters after me. Guess it was just easier to chop one off."

Hiram nodded.

"Well," he said, "it appears I have sufficient time in my day for extraneous letters. So if it's all the same to you, I'll tack it back on."

I didn't say yes or no. Truth is, I'd never figured such a thing for being possible. Putting a name back to where it had been.

"Good night," he said. "Good night, Amelia Hoyle."

He held down the clutch till the engine was of a mind to go.

"See you in the morning," he said.

• • •

An hour after he left, the rain come. One of them *sincere* rains that wants to claw up every last smell from the earth. Most of the time, Earle and Janey love to go to sleep to the sound, but that night, they was on edge and kept asking for more Sinbad stories. I had to really put the poor feller through his paces—crocs and apes and man-eating giants and I don't know what else. *Enough*, I said finally, but even then, they wouldn't go off.

"Where's Washington?" asked Janey.

"Oh," I said, settling into the bed space between her and Earle. "It's due east of here."

"Is it far?"

"Two, three hours by car. We'll get there ourselves someday."

"Franklin Delano Roosevelt lives there," said Earle.

"That he does."

"Mrs. Roosevelt, too."

"When she ain't busy."

They was quiet for a bit, but Earle spoke up again.

"That fortune-teller throws any evil my way, I'll send it right back."

Seems I wasn't the only one troubled by that picture.

"She don't really look like that," I said. "That's just, you know, art."

"I'll give 'er what for," said Earle.

They finally nodded off around midnight. Me, I was up another hour, listening to the rain. Don't know how long I slept before I jerked up in the bed. A pair of lights was sweeping across the front of the house.

I crept to the door. In the driving rain, I saw two shadows, queerly joined, rising and falling together.

"Hiram?" I whispered.

"Give me a hand," he said.

"Where?"

"Up to my room."

It was very near a relief, rummaging in the dark for the keys. Meant I didn't have to look at her head-on. Wasn't till we was all standing at the bottom of the stairs that I dared a peep.

She was slumped against Hiram's shoulder, so all I could see at first was a blue kimono and a pelt of wet hair, reddish brown with worries of gray. Then her head tipped back, and I saw a round face caked in white powder—like a pork chop dredged in flour. On her mouth was a painted Cupid's bow.

"Say, now," she said. "What *is* this dump?"

"Why, it's the Willard," said Hiram.

"For real?"

He give me a signal, and I took her by the left arm, and between us, we got her up the stairs. She was lighter than she looked, but she rattled the whole way. Brooches and pins and necklaces. Rings on near every finger. Fumes of bourbon rising off like swamp mist.

"Geez," she said. "What happened to the damned elevator?"

"Broken."

Took some doing, but we lowered her onto Hiram's mattress. She laid there, still jangling, eyelids aflutter under penciled-in brows.

"Hiram, honey. Tell 'em not to wake me before noon. I can't do a thing before noon."

Then she rolled onto her side. The jangling stopped. Half a minute later, she was snoring.

"Go back to bed," Hiram told me.

"Where you gonna sleep?"

"Floor's fine." He looked at me. "Don't worry. Nothing un-Christian is gonna happen."

"It ain't that."

But I couldn't say what it was, neither.

"You'd best get some shut-eye," he said. "We open in a few hours."

Well, naturally, I didn't catch a wink from then on. When dawn come, I was already up, watching the mountains bleed out of the dark. No eggs for breakfast, so I made myself eat some old coconut macaroons. Even with the moldy edges cut off, they was dry as bark, but it was all my stomach could get down.

To my surprise, Hiram was up, too. Washed and shaved and setting out the old root table in front of the store.

"You didn't sleep, neither," I said.

"Too much coffee in Warrenton."

He reached into an old turnip sack and pulled out an oilskin cloth and arranged it over the table. Then he pulled out a crystal ball and a deck of tarot cards.

"We'll need a chair," he said.

"I'll get one from the house. This where she's gonna sit?"

"Yes, ma'am."

I ran my finger round the table's rim. "When's she planning on comin' down?"

"When the time's right."

"You don't mind my saying, she looked pretty tight."

"I've seen Barrymores tighter than that. She'll come through."

Problem with getting up so early was there wasn't too much to do right off. I fed the kids two bowls of Aunt Sally rolled oats and a couple slices of bread soaked in Wesson. ("Can't you at least fry it?" Janey said.) I made sure the pumps was in order, made sure Earle knew how to work 'em. Mostly I roamed. Up the road and back. Some point or other, I swung a glance over toward the front porch and saw Janey, hunched over some pasteboard, with a box of crayon stubs by her elbow.

"Melia!" she called. "How do you spell *haunted*?"

"Who wants to know?"

"Me."

"To what end?"

"I'm gonna make me a haunted house."

"No, you ain't."

"In the root cellar."

"I said you ain't."

She jumped to her feet. "Don't you *dare* tell me no! There ain't nothing in that root cellar 'cept for mice and rotten parsnips and Emmett Tolliver's moonshine, and even *you* don't like going down there, so there's something gotta be haunting it. And Earle's already helping with the gas, and Daddy Hiram's got the store, and I mean to pull my weight."

I could see there weren't no turning that child's mind. She even drug me down to the cellar and made me stand there in the dark while she hid behind an old joist.

"Ready?" she said.

Into that dark, musty, dripping space, she sent scream after scream, each higher in frequency than the last, bouncing off wall and ground and ceiling and shredding every last nerve. When she was done, she stepped back out, grinning and bashful.

"What do you think, Melia?"

"It's just gonna be you screaming your fool head off?"

"Well, sure. Don't I sound fearsome?"

Had to admit she did.

"But you ain't gonna have no voice left by day's end."

"That's okay, it'll get me out of school."

"Well, okay. But you can't charge more 'n a penny."

"Make it two, and we got ourselves a deal."

• • •

The cars started pulling in after ten. Not much at first—wagons and delivery vans. It was around eleven when a new crowd started rolling in. Adler Standards and a Hudson Greater Eight and a

Pierce-Arrow and the cutest ol' Nash Ambassador, but there was Buicks, too, and Plymouths and Ford coupes. Some of the cars was driven by folks I knew—Basil Buckner, Ella Preston, Minnie-Cora Harper and her latest beau. Some I'd never seen in all my days.

Earle was mighty pressed to keep the gas flowing, and since a good third of the customers wanted the lubrication deal, I ended up in the service bay for the rest of the morning. Somewhere around eleven thirty there came a lull, and I stepped out of the bay, smearing the sweat off my face with my forearm and looking round.

It was a whole new world.

All those cars that had driven in . . . well, they hadn't driven off. They'd parked themselves. On the gravel, on the shoulder, wherever they could find a spot. And from those cars had spilled out half of Walnut Ridge.

Women talking in low, bustling tones. Men with their hands in their overalls, chewing their quids. Earle striding from car to car and Hiram calling out "Lemonade! Coffee! Iced tea!" Kids *everywhere.* Rocking themselves dizzy on our tree swings or rotting their teeth with our Coke-and–Life Savers cocktails or stumbling white-faced out of Janey's haunted house, grabbing at their chests.

And that didn't count the two dozen or so folks who was lined up for Madame Ouspenskaya. Persons of every age and station, waiting with that air you see sometimes outside a WPA office. Quiet, but tensed like arrows. I thought of the woman I'd helped up the stairs that morning, and I thought, *There's no way these folks is gonna walk away happy.*

Hiram was already working the line like some small-town mayor, shaking hands, tousling kids' hair. "Don't you worry," I could hear him saying. "She'll be down here before you know it. And it'll be the best nickel you ever spent, I guarantee it."

But noon came, and she wasn't there.

"Aw, you know how women are," Hiram chuckled. "Let me go check on her. Don't go anywhere, friends."

If it were me, I'd have gone home, but those people stayed where they was, and by the time Hiram come back down, there was a good hundred folks lined up. And now they really *was* starting to stir and grumble, and it was all I could do not to go up to each and every one of them and tell 'em how sorry I was and would they go away if I give 'em each a nickel?

Then the door to the store opened, and out she came.

Thought I was pure dreaming at first. The woman who'd come staggering in out of the rain had changed into someone else altogether. Someone bigger, for starters. What with her heels and her crazy black wig, she must've grown half a foot. Her face was even whiter, and she'd rimmed her eyes in something that looked like charcoal, and she'd switched out her kimono for a long black robe with half-moons and stars. Oh, and her Cupid's bow was now a gash of purple that only kinda resembled a mouth.

"It is she!" cried Hiram in a ringing voice. "The one who sees all! Madame Ouspenskaya!"

With great dignity, the fortune-teller set herself at that table, settled her robe around her, then turned on the crowd and said, in a low growl, "Who weeshes to see the trroooth? Who *dares* to see the trroooth?"

A shudder went through the citizens of Walnut Ridge. It was some time before the first person in line worked up the nerve to come forward. She was a heavyish lady with gold spectacles hanging from a cord, and before she'd got out two words, Madame O stopped her.

"Please to deposit five cents," she said. Then she swung her head back toward Hiram. *"And please to bring Ouspenskaya her tea!"*

Hiram had the thermos already waiting. The fortune-teller took a sip, winced a little, then took another. From the way it went down her, I suspicion it was something other than tea.

"Now, my dear," she said. "Tell Ouspenskaya all your troubles."

Just when I thought the world had no more bodies to offer, more kept coming. From Riverton and Riverside, from Waterlick and Nineveh, from Chester Gap and Happy Creek. By mid-afternoon, cars and trucks was jammed along both sides of the road—two hundred yards in each direction—barely enough room for a tricycle to get by. It was like a county fair or a carnival, and, for the first time in our lives, we was in the heart of it. All these grinning, chattering, back-slapping people. All these children, swinging by the half dozen or going back for more of Janey's wails or running in circles like guinea hens.

The gas and lubricant kept flowing, the store shelves got emptier and emptier, and the line to see Madame O showed every sign of being perpetual. Even from the service bay, I could hear her snarling at her customers.

"A dreadful curse hangs over you! Only blood can remove it! . . . The devil and the moon sit opposed! You must give up this man you call Billy Bob! . . . Make peace with your dead grandmother now, for tonight *you yourself will die!*"

Didn't matter how dire the forecast—people wanted more. I'll confess I wished for a couple minutes myself, but I had too much going on with batteries and spark plugs and fan belts.

There was a few locals who declined to partake in the day's festivities. Chester Gallagher swung by for a couple gallons and a hello, but Mina stayed in the car with the windows closed. Pastor Goolsby drove by, real slow, like someone taking the measure of Gomorrah. (Mrs. Goolsby had already snuck in to get her palm read.) And somewhere round three in the afternoon, the butternut Chevy Eagle of Harley Blevins come rolling past.

Dudley was back at the wheel, in his Buck Rogers outfit. I saw the car stop for a few seconds, long enough for Harley himself to push his head out the window and take in everything he needed to see. He snapped his fingers, twice, and the car drove on. Dudley never took his eyes off the road.

I can't tell you how many thermoses Madame O downed over the course of that day, but by four o'clock, her head was tilting hard south. It'd lift a little when someone set down next to her, but then it'd start sinking all over again—till finally it was resting right on the table.

"Madame Ouspenskaya!" cried Hiram. "Are you all right?"

From somewhere in that tangle of black hair come a low droning.

"What'd she say?" someone called.

"The shadow world has grown dim," said Hiram. "No *more* can Ouspenskaya see."

"But we ain't heard our fortune," said someone else.

"It's a rotten deal," allowed Hiram. "If I could make the spirit world operate like a business, you bet I would. But tell you what, everyone still in line is going to receive a chit. The next time Madame Ouspenskaya's in town, you'll *all* get a free reading, you've got my word on it. Till then, how about some saltwater taffy, folks? It's on the house. . . ."

Funny thing. For all the people who'd lined up to see her, nobody paid her much mind once she was conked out. Me, least of all. It was only that night—when the crowd had finally cleared out and taken their cars and kids and left behind all their wrappers and bottles and straws and paper cups—that I saw Hiram bending over some bundle and realized the bundle was her.

"Tell me she's alive," I said.

"She is."

"What are we supposed to do with her?"

"Same as we did before."

Only she was a lot heavier this time. Weren't no point dragging her back up the stairs, so we took her into the house and laid her in Mama's bed. By now her wig had fallen half off her head, and her string of beads had somehow wrapped itself round her forehead like a rani's headdress.

"Hiram," she muttered. "Put a sign on the door, would you? I don't want any maids waking me up."

"We don't got no door," I whispered.

"She won't notice."

True to form, she dropped right back to sleep. Like some anchor come and dragged her down.

"How do you know her again?" I asked.

"My theater days."

"She an actor, too?"

"Wardrobe mistress. I figured, with this kind of thing, the clothes are more important than the acting."

Watching Madame O laying there, with the snores pouring out her open mouth, I got a little stab thinking on Mama. Only 'cause she would've got such a laugh out of it.

"Guess it's okay to leave her," I said.

"She wouldn't have it any other way. Got something to show you."

The bag of change was sitting behind the store counter under Hiram's stool. He picked it up, hefted it in his hand with a tiny cracked smile.

"You want to count it yourself?" he said.

"Just tell me."

"One hundred ninety-four dollars and fifty-six cents."

I had to sit down, but there weren't nowhere to sit.

"You ain't shitting me, are you?"

"I should add that eight dollars and seventeen cents of that came directly from Miss Janey Hoyle. Who can no longer speak."

"Oh, my," I said. "Oh, Lord. What are we—what are we gonna—"

"We're going to start by paying the good madame her salary. Thirty-five dollars, with board and lodging thrown in."

"Okay."

"Then, on Monday morning, I suggest you and I bring one hundred and thirty dollars—in little stacks of coinage—to one

Wallace Paxton of First Bank of Virginia. See how he likes *them* apples. As for the remaining twenty-nine dollars and change . . . that's up to you."

At first I was stumped, but then I got the brightest picture in my head. Me and Janey and Earle walking into Pastor Goolsby's church of a Sunday morning. Pouring those twenty-nine dollars right into the collection plate and daring the whole congregation to take 'em out again.

Oh, I knew it'd never happen, but it give me some satisfaction. "That'll teach 'em," I said, half under my breath. "Best not mess with the Gas Station Pagans."

Hiram's face got an extra crease. "What's that?"

"It's just a name they give us in town. They meant it like an insult, but we figured we'd just turn it on its head and make it our own."

Hiram nodded slow. "I like the sound of it myself," he said.

"Well, you better," I said. "You're one of us now."

Chapter
FIFTEEN

All in all, it was a good thing we weren't church folk, 'cause the four of us was so beat, we slept near to noon. I'd have slept later if Madame Ouspenskaya hadn't commenced to tugging on my ankle.

"Hey, kid. Is there a cab in this joint?"

Hiram took her back to Washington and didn't get home till six. All we had it in us to do that night was get our weekly baths and listen to *Amos 'n' Andy* and Fred Allen. Next morning, I woke up figuring I'd dreamed the whole business. The fortune-teller and the kids on the tire swings and Janey screaming in the root cellar and Hiram lifting up that sack of money—none of it could've happened, could it?

But after the morning truckers had cleared off, Hiram went up to his room and came down in Chester's old suit.

"We'd best be off," he said.

"Where?"

"First Bank of Virginia."

So I put up the CLOSED sign in the window, and we drove into Front Royal and set down with Mr. Wallace Paxton, whose mustache had yet to crawl off his face (though it dearly wanted to). Hiram hoisted up the turnip sack and set to stacking every last nickel, dime, and quarter in columns on the banker's desk. Took him near ten minutes, but he enjoyed every second of it.

"Feel free to check my figures," he said.

Well, Mr. Wallace Paxton was looking a little green in the gills by now. He reached out one arm of his seersucker suit and dragged all those stacks into a big patent-leather pouch.

"Pardon me," he said to Hiram. "Have we met before?"

"We have not."

"And you would be?"

"The girl's father," said Hiram, his voice deep as a coal seam. "You're telling me you don't see the resemblance?"

"Spitting image."

"That's what I've been told."

"It goes without saying"—Mr. Wallace Paxton pressed that pouch to him sweet and tender—"that First Bank of Virginia deeply appreciates your continued business, and we bid you both good day."

"There's just one more thing," said Hiram.

"Yes?"

"Next time you send one of those viperish little letters of yours, you address it to *me*, do you follow? And we'll take care of it man-to-man."

Now, I'd have said Mr. Wallace Paxton had ten or fifteen pounds advantage on Hiram, but you'd never of known it.

"Of course. Naturally. And may I say what a relief it is to do business with a gentleman of your obvious sagacity."

We took our leave with no more fuss, and we was just about to climb back in the truck when I remembered we'd left our empty sack behind.

"Just leave it," said Hiram.

"I ain't giving them nothing they ain't earned."

So that's how I come to walk into the bank just as Mr. Wallace Paxton lifted his head off his desk and shouted to his secretary in the next office.

"Miss Stanhope! Get me Harley Blevins on the phone."

I figured it was okay to leave 'em our turnip sack.

One way or another, we was feeling mighty merry when we pulled back into the station. I was just about to get out of the car when Hiram put his fingers on my arm and said, "The bills are for you."

Dollar bills, he meant. He counted them, one by one, into my palm. Eleven.

"What the hell is this?" I said.

"Your salary."

"What are you talking?"

"Amelia." He put his one good eye level with my two. "You've been working like a dog all these years, and nobody's ever given you any wages?"

"Wages is for chumps," I said.

All the same, I will confess that the paper felt good in my hand.

"What are you going to do with it?" said Hiram.

"Save it."

"Toward what?"

"Well, that's a good question. New piston grinder runs twelve hundred, so that ain't about to happen. Westinghouse refrigerator these days is running hundred and nine with no extras. I'm thinking plate-glass window for the store. That's no more 'n a hundred, and I'm pretty sure I could talk the glazier down 'cause he's a hopeless drunk every day but Sunday."

"Nothing for yourself?"

"What would I get for me?"

"I don't know. A new dress, maybe. A pair of shoes."

I was all set to tell him about Joan Crawford's sandals, but then I remembered they was still in the back of the broom closet, covered in mud. Hadn't had the heart to touch them since that afternoon with Dudley. If they hadn't been Mama's, I'd have pitched them out with the Monday trash.

"Well," said Hiram, "you think on it. Meantime, how about we all go to a picture show tonight?"

"Picture show?"

"Sure."

Well, it's a strange fact about the Gas Station Pagans that we will read *Modern Screen* and *Photoplay* and *Movie Mirror* front to back and tell you what Wallace Beery's pool looks like and where Norma Shearer spent her honeymoon, but when it comes to actual *movies*, well, we tend to steer clear.

Mama, she just hated to spend the money, and Earle favors the radio. Me . . . I don't know, there's some part of me hates all forms of cunning, so soon as the lights go down, I can neither stop myself from seeing every crummy trick that's being played on me nor can I forgive.

Janey's different, though. Once she saw Gary Cooper nursed back to life by Helen Hayes in *A Farewell to Arms*, she was hooked. And when Hiram said the Park Theatre was showing something called *Men in White*, first thing out of her mouth was, "You mean like doctors?"

"Sounds it," said Hiram.

"Gee," she said. "This one have Gary Cooper, too?"

"Clark Gable."

"I'll give him a try."

We'd have never gone to that picture but for her, 'cause the Murphy Theatre was showing *Death Takes a Holiday*, and Death was played by Mr. Fredric March, who is okay by me, but Janey had to have her wounds, and seeing what little voice she had left, we couldn't stand in her way.

It wasn't but a twenty-minute drive to Front Royal, but parking the truck was harder than we figured—the only space big enough was over by the Presbyterian church. The theater was mostly full by the time we got there. The only row that had four seats together was all the way in the front, and the only way it had four seats was if the woman sitting at the very, very end of the aisle weren't expecting no one else to join her.

So Hiram, he did the natural thing. He leaned toward the woman in question and said, "Ma'am?"

Well, she jumped like a quail, and who could blame her? I'd seen three-hundred-pound truckers grow alarmed at the sight of Hiram.

"Didn't mean to startle you," he said. "Is it all right if we sit here?"

She stared at him.

"I mean, you're not expecting anyone?" he said.

A flush stole into her cheeks, then into his.

"We'd be grateful for the company," he said, pressing on.

She spoke. Not a timid voice at all, but low and full.

"Why, of course," she said. "Please."

Earle stepped on past her, and I was all set to follow Hiram when Janey grabbed my arm.

"Melia," she whispered. "That's Crazy Ida."

"Who's that?" I asked.

"Oh, for the love of Pete." She dragged me back into the aisle and hissed in my ear. "Crazy Ida Folsom is the daughter of some local quarry owner. Got her heart broke twenty years back by some feller."

"Big deal. What'd he do, leave her at the altar?"

"Left her the day *after*. On their honeymoon."

"Well, that is peculiar."

"Now, some say she kilt him, but there's others say they seen him shacking up with some hotsy totsy in Harrisonburg. Which makes him a two-timer and maybe even a bigamist."

Two-timer. Bigamist. Hotsy totsy. Where'd she ever find these words?

The house lights was still up, so I could see Ida's face tolerably well. Heart-shaped in its youth, I guessed, but going soft round the edges, with curd-white skin that blotched in the oddest places.

"She don't look crazy to me," I said.

"Oh, but she never got over losing her feller, and ever since, she goes round town all on her lonesome. Square dances, church

156

socials—*movie* theaters. Wherever you'd take a husband, only it's just her."

"Ain't nothing wrong with a woman going off by herself. She don't need no damn man."

"But Melia, her *hair* . . ."

Can't explain why I didn't notice right off. All I needed was another second or two, and I could see that weren't no cape or shawl hanging all the way down to the floor. That was Ida Folsom's by-God hair. Long as an Indian squaw's . . . mighty as a river. Draped cross her lap like some rich lady's dog. *Dear God,* I thought. *How much time would it take for a gal to grow hair that long?*

Then it hit me. Twenty years.

Ida Folsom's hair had been growing for twenty years. And it'd keep growing till that man of hers come home.

"What's the holdup?" called Hiram. "Show's about to start."

So we filed on in, Janey and me, and you'll have to believe me when I say that, hard as it was not to look at Ida's hair, it was even harder not to *step* on it. I was relieved, honestly, when Hiram took the seat next to her. Even more relieved when the lights went down.

It was a full bill that night. Krazy Kat cartoon, then a newsreel on the emir of Yemen, then a Charley Chase comedy, and only then did *Men in White* get around to showing itself. It was mostly pretty dumb. Clark Gable walks around in white scrubs—whitest you ever seen—and saves little girls and old folks, but he spends too much time at his work, so his rich girlfriend gets all hot in the collar. "How come you can't have some vittles with me, and how come you don't love me like I love you?" and on and on. So along comes this pretty little nurse who's English. . . .

157

Well, that's 'bout as much as I can tell you 'cause it was right around then I noticed Hiram's head tipping. Just ever so slightly in the direction of Crazy Ida.

At first I figured he was falling asleep, only the head tipped itself back like nothing happened. Couldn't make sense of it, but then I heard him talking. In the most low-down secret kind of way. I was sitting right next to him, and I had to work to hear him.

"Get a load of that hospital. It's like something on Venus. . . . Never seen a patient with so much makeup. . . . It won't do letting Myrna Loy into your operating room. . . ."

Looking back, I can see it's the kind of thing I do at the movies, too, always seeking out the foolishness. But I could tell that he meant his little wisecracks for one pair of ears, and they wasn't mine.

Now and then he'd say something so amusing she'd have to put one of her gloved hands over her mouth to keep a laugh from coming out. Before long, she started whispering back to him. And something she said must've been funny, too, 'cause his head tilted back and his lips stretched wide.

Dear God, I thought.

From there, that dang movie couldn't end quick enough. Soon as the actors' names come crawling up the screen, I was calling over to Janey and Earle.

"Hey, now! We'd best get going! Scoot!"

"Oh, what's the hurry?" said Hiram. "Think I saw a soda counter down the street."

Before I could talk him out of it, he was leaning his head back toward Crazy Ida. "Maybe you'd care to join us," he said.

Long as I live, I don't think I'll forget the look on her face. Or the way the words come rushing out of her, like they was afraid of being called back.

"I'd be delighted," she said.

Wouldn't you know? Shiner's Drug had four open stools. Hiram sat the kids first, then he offered Crazy Ida the third, and he motioned for me to take the last, but I said I'd rather stand.

"Daddy Hiram," said Janey, "can I get a cherry Coke?"

"Why not?" said Hiram.

But she was too cranked up to drink a drop.

"Daddy Hiram, what's an appendix?"

"It's something that, when it gets good and ready, wants to come out."

"What's the point of having one in the first place?"

"Heck if I know."

Just then, Crazy Ida said, "Darwin."

It came dribbling out one side of her mouth. She flushed a little and swung that river of hair and, with the most apologizing eyes I ever seen, she said, "Well, *Darwin*."

"Oh, brother," I muttered.

"You mean Darwin had a theory about the appendix?" said Hiram.

"Well, yes," she said, flushing brighter. "He suggested it had a job once. To digest leaves. You know, back in the days of the primates. But now that we don't eat leaves, we don't need it quite so much. So we—we only miss it when it's gone."

Nothing but quiet. And through the quiet, Hiram's eyes, the good one and the bad, all shiny with wonder.

"What's a primate?" said Janey.

"Who the hell is Darwin?" said Earle.

"A great man," said Hiram. "Beloved of Gas Station Pagans everywhere."

"I believe," said Janey, "I will call my first child Darwin."

The next five or ten minutes is mostly lost to me now. Earle, I seem to recall, drained a strawberry phosphate in record time. Janey probably nursed her Coke. Hiram and Ida, I'm pretty sure, drank their chocolate shakes. Hiram's hat was off and, as he spoke, he ran his finger round the sweat band.

"*Melia!*"

It was the woman at the very end of the counter. Who, upon further looking, turned out to be Mrs. Frances Bean.

Now, I hadn't seen her since Mama's wake, and any other night, I might've asked myself what she was doing sitting alone in Shiner's Drug with a big ol' birch-beer vanilla ice cream float. Where in hell was Mr. Bean? But tonight, all I could think was how to keep her from seeing the spectacle at the other end of the counter.

"What a pleasure," I said.

"You know, I thought it was you."

"And you was right."

"Oh, and there's Janey! And Earle, and that dear old daddy of yours. It does a body good seeing the four of you up and about, with a little pep in your step. It's like I always say. Just 'cause trouble knocks on your door, you don't have to ask it in and set it in a chair."

"God's truth."

Then she motioned me toward her.

"I want you to know, Melia. I consider it downright sweet."

"What is?"

160

"How quick your daddy's gettin' over your mama."

I swung my head back toward Hiram and Ida. There they was, leaning toward each other, their elbows on the counter, their chins propped in their hands. Laughs tinkling in the electric light.

"I don't care how far menfolk get on in life," said Frances Bean. "They *always* need taking care of." She lifted her spoon an inch or two above her saucer. "'Cept mine."

Chapter
SIXTEEN

On the drive home, Janey was still peeling that damn movie open.

"So where did the English nurse go?" she said. "First she kisses Dr. Gable, then she goes away, then she comes back sick as a dog. What from?"

"Dr. Gable just needed something to feel bad about," said Hiram.

"But he tried to save her."

"*I'd* save her," said Earle. "I'd save her but good."

Hiram thought that was funny.

"Dr. Gable's got big ears," said Janey.

"Always has," said Hiram.

"What's that s'posed to mean?"

"I mean he had them the one time I met him, and that was, oh, nine or ten years ago."

Janey set up in her seat. "You knew Clark Gable?"

"Well, I met him is all. When he was still trying to break into the business."

Earle was sitting up now. "You was out in Hollywood?"

"For a time."

"Was you in pictures?" asked Janey.

"*In* them, no. Once they got a load of my lazy eye—well, that'll pass on the stage but not on the screen. So I became a scenarist."

"What in tarnation is that?"

"Why, he's the fellow that writes the thing. The dialogue and the situations and so forth."

"You wrote movies?"

"For a bit."

"And ads, too," I said. "And sold hats. Ain't no limit to Daddy Hiram."

The truck got quiet.

"Lord," said Janey.

"What climbed up your ass?" said Earle.

Well, I didn't say nothing right off, but soon as we got home, I told those two young 'uns they could pack it right in.

"How come?" said Earle.

"So I can speak with Daddy Hiram."

"On what subject?"

"The subject of how I'm about to tan your hide."

They was still fearful slow about going. Zigging and zagging and circling. But I stared 'em down till they was inside. Hiram, he just leaned back against the truck, fishing in his pockets for a Zippo.

"There a problem?" he said.

"Not unless you count being shamed by Frances Bean."

"Shamed how?"

"On account of you courtin' a crazy old maid."

He lit himself a Lucky, took his sweet time with the first draw.

"Miss Ida Folsom," he said, "is one of the more balanced specimens I've met in my lifetime. As for being an old maid, I believe she has herself a husband somewhere."

"And *you* got a wife in the ground. Who you're supposed to be grieving on."

He smoked a while longer.

"Only I don't have a wife in the ground. I thought we understood that. All I'm supposed to do is tell people I'm your father."

"Well, how are they gonna believe you if you don't act like it?"

"So you want me to pretend to be torn up over a woman I've never met? Just how am I supposed to do that?"

"I don't know, maybe Clark Gable can help you out."

He studied me. "So I'm not even allowed to have a past anymore, is that what you're telling me? I've got to erase my whole history."

"All I'm asking is—show some *respect*, that's all. A little goddamn *respect*. Even if you never did meet my mama. 'Cause I'm telling you if you *had* . . ."

My eyes was stinging, so I cut them toward the house. Earle and Janey was watching us from the front window, with their hands curved like binoculars round their eyes.

"If you'd of ever met my mama," I said, "you'd be torn up about her. Every hour of every day. There'd be times you couldn't hardly breathe."

"Amelia," he said, "I know what you're going through. I lost a mother, too. But you can't ask me or anybody on God's green Earth to . . . to stop *living*. Just to keep your little house of cards from falling down."

I turned round real slow. The heat was climbing up from my chest.

"House of cards," I said. "That's what you think this is."

"From some angles, yes."

Now the heat was rolling up my throat. Coming on with such force, I knew if I let it out, it would travel all the way to the moon.

"Listen here, Mr. Hiram Watts. If that's how you feel about this house—this *family*—maybe you should just hightail it on out of here. I bet there's a coal truck comin' along any minute."

He looked at me a long time. Then he dropped his cigarette on the ground, mashed it with his boot. "Is this how you're gonna be your whole life, Amelia? Driving people off when they don't do what you tell them?"

"I ain't never driven off a body who weren't rarin' to go."

"Jesus." He flung up his arms. "There's no winning with you, is there? Only losing and more losing. And by the way, it's none of your goddamned business who I talk to. Or do a goddamned thing with."

"Is too my business!"

"You may have seen your share of struggles, but there's a whole lot about life you don't know, and I am *way* too far gone in years—"

"To be acting like a lovesick chump."

"To have my last string pulled by a bossy-ass child. That I will not abide!"

He started walking toward the store. Then, a few feet shy of the door, something switched in him, and he kept walking. Past the store, past the house. Moving at a tight fast clip, like he'd just re-called an appointment.

"Hiram . . ."

Can't be sure his name even left my lips, but it hung there all the same as I watched him slip off into the darkness.

The lights was mostly out when I come toeteetering into the house, and Janey and Earle was both lying in bed. They still had their clothes on, though, and they was most definitely not asleep.

"Let's call it," I told them.

Nothing.

"Come on," I said. "You only got but the two days of school left."

"Where's Daddy Hiram?" said Janey.

"He's taking a walk."

Only Hiram never went for walks, I realized all of a sudden. He was about the sittingest body I'd ever known.

"We had words," I said, "but it's all right."

Earle's hands curled into fists. His face squeezed down.

"That's what family does," I said.

Too late. A river of tears was rolling down his face.

"Oh, for all that's holy," I said. "Quit it."

"You made him go away."

"No, I did not."

"Yes, you did. You and your evil tongue and your nasty disposi-tion. You drove him off, and he ain't never coming back."

I looked at Janey, but she weren't about to disagree.

"You two are the dumbest hillbillies I ever seen," I said. "He can't run off without his clothes, can he? And his—his *comb*. His razor . . ."

In my head, I went through his room, item by item. "His Luckys. His shaving cream . . ."

And his what? Whatever cord still bound him to us got thinner and thinner the harder I looked.

"Come on," I said. "You think he'd bail on us without even a word of good-bye?"

"Why not?" said Janey. "That's what *our* daddy did."

Well, that just made Earle sob all the harder. He covered his face with his pillow to stifle the sound, but the bed shook on every side of him. I could've promised him two dozen Sinbad stories and a month of ginger ale, and it wouldn't have made a lick of difference.

"Janey," I said, "I'm gonna sleep in Mama's bed tonight. Make sure Earle don't smother hisself."

I pulled the curtain after me.

Amazing thing. Mama's sheets still had her blackberry scent, and the shape of her body was still carved in the mattress, no matter how hard I laid on it. The dark folded round. Even when Earle had gone silent, my eyes was blazing and my mind circling. Like an old buzzard with nowhere to land.

Must've been two when I finally nodded off. Mama come to me on the nearest dream. We'd missed the last ferry at Dickerson, and night was falling fast, and Mama was laughing and saying, "Time to get us wet." Before I could stop her, she'd thrown herself in the Potomac and started swimming to the far side. Nothing for it but to jump in and follow her.

In real life, you'll learn this, I ain't much of a swimmer, but in the dream, I was pretty damn good. Long, smooth strokes, parting the river. Water warm on my skin. I was probably fifty yards from shore when it hit me. Mama wasn't in front.

I jerked my head round. The river was rolling now, like an ocean, and way off in the spray and froth was Mama. Not drowning, exactly, but bobbing and dipping. Only with each dip, she dipped deeper. The last part of her to go was her hair—beautiful dark red, like fox fur. Queerest thought come over me when she finally dropped under.

At least she give Janey her hair.

I woke with a gulp, thinking I'd swallowed half that river. But the bed was dry.

I sat up. Squinted at the clock. Five thirty-two.

Quiet as I could, I stumbled over to the kitchen and dug out the Rayovac flashlight from under the sink. Crept outside.

It gets fearful dark in Walnut Ridge when the stars ain't out. I had to feel my way round the house, swinging the flashlight in front of me to make sure I didn't fall headlong over something.

The root cellar was open.

Now, what Janey said is true. I do tend to steer clear of that place—specially at night—but I had a hunch, and the only way to know if I was right was to go in.

Didn't need to stay long, that was the good part. Just had to swing the light around for a minute to see what was there and what weren't.

I closed the door after me. Turned round. There was but the one way he could've gone. Up what we call the Snaky Path. Hardly even a path, really, just a kind of gap that winds through a mess of rhododendrons, climbs higher and higher till you meet the rock face and there's no more climbing.

The air was cold, and the grass was clammy on my bare feet. Owls had all gone to bed, but there was a whip-poor-will calling for all he was worth, and some mockingbirds. Wish I could say they made for good company, but the louder they got, the more alone I felt.

It was slow going. What with the bushes and brambles blocking the way, I had all I could do to keep my arms free of scratches. Which is why I didn't pay near enough notice to what was going on below and ended up flat on my side, with a sweet old knot in my shin.

Lordy, but it hurt. And no wonder. I'd gone and tripped over the earthenware jug that held Emmett Tolliver's moonshine.

Well, I knew Hiram couldn't be far off, but the dark was still so thick, I had to *hear* him before I knew where he was.

Wasn't his usual snore, neither. An angry old buzz, like a fly caught under a jar. I picked up the jug. Grunting under its weight, I carried it toward him, stood over his head, and poured. The booze rolled down his face in a cold lather.

"*Huhn . . .*" He jerked up, hands shielding his eyes. "*What the hell!*"

His legs swung under him as he made to stand, but he fell back on his hands and dragged himself clear. I set down the jug. Then I picked up the Rayovac and aimed it at him.

"You too hungover to talk?" I asked.

His hands made a web round his face. "Stop shining that damn thing."

169

I laid the flashlight on the ground, but I set it at an angle so I could still pick him out of the shadows.

"Got any cigarettes?" he asked.

"Naw."

"That's too bad."

With his face still covered, he leaned his elbows on his knees and set to rocking.

"Christ," he said.

"I'll bet," I said. "Must've tasted right awful."

"I'm not so used to it as I was. . . ."

The whip-poor-will was quiet now, but the frogs was twanging their hearts out. First streaks of purple was stealing out of the black.

"Listen here," I said. "I know we didn't put nothing down in writing, but I could swear we agreed on no drinking. If I weren't clear on nothing else, I believe I was tolerable clear on that."

"I believe I was still a little drunk when I agreed."

"You think this is funny."

"No," he said. "I don't."

I looked at him.

"Honestly, Hiram, it ain't even me I'm thinking of, it's Earle. He ain't had a lot of menfolk to look up to. If you gotta know, you're kind of *it* in that department, so . . ." I stared down at my feet. "So I guess I don't want him ever finding you like this."

"I'm grateful he didn't."

He stopped rocking and started in to rubbing at his face, but that just seemed to make things worse, so he let his hands drop to his sides and rested his face on his knees.

You won't believe this, but in that moment, I was really wishing

I could sew. Oh, I know that sounds crazy, but I'm telling you it takes the awkwardness out of things. I've seen more than one woman pour her terrors into a piece of calico.

"Funny thing about that moonshine," I said. "I always tell Janey and Earle it's been sitting in yonder cellar since—well, since the night Emmett Tolliver brung it. Ain't nobody's ever touched it, that's what I always say, but that ain't true."

His face cut a little my way.

"Toward the end there," I said. "With Mama, I mean. Well, you know there ain't much space 'tween her bed and ours—just a curtain to block out the sound. So when the pain come grabbing at her, I don't know, it was like she was right there in bed with us. I couldn't sleep through it. Neither could the kids."

He watched me through the slits of his eyes.

"There was one night," I said, "the sound got so bad, I figured I'd best do something about it. So I went down to that there root cellar and drug up Emmett Tolliver's moonshine. Lord, it's heavy! I don't rightly know how you carried it as far as you did. But I managed to pour some in a milk glass, and I mixed it with some flat Dr Pepper. Mama's mouth was already kinda *swung* open, so all I had to do was pour a little inside. She didn't gag or nothing, so I poured in a little more, then a little more, and she swallowed the whole damn brew.

"Well, sure enough, the groaning stopped, and her breathing got easy and, a few minutes later, she was down. Slept straight through till morning, too, which was a miracle. I 'member I woke in a fright, thinking something was wrong, but she was just sleeping.

"So that's how it took. Every night I'd give her some of Emmett

Tolliver's medicine and some Dr Pepper, and she was glad to have it. And what with the jug doing its work—well, Janey and Earle could go stretches not even pondering on things, 'cause I'd pack 'em off to school at dawn, and when they come back, I'd just load 'em down with chores, and after supper I'd send 'em out to play and only bring 'em in when Mama was dosed up but good.

"Won't deny I felt guilty some nights. Owing to that she'd sworn off the booze and all. But I reckoned this was a special case."

Slow as he could, he raised his head. "Why are you telling me all this?"

"'Cause the only other person who needed Emmett Tolliver's medicine as bad as you? She was in the business of dying. So whatever pain *you're* in, I'm guessing it's rough."

He closed his eyes, dragged the skin back from his face.

"Listen," I said. "If this is any way my doing—"

"It isn't."

"Then what?"

"I guess"—he opened his eyes halfway—"I guess it's what comes of thinking on things."

"What kinda things?"

"Mortal things."

"Like death, you mean?"

"Like love," he said.

"Love?" I said.

He curled his arms round his chest.

"That first flutter, Amelia. It's like nothing else in the world. Never even knew how much I missed it."

"That what you felt with Ida?"

"Mm." One shoulder shrugged up. "No more than an echo, probably. What it *is*, you see, it's looking in someone's eyes and having them look back. Oh, I know, you're thinking a fellow as ugly as me, he won't ever know that."

"Don't go putting—"

"Well, I'm here to tell you I do know, and it beats any liquor I've ever tasted. Only it goes away."

Couldn't help but think of Dudley. Me watching him watch me.

"I was wrong," I said. "Going and poking my nose in your life. You can see Ida all you want, I don't care. Hell, you can marry her tomorrow. I'll throw Rice Krispies."

Half smiling, he lowered his head. "I believe that would be a waste of store inventory."

"And if you're feared of townsfolk wagging their fool tongues, well, you oughtn't be. They's been wagging since we got here, and we don't pay 'em no never mind."

"Well, now. If I were to concern myself with local gossip, I'd be an even poorer excuse for a man than I already am."

I picked up the flashlight, turned it off.

"You ain't the worst excuse I seen," I said.

He give that some study.

"Tell you what," I said. "I'll get us some coffee going."

"Would you?"

"Hiram."

"Yeah."

"What if I went and proposed something? Like in the way of a business arrangement?"

"Yeah?"

"Thing is, here it is getting on high summer, and I reckon that room of yours will get to roasting before long."

"Already has."

"So it occurred to me you might, you know, think about coming on down and sleeping in the house. In Mama's bed, I mean. Like, from now on."

My two eyes met his one good one, then sidled off.

"'Cause think about it," I said. "Nobody's using her bed, it's just going to waste. And it's gotta be a hell of a lot easier on the body than that nasty ol' tick mattress. God knows what's crawling inside it. I mean, it's just plain common sense."

He was quiet. "You make a good case, Amelia."

"'Course I do."

"Consider me sold."

"Well, okay, then."

I bent down, give the bruise on my shin a light rub, then stood up again. To the east of us, red was piling on top of the purple. I could hear goldfinches.

"Coffee in ten," I said.

"I'll be there."

I was nearly out of his sight when he called after me. "Amelia . . ."

He was standing now, but just barely.

"Did you empty the whole jug?" he said.

"No."

"Then I'll carry it back. And we'll save what's left for the next poor sap who needs it."

Chapter
SEVENTEEN

All things considered, I was ready to give Hiram the day off. But a few hours later, he come trudging down the steps from his room—his breath clean, his face and hair washed—carrying what few belongings he had. The comb and the razor, the shaving cream, and I'd clear forgot about the root table, which was just small enough to fit over his right shoulder. He carried them all into the house, arranged them round Mama's bed. Then he come out again and set himself behind the store counter. Other than taking a longer nap than was customary, he didn't treat that day as different to any other, and neither did I. Even that crazy old redbird was back at work, hammering on the store window.

But that night, Hiram did something that hadn't been done in our house in a very long time. He cooked dinner.

I didn't even know what he was up to. First he lit the stove. Then, from the pie safe, he pulled out a big old cast-iron skillet, scabby with old food. He scraped it down and then rubbed it with some shortening. Then he opened up some old pork-and-beans cans, scooped out the pork pieces, threw them into the pan, and set the flame to high.

It was the sound drew us as much as the smell. The sound of food cooking. Had a far-off note to it, like a train crossing a trestle. Silently we stood round him as he cut up an onion and a stalk of celery and threw them in the pan, too, and then tossed some salt and pepper after.

"Janey," he said, "hand me that wooden bowl, would you?"

He mixed up some water and a little cornstarch and sugar, then he threw that in the skillet, and he stirred and stirred. No more than five minutes later, it was done.

Janey frowned. "What is it?"

"Chop suey," said Hiram. "Or as close as I can get."

He set a trivet in the middle of the table and put the skillet on top, and then he ladled the stuff onto each of our plates. Earle took one forkful and closed his eyes.

"Sweet Jesus."

"Where'd you learn this?" Janey said.

"When I was not much older than Earle over there, I met a man named Yan Sing in Hong Kong. Best cook I ever knew."

"What the hell were you doing in Hong Kong?" I asked.

"Machinist's mate," he said. "With the navy."

"U.S. Navy?" said Earle.

"Some other kind."

Well, that's how Hiram worked—throwing you off the moment you'd picked up his scent. When I look back on that summer,

I remember him moving as little as a human can move, but in his accounts of himself, he was always on the go. Hong Kong, Chicago, Los Angeles, New York.

It gave me some disquiet, honestly, to see how built for speed he was. Everything he owned was in arm's reach. He could go hours without moving, then slip away the next minute like a cat. Many's the time he'd push a yawn back with his fist and wish us a good night and close Mama's curtain after him, and you'd roll right off to sleep and wake up next morning and find him long gone—the clothes never shed, the bed never slept in. Ten minutes later, he'd come strolling back down the south shoulder of Route 55, calm and easy, like the iceman pulling his wagon.

He'd never tell me where he'd been, but there was no denying the smell on him. Talcum and dried apricots and orrisroot. If you could've peeled the paper lining out of some lady's chifforobe, it'd have smelled like that.

Ida.

Only Hiram never looked like he'd been hugging and rubbing on some gal. More like he'd spent the whole night pushing something through his brain—till at last he'd be rolling a cig or shining his shoes or brushing his teeth in front of the washstand mirror, and the idea would come dropping out of him, quiet as a mitten.

"Hot dogs," he'd say.

Which meant, what better way to lure back the kiddies of Warren County for another Saturday outing than with hot dogs?

"Popcorn . . ."

Which meant next Saturday, let's offer free popcorn.

"Compasses . . ." And the following Saturday, it was compasses.

And after that board games and cutout kites stamped with BRENDA'S OASIS, and why stop there? Free matchbooks and spinning tops. Harmonicas and dice and bingo cards and Swedish yo-yos and Blue Eagle decals from the National Recovery Administration. Whatever could be got cheap and snapped up quick, Hiram would turn it into a premium and advertise it every Sunday in the *Warren County Register*, where, for seventy-five cents more, we could put our ad right on top of Harley Blevins's.

"I want him to *feel* us," Hiram said. "Squatting on top."

So if you're asking why I never squawked when Hiram went sneaking out of a night, it's 'cause I knew he'd be back the next morning with some new idea for the place. Maybe ten. *Let's get us a bigger Coca-Cola sign . . . rearrange the hunting-knife display . . . offer free iced tea for first-time customers . . . use a squeegee to clean the car windows. . . .*

"Oh, and let me tell you where we're losing money, Amelia. That air pump. From now on, unless you're a customer, it's going to cost you a nickel. The Lord's air is free, ours isn't."

Some of his dreams was easy to make true—taking down written orders, say, for every repair. Some, like the row of ten billboards he visioned between Walnut Ridge and Strasburg, well, they'd never come to pass in a million Julys. But whenever one notion fell away, another rose to take its place.

"Janey," he said one evening, "how many wildflowers can you pick and bring home in one trip?"

"Queen Anne's lace or lily of the valley?"

"Either. Both."

She stretched out her arms like a cross.

"That's fine," he said. "That's how many I want you to bring

178

home tomorrow morning. And then I want you to strew them all around. Alongside the road, in front of the store. Whatever looks gray and beaten down, lay some flowers on it."

"What happens when they die off?"

"Get new ones. Now, Earle, you know a thing or two about planting, don't you?"

"Yes, sir."

"Gonna grow your own crops someday?"

"Maybe."

"I want a dozen flowerpots. Petunias, geraniums, marigolds— whatever the car exhaust won't kill. I know the heat's getting fierce, but do you think you could manage it?"

"Easy."

"We're going to put them all around the store, maybe a couple by the pumps. And when fall comes, I want some pansies along the walkway to the house. They'll pop up next spring, just when we'll be wanting them. Oh, and let's dig up that nasty forsythia bush. It only blooms three days of the year. . . ."

"Hiram," I said, "we're a filling station, not a flower shop."

"We're a business for gentlemen *and* ladies. Unless we start making this place more becoming, every woman with an ounce of delicacy is going to pass us right by. And that's another thing. We need a separate ladies' room."

"Oh, come on."

"Listen now, no lady worth her silk stockings will go anywhere near that little outhouse with the door half hanging off. We need a nice little *retreat*. Set back from the store."

I pointed out that nine out of every ten drivers was a feller.

"And who do you think is sitting alongside that fella? Some woman, that's who, leading him by the nose and telling him where to get off. If *she* doesn't feel at home, *he* won't stop."

Well, it took Hiram a weekend to lay the water and sewage lines, another three weekends to build. But he got his restroom. Painted all in white, with a trellis in front and half-moon carvings on every side. He put in a liquid-soap dispenser, and Janey made a sachet of dried flowers, and Earle kept it scrubbed, and it didn't take too long for the ladies to find it. They was posh, too, some of them, gloves and pince-nez and pearls down to the waist. They ducked in there with tiny smiles and come out with bigger ones.

Word must've got out 'cause before long there was two dozen ladies stopping in each weekday, more on weekends. I reckon, if you been driving over the Blue Ridge for that many hours, that white trellis of Hiram's must've looked like a pillar of cloud.

Well, he was mighty pleased with himself, but he wasn't the type to quit when he was ahead. Sometime in July, he got it in his mind in the worst way that we needed uniforms. Now, me, I'd never worn nothing but a denim shirt and black overalls and didn't see no point in changing. But night after night, Hiram kept at it.

"Amelia," he said, "what's the first thing you see at one of Harley Blevins's stations?"

"Hell opening up."

"Uniforms, that's what you see. The sign of trained, professional mechanics. And that's the moment you relax because you know, whatever happens, you're in good hands."

"Well, you're wrong."

"Doesn't matter. In that *moment*, you believe. That's all the uniform is for, creating the impression of trustworthiness."

Night after night, he went at it, and hard as I dug in, he came back that much harder. Till, finally, all I wanted to do was shut him up.

"Jesus," I said. "I will wear it for *one day*. And if you make me look like Dudley, I will kill you."

Wouldn't you know those uniforms came the very next week by parcel post? Four jumpsuits, the color of goldenrod. I give the fabric a good hard pinch.

"Cotton?"

"Reeves Army Twill," said Hiram. "Sturdy, but it breathes."

"I don't know about this. . . ."

"And you *won't* know until you try it."

Well, I'm a woman of my word, nobody can tell me otherwise, but I'm telling you I couldn't even look at myself in the mirror when I was putting that thing on. Even harder to look my truckers in the eye. But as the day wore on, I found I wasn't so hot as usual, and I didn't have to roll up my sleeves, 'cause the uniform stayed nicely bunched round my wrists and never snagged on nothing.

But here's the best part. I clear forgot I was wearing it. Till Hiram come wandering over at the end of the day with a sly old grin.

"Let me think on it," I told him.

All through supper, he kept trying to catch my eye. It was only when we was getting ready for bed that I broke down and said, "Okay, this ain't the worst idea you ever had. But if you ever sew my name over the shirt pocket, I will set the whole thing on fire."

Funny thing about Hiram. Any little failure he could sweep right out of his head, but success took root like a dandelion, wanted more of itself. He took to reading. Rooted through Earle's Great Heap o' Treasure for back copies of *Time* and *Fortune*, *Advertising Age*. Ordered books through the mail like *Automobile Service Shop Management* and *Grouches Lose Business!*

One morning, he dragged us out of bed an hour early. "Today, we're going to work on our greetings."

"For the love of—"

"Now, according to that sign up there, we all work in an oasis. So our job is to make it feel like one. Earle, when a car pulls in, what's the first thing you do?"

"Uh . . . I ask if they want me to fill 'em up."

"No. First, you tip your hat. And then you say?"

"Uh . . . *hey.*"

"Hay is for horses. You say *morning* if it's morning. *Afternoon* if it's afternoon. Then you say, *How can we help you?*"

"*How can we . . . help you?*"

"The *we* part, that's important. They've got to know you're part of a whole family of folks wishing to serve."

Earle's mouth folded down. "Melia, too?"

"We'll work on her later. Just remember *you* are the first face customers see when they pull in here. The success of our business rests in *your* hands, do you follow me?"

"Yes, sir."

"So I don't want you strolling out to customers like you just woke up from a nap. I want you *running*, you hear? Go on. Show me how you run."

Well, Earle got tolerable good at running. So good, in fact, that more than one driver took fright at the sight of him. There was a trucker named Wendell who figured Earle for a robber and whipped out his shotgun. Mostly, though, folks was charmed. And with him doing such a good job at the pumps, I could spend most of my day in the service bay—refacing valves, aligning wheels, charging batteries. Truth be told, it was the way I liked to work—nobody I had to smile at or bend an ear to—and if I ever get a notion I was needed elsewhere, Hiram set me straight.

"The less I see of you," he once said, "the happier I get."

I told him he weren't the first to say that.

"Melia, pumping gas gets us barely three cents on the dollar. Accessory sales and repairs are where the profits are. Now, sales I can handle, but the repair is all on you. Think about it this way. Earle gives them the gas, *you* give them peace of mind."

Nobody'd ever put it quite like that before. It was a queer sort of comfort. More than once during those dog days of thirty-four, with the hot wet air pushing down on me like a fist, oil and grease dripping down my neck, carbon crawling through every crevice of skin, I'd close my eyes and say just the three words. *Peace of mind.*

Sometimes, when I had a free moment, I'd stand in the garage doorway and see Earle jogging over to greet a car . . . Janey coming right after with Dixie cups and a pitcher of lemonade . . . Hiram calling from the doorway, "Morning, folks! Come on inside where it's cool." And I'd think, *This is the place Mama would've made. Only she couldn't see it yet.*

'Cause that's the whole trick. Imagine, say, you're flying in an airplane. (I have to imagine 'cause I ain't never done it.) You start out on the ground, where you always been, the world nagging at you like it always does. But then you lift off, and before you know it, that old world drops away like it was never there, and this new world comes rising up at you. All these shapes and patterns and colors that was there the whole time, only you never knew it.

Well, that's what happens when you get a fresh pair of eyes on your life. You see things. Possibilities. Even if the eyes in question belong to a crazy old coot and one of 'em is on the lazy side.

Chapter
EIGHTEEN

Well, all the while this was going on, Hiram was getting new takers for his elocution lessons. You wouldn't have thunk it, but Warren County was crawling with folks who wanted to talk better. Druggists. Funeral directors. Beer distributors. Schoolteachers. The daughter of a Nineveh horse farmer. The father of a Riverton Lime plant manager. Grown men and women shelling out a buck an hour in the middle of a depression to have Hiram chip away at their vowels.

The only trouble was, with all the work around the station, Hiram had to squeeze his lessons into Sunday afternoons. So right round the time that Walnut Ridge's Christians were dragging themselves back from church, Hiram was climbing into the truck and making his rounds. There was times he was lucky to get back before nightfall.

Well, it was on one of those Sundays in early August that Ida came.

The heat was so thick, even the locusts had taken a breather, and every horse was snoozing in the shade of an old elm tree. Even the flies had gone quiet, so the sound, coming in from the east, lodged straight in my ear. A soft sweep, like leaves blowing up from a well. It built and built, without getting much louder, so there weren't nothing for it but to turn my head.

And there was Ida Folsom, shuffling down the side of the road.

Almost not to be recognized from the lady who'd sat next to us at the Park Theatre. *This* Ida was wearing a dress that looked more like a feed sack. Her legs was bare, her head was bare. Not a speck of jewelry, and that river of hair hanging down every side of her, like a ratty old comforter.

She must've known where she was going 'cause once she got abreast of the gas tanks, she veered straight for the house. Step by step, dragging the gravel as she went.

"It's Amelia, isn't it?"

"Yes, ma'am."

"How do you do? I was . . ." Her head did a slow turn. "I was wondering if Mr. Watts is at home."

"No, ma'am, he is not."

The news didn't seem to hit her one way or another.

"I can tell him you stopped in," I said.

"Would you?"

She smiled, very sweetly, but didn't move.

"Uh, maybe you'd care to wait inside," I said.

"I'm fine. Thank you."

I looked at her a little harder now. "Miss Ida?"

"Yes?"

"I believe you're bleeding."

It was fresh blood, too. Dribbling out from under her soles, caking round her toes and heels. She'd gone and walked Lord knows how many miles without so much as a scrap of leather between her and the road.

"Oh," she said.

It took me no more than a minute or two to find some strips of gauze and an old bottle of hydrogen peroxide.

"Thank you," she said.

And then, before I knew it, she was setting. Right there in the gravel. Mopping the blood off her feet and humming something low and tuneless.

"Is there anything else I can get you, Miss Ida?"

"No, thank you."

I got Janey to make her some lemonade, and Earle, he fetched an old umbrella of Mama's to keep the sun off. Ida thanked them both, but nothing on Earth could dispose her to come inside. It was like she had just enough in her to get this far and no farther.

A little past eight, our truck come rolling down the road. What must Hiram have thought, I sometimes wonder, when his headlights carved out that queer figure setting in the gravel in a sack dress? He shut off the engine and jumped out of the driver's seat.

"Ida?"

"Why, hello," she said, rising to her feet.

As he wrapped his arms round her, she made a soft kittenish sound and rested her head on his shoulder. He whispered something in her ear and then led her to the truck, and he'd just about got her into the passenger seat when I heard her say, "How charming they are, Hiram."

He peered at us through the beams of the headlights, then bundled himself behind the wheel and drove away.

He didn't get back till six o'clock the next morning, but come seven, he was washed and dressed and in his customary place. And that night, he made chop suey again—the "real kind," he said. (One of his students had paid him in pork shoulder instead of cash.) To look at him, you'd never of figured anything was off. Yet, when I think back on that night, I wonder if that wasn't the point he began to draw away.

It ain't nothing I can prove. Just a feeling I had that some *space* had opened up behind his eyes. Where we couldn't go in.

"Everything okey?" I asked.

"Why wouldn't it be?" he said. "Now listen up, pagans, I'm taking a break from elocution next Sunday 'cause I've got a new project in mind. And I'll need all the help I can get."

It rained most of that day, but come three o'clock, we brought out Mama's tool bucket and set down a tarp and got to work. We was still at it two hours later when Chester Gallagher came driving up.

"Melia," he said. "A minute, if you'd be so kind."

I poured a couple glasses of well water, and the two of us set just out of the sun in the Adirondack chairs in front of the store.

"You going to tell me what you're building out there?" Chester asked.

"Well, it's a—it's a porte cochere."

"I'm not even sure what that is."

"Geez, Chester, it's one of them—*porchy* things. I mean, you put it over a stretch of sidewalk or road, and it damn well covers it."

"But why?"

"*Why?* Well, say it's raining, and some folks drive on up. They can pull up under that there porte cochere and stay dry all the way to the store and back. It takes a load off folks' minds is what it does."

"Does it now?"

"Why, sure."

Chester sipped his water slow, like it was new whiskey.

"Two days ago, I had a most pleasant conversation with Miss Wand of juvenile court."

"Can't rightly see how that would've been pleasant."

"Oh, hold on. I meant unpleasant." He give his glass a light swirl. "It seems they've uncovered your birth certificate. The original."

I stared down at my ankles. Watched them cross and uncross.

"Well, so what? Who cares?"

"Just to be clear, Melia, the Warren County Juvenile Court now has two birth certificates in their possession. One claims that Hiram's your father, the other claims nobody is. Our good civil servants will likely conclude that one of those documents is a forgery. Experience and plain old common sense will tell them it's the one that appeared out of thin air."

"Experience and sense. They ain't proof."

"How about we call it a headache and leave it there?"

"I can take headache. I can take it for . . . six years and four months. What do you think, Chester? Can we hold out till I'm twenty-one?"

He tipped his head to one side, half shut his eyes. "I think we'll be in court before this year is out. And if I still have a law license by this time next year, I'll be politely surprised."

"We can get through this, Chester."

"I don't see that we have any other choice."

Off in the distance, Earle was sawing off the end of a two-by-four, and Janey was pounding a nail into submission, and Hiram was wandering between them, bending now and then to pass on words of instruction.

"Maybe there's another way out of this," I said. "Supposing we make Hiram an honest-to-God daddy."

"Whoa, now."

"I mean, we been calling him that long enough, it's kinda starting to stick."

"You mean have him adopt you? All three of you?"

"Well, why the hell not? Wouldn't that keep the dogs off us?"

He looked at me. "So you're thinking Hiram's here to stay."

"Don't it look like it?"

Chester raised his glass to his lips, took a tiny sip, and set the glass back down on his thigh.

"The judge would have to sign off," he said.

"Well, that's where you come in."

"It's not that simple, Melia. They'd have to ask questions. Conduct an investigation."

"What for?"

"To make sure he'd be a fit guardian." Chester paused just a fraction of a second. "And to see if he was guilty of any criminal activity."

I stared at him so hard he actually wiped his brow.

"You know something I don't?" I asked.

"I don't know anything. Neither do you."

I frowned, stretched out my legs. "When you say *activity*, you mean like what? Like being a vagrant or something?"

"Trespassing. Assault and battery. Theft. Uh, *fraud*."

We was quiet.

"It's the kind of thing they'd look into," said Chester.

But he sold hats to ladies in San Francisco. And made up ads for J. Walter Thompson. And met Clark Gable and learned how to cook from Yan Sing and . . .

And was any of it true? When it come right down to it, what the hell did I know about Mr. Hiram Watts?

All I could say for sure was that, a couple months ago, he'd been a bum. No different from any of the millions of others riding the rails and roads. He might've been living that way for years, and if that were so, then what had he needed to do to stay alive? How many scrapes did he fight his way out of? How many jail cells did he see the inside of?

And how much of *any* of that did I really care to know? It was like Mama used to say: *If'n you don't like the sight of worms, you'd best not turn over any rocks.*

So I set there a while longer, watching Hiram and Janey and Earle bang that porte cochere into shape.

"Know what, Chester? Forget I spoke."

Chapter
NINETEEN

Now, I can't say for sure if it was on account of Hiram, but by the end of the summer, Brenda's Oasis was starting to do a little bit of okay. Oh, we was still up to our assholes in debt, but for the first time ever, the ground was rising beneath us.

Bills was getting paid, debts whittled . . . hope planted. I could see it in Earle's step, when he went sprinting out to greet a car. I could see it in our customers. Drivers who, in days of old, would've hurried past us without a second look—they was stopping now. Saying things like "How you?" and "Nice day overhead" and "Living good as common." They was greens peddlers and hog farmers and shoe-store clerks. Firemen and laundresses. Schoolteachers. Drill instructors.

They come every hour of every day, in every manner of jalopy and wagon and coupe. So many of 'em, at times I couldn't keep their faces straight. But Hiram could. Their names, too. Jobs and hobbies. Every vanity and earthly desire.

"Farmer Stokes! Got a new shipment of Prince William snuff just for you. . . . Say now, Floyd, how'd the missus like those glacé cherries I sent you home with? . . . Why, as I live and breathe, it's Ella Preston! Got your Schweppes Lemon Squash waiting for you at the bottom of the icebox. Colder than a polar bear . . . Why, Mrs. Grubbs, there's some fresh strawberries on sale, and it just so happens they remind me of your complexion, that's no lie. . . ."

Frances Bean got to be quite the regular. So did Mrs. Hicks and Mrs. McGuilkin. Basil Buckner said Hiram's coffee couldn't be beat this side of the Shenandoah, and every time Minnie-Cora Harper started seeing a new feller, first thing she'd do was bring him round for Hiram to look over.

"Well, this one looks most promising," he'd tell her. "Boy's got a good head on his shoulders. And Lord, is he smitten!"

Now, at the risk of bragging on myself, it wasn't all Hiram keeping us afloat. One morning, we got a visit from the mayor of Walnut Ridge. Big red-throated gingery feller, ready to tear out the few wisps of hair he had.

"My damn brakes won't quit squeaking!"

All it took me was five minutes with castor oil and an old paintbrush, and those brakes was quiet as a queen's fart. Mayor shook his head and said, "Young lady, you live up to your reputation."

From then on, he was a regular, and I knew our luck had turned for real when Pastor Goolsby did us the favor of stopping in.

"Melia," he said, "my engine keeps shutting off when I least expect it. I'm in mortal peril every second."

"Is it shutting off quick or slow?" I asked.

"Quick."

"What'd the other mechanics say?"

"The other—"

"Harley Blevins's boys."

His cheeks colored. "They kept telling me it was jammed. Bled me for a new gear key, but it didn't change a thing."

I was back a half hour later.

"Engine was jammed," I said. "But it weren't no gear key, it was the connecting rod bearer."

"You sure on that?"

"Tell you what—you drive it around a few days. If it shuts itself off even once, you don't owe me a red cent."

Well, next week, who should come driving in but the good pastor?

"Melia Hoyle," he said, "the Lord must be working through you."

"That'll be three dollars and seventy-five cents."

From then on, Pastor Goolsby was a regular, too.

• • •

So against any betting man's odds, Brenda's Oasis was hanging on. Business had got to the point that Hiram and me could talk about staying open an hour later. Hiring extra help in the fall when Janey and Earle went back to school. Buying us a tow truck.

We could talk about plate-glass windows.

And maybe it was the *wishing* that finally brought Harley Blevins out of hiding.

He started small at first. Trash cans turned over. Gas nozzles left dangling. Shaving cream on the windshield of our truck.

Then it started to build. Newspaper stuffed in the men's toilet. Chewing gum wadded into the coin slot of our pay phone. An old rocker swiped off the front porch of our house.

Then one of our gas hoses was slashed—slashed so fine we didn't even know it'd happened till the gas was flowing.

Hiram insisted on calling in the police, but the deputy who come by just lowered his chin to his chest and said, "I don't rightly see what we can do for y'all."

"How 'bout you tell your boy Harley there to—"

But Hiram was already cutting me off. "Maybe you could swing a cruiser by every hour or so. Just to let them know they're being watched."

"Can't promise every hour. We got a heap of ground to cover, Mr. Watts."

"Whenever you can, then."

The next couple nights was quiet. Then, Saturday morning, I come out to find the door to the service bay jimmied open, and ten new whitewall tires laying all over the ground. Each and every one of them slashed.

"Looks like we've got ten new tire swings," said Hiram.

"At sixty bucks a swing," I said, hocking spit on the ground.

That afternoon, Hiram drove into Front Royal to buy a heavy-duty padlock and a length of chain. While he was gone, Harley Blevins come driving on by in his butternut Chevy Eagle. Slowed the car to a halt, then pushed his head out the open window and looked at me straight on. Tipped his hat and drove away.

That night, over dinner, Earle said, "Ain't none of this'd happen if we had us a dog."

"Oh, don't start," I said. "Dog's just one more mouth to feed."

"It'd earn its food ten times over," said Hiram, "if it saved us the cost of new whitewalls."

"Well, maybe if everybody here didn't sleep like the dead, we wouldn't need us a watchdog."

"It's a wonder we sleep at all," said Janey, "you snoring like an alligator."

"I'd sooner have an alligator than a mangy old fleabag."

Looking back on it, I should've just fessed up. Me and dogs'd never really taken to each other. I weren't feared of them, exactly, I just didn't cotton to 'em, and I took it kinda amiss when they come at me with their nose or tongue. If the universe could've brought me a dog I didn't have to wipe off me ten times a day, I'd have given it a thought.

"Never mind the pooch," I said. "I'm gonna take care of this problem by myself. You wait and see."

Well, that very Sunday, we put up the porte cochere. I'd figured it for a five-hour job, but Hiram had everything measured so careful, it went up like incense. The posts, the roof, the arches . . . all sliding into place so sweet, you'd think they'd been searching for each other all their lives.

'Course Hiram kept fussing. Repainted some of the trim and checked the angle of the gutters and taped the joints and beveled the molding. But from the second we pushed it toward the sky, that porte cochere was one of the finest works I'd ever set eyes on. Every so often Hiram would step back and let his face go slack with wonder.

I thought, *Harley Blevins is gonna take this, too.*

Hiram went to bed early that night, and Janey and Earle, they wasn't far behind. Me, I got a pillow and a blanket and went outside and laid down on the porch swing. Brought the Rayovac flashlight with me, plus an old police whistle.

I laid there a long time, squinting into the darkness. After two or three hours, my eyes got so tired, all the stars took to wheeling like fireflies. Had to roll down my lids to make it stop, and I guess I must've closed them too hard 'cause I went right off. Woke up with a wheeze and a cough right at the pitch of dawn.

The sun was just starting to dribble down, and off in the distance, some cows was grousing, and a mockingbird was getting sassy. I tiptoed out toward the porte cochere, flashing my Rayovac, but the daylight was already swallowing it, so I set it on the ground and kept walking till I was standing under the porte cochere.

Still here, I thought, leaning my hand against one of the columns.

Only the hand wouldn't pull away right off. I looked down at my palm and saw a strange smear of black. Dipped my finger in it and raised it to my mouth.

Tar.

From there, all I had to do was take three steps back to see the tar was everywhere. Every column, every arch, every molding. Staining every last stretch of white.

And there, on the column just beneath the Brenda's Oasis sign, a message.

To this day, I can't rightly say if they spelled the word wrong or just meant to drag it out a little. *Sluuuuut.* Or else it was too dark to see what they were doing.

The police whistle was still wrapped round my neck on a chain. I raised it to my mouth, but no air would come out. I believe it was still hanging off my lower lip when Hiram come walking toward me. He told me later that, as he folded his arms round me, I kept saying the same thing.

"I'm sorry. . . . I'm sorry. . . ."

Chapter
TWENTY

If I can learn you one thing about tar, it's this. Don't try to paint over it.

Not on a summer morning when the mercury on the shop window's already reading eighty-seven. Tar don't want to be covered up, it wants to bubble and ooze. Throw a brush at it, and it'll just grab on.

Only thing you can do, really, is cool it down with ice till it gets brittle. Then scrape off what you can. Cool it down some more. Scrape some more. Then rub in some Wesson oil, real hard, till the last specks is gone. It ain't the work of a few minutes, believe you me, and here it was Monday morning and the first truckers half an hour off.

"Unless my eyes deceive me," said Hiram, "it was just the columns that got hit."

"So what?"

"So grab all the tarps you can find from the garage. I'll grab some rope. We're going to wrap these columns up but good."

"Supposing somebody asks what's underneath."

"Tell them it's a *surprise*."

Well, off we went, the two of us, and it were that very morning that Earle Hoyle decided to wake his damn self up. Guess he couldn't live another second till he'd shared that porte cochere with humanity. So he come running on out, eyes sprung wide. It's the one time I was ever sorry he could read.

"That weren't for you to see," I said.

He didn't say nothing.

"That's just fools talking. Ain't a lick of truth behind it."

Still nothing.

"You ain't to tell Janey now," I said. "You ain't to breathe a word."

Well, me and Hiram set to wrapping, and I'll say this. Once we was done, there weren't a splash of tar to be seen. Hiram checked his pocket watch.

"Six fifty-five. I suggest we put some smiles on our faces. What do you say, Earle?"

The boy was nowhere to be seen.

We checked round the house, went calling up and down Strasburg Pike. Not a sign.

Now, Earle was famous for lighting out whenever he got in a stew, but morning passed into afternoon, and he was as gone as ever.

It was fearful hot that day. The air sharp as copper, steam rising off the asphalt. Mamas running from the sound of their own babies, and drummers and preachers chasing sales that weren't never coming, and good old boys strutting round with cigarette packs in their rolled-up undershirt sleeves, looking for a fight. Ain't no easy living to be had on a day such as this. More than once, I confess, I was moved to curse Earle's name for leaving us in the lurch, but each time, I thought back to how he'd looked, reading those words.

Five o'clock rolled by. Then six. A little after seven, I told Hiram I was going to take a walk, but all I did was stroll to the edge of the road and swing my head every which way, trying to picture where he might be. Lake John? Squabble Creek? Cauthorn Mill Road? Could've been any of those places or none.

Just when the sun was starting to drop, I saw a figure far down the road. A lank, rawboned thing with a boy's shoulders and man-sized arms. His face was in shadow, and he kept turning his head like he was talking to somebody.

Dear God, I thought. *That brother of mine has gone and lost his marbles.*

By now, Hiram and Janey had followed me out to the road. Earle saw us, I guess, 'cause his hand shot up. Then something came skittering out from behind him, and I knew that whatever he'd been talking to was flesh and blood.

Four spindly legs, brittle as peppermint sticks. A coat the color of dead grass. A saggy head with black-rimmed eyes and ears at wrong angles to each other. And, sprouting from those ears, fringes of old-man hair.

"Why, that little devil," said Hiram.

'Bout ten feet away from us, the creature stopped and drooped its head so low you couldn't even see its eyes.

"This here's our new guard dog," said Earle.

"Walks funny," said Janey.

"He can't help that, he's bowlegged. Look, I already taught him a trick. Hey, you, roll over!"

Critter did just like it was asked, and it was the saddest thing you ever seen. And then, instead of springing back up, like a normal dog would do, he just laid there on the side of the road, scrunchy with fear.

"*Guard dog* written all over him," I said.

"He ain't never had nothing to guard before," said Earle. "We give him a home, he's gonna look after it."

"Don't look too smart," I said. "Probably wouldn't know his own name."

"We ain't named him yet."

"Or find his own food."

"I'll feed him."

My eyes twitched down to that pale yellow belly, patchy and scabby.

"I reckon he's crawling with ticks and fleas," I said. "We'll all come down with lice before the week is done."

"I'll brush him out."

Janey knelt down and commenced to scratching behind the thing's ears. "Why," she said, "he looks like a little deer, don't he?"

And now it was Hiram, running his fingers along the thing's spine. "He just needs a job. Like any other working stiff."

I reckon I could've held out a while longer. 'Cause if only you could've seen this mutt—I mean, life had gone and washed its hands of him. But then I made the mistake of asking myself what Mama would've done.

"He damn sure needs a bath," I said.

"'Course," said Earle.

"And I ain't lifting a finger for him. Y'all can feed him and pick up his shit and whatever else."

"What're we gonna call him?" said Earle.

Janey didn't miss a beat. "Gus."

"Why Gus?" I said.

"Lord, Melia. That's what he looks like."

I'm sorry you're so dumb.

"He don't look no more like a Gus than a Walter," I said. "Or a Pierre."

But the seed was already planted, and before I knew it, the other three was whispering it in his ear. "Hey, Gus. . . . You hear that, Gus?"

Feeling a little encouraged, the dog made his way toward the store. Sniffed around by the door, then pushed his head under the stoop and come back out with something in his mouth.

"Would you look at that?" cried Earle, eyes blazing. "He's hunted down his first critter."

Whatever he'd hunted down, he weren't in no hurry to show us. Dropped it at our feet like an apology.

It was the redbird. The one that'd been pecking away at our window for all these weeks. Hardly a mark on him now—he'd gone to his maker long before Gus ever got there.

I stood there, staring down at his stubby carcass, thinking, *You should've quit while you was ahead.*

"Well, now," I said, feeling my jaw go tense. "Maybe next time this fool dog will catch us something that weren't already dead."

Chapter
TWENTY-ONE

First thing Earle did when we got in the house was serve that dog a plate of leftover chop suey. Gus wolfed it down in two seconds, threw it up a minute later.

"We've got a shoulder bone left," said Hiram.

But the creature just squinted at it like it was Satan's trickery. Finally, he drug it into a corner, but even then he wouldn't gnaw at it. Nor bring himself to part with it. Just huddled over it, glancing back from time to time to see if we was coming to snatch it away.

"He's about the cowardliest dog I ever seen," said Janey.

"You don't know nothing," said Earle.

Well, when bedtime come, I opened the front door and said, "Okay, Yellow Belly. Out you go."

"What you talking 'bout?" said Earle.

"If he's gonna earn his keep, he needs to be where the action is."

"You can't just put him out like that."

"The hell I can't."

Earle was about to come back with something smart, but Hiram put a hand on the boy's shoulder.

"Gus'll be fine. We'll leave him some food and water, and I'll check on him every hour, how would that be?"

Well, Earle didn't like it one bit. Couldn't even look when we tied the dog to the chain and set out a bowl of Chappel's Ken-L-Biskits and closed the door after. When I went out a few minutes later, Gus was right where we left him. Still staring at the door. I turned his head toward the road, but the moment I stepped away, that head spun right back toward the house.

Best solution we could come up with was to have Hiram sleep out on the porch swing that night. Having company seemed to ease the dog's mind, and when I come out the next morning, he was curled up like a radial. Not a single biscuit eaten.

"Ain't one bad thing happened all night," said Earle. "That makes Gus a keeper."

"Makes him lucky is all."

Gus ate a little more that day, more the next, but he still treated food like it was going to turn around and eat him. He didn't take well to being petted. Or looked at. Yet he didn't mind a collar being put on him, and he didn't snarl or fuss when he was washed or combed. And oh, did he love the sunlight! He'd lay on the porch for half a morning and all of an afternoon, the boards baking beneath him, the slits of his eyes trembling.

"I believe he is a lizard," I said.

Day by day, we learned something new about him. He could

spend an hour sniffing a cinder block or a downspout. He'd chase mice but wouldn't kill them. He didn't care for licking you (that were a relief), but he liked having his face right up in yours. If he was keen on you, he'd climb you—like you was a mountain. For exactly three minutes every day, he liked to run in circles, the faster the better, then flop down in a faint.

He sipped his water dainty, but he wolfed down golden malted milk, and he chewed on Oxo bouillon cubes like they was opium.

He never growled. And he never, ever barked.

"Told you he weren't no watchdog," I said.

Earle liked to point out that nothing bad had happened since Gus come along. I explained that was 'cause Harley Blevins was just waiting on his next chance.

"So is Gus," said Earle.

The dog still needed someone to sit outside with him before he'd consent to go to sleep. Some nights it was Hiram, but on those evenings when he was at Ida's, I'd just drag out a pillow and lay there on the porch swing.

These were late-August nights. The scatter of bat wings and the screeching of cicadas and, off in the distance, the Southern Railway, heading for the same old parts. Most nights, it was hard to sleep and just as hard not to. I'd doze in and out, and sometimes I'd wake with a little snap, and the first thing I'd see, in the light from the front hall, was Gus staring back at me. Still not looking where he was supposed to.

One night, I was sleeping full out when the swing give a lurch. My head jerked up, and my feet went scrambling for purchase.

"Easy," said Hiram.

I set up, give my eyes a rub. "You're back early."

I slid over to one side of the swing, and he set on the other. He pulled out a pack of Luckys. In the flare of match light, I could see Gus rolled up like an apple turnover, his chest rising and falling.

"Say, what's this?" said Hiram.

Before I could stop him, he was snatching a book from under the swing. Green leather with gold-rimmed pages.

He let out a soft whistle. *"Thousand and One Nights."*

"Well, what? You think I don't know how to read?"

"I just figured you didn't have the time."

"I gotta make time. I got me a very demanding audience."

He took a drag off his cig. "Earle and Janey?"

"Every blessed night."

With his thumb, he leafed through the pages. "Aren't they a little old for this stuff?"

"They was off it a good while, but once Mama took sick . . . well, to keep 'em easier in mind, I started telling the old stories. The ones *she* used to tell. Only I couldn't bring 'em all to mind, so I ordered this here book through the mail. Now every time my tank's running dry . . ."

"You fill 'er up again."

I shrugged. "Those two are very particular when it comes to their *Arabian Nights*. You can't just tell 'em the same tale over and over. They always want the next one."

"Why, Amelia Hoyle." The ghost of a smile on his lips. "You're practically Scheherazade yourself. Coughing up a new story every night."

"Least I don't got no fool man threatening to kill me if I don't."

"There is that." He stretched out his legs, flexed his feet. "My mother used to read to me from the same book. Sadly, it had the wrong effect."

"How so?"

"Well, I figured the world would be just like the book—never-ending adventure. So I dropped out of school after fourth grade and never looked back."

"Yeah? I made it halfway through fifth."

"Always have to show me up, don't you?"

I gave a low chuckle and stared out to the road. "School and me weren't right for each other. All that do this, spell that, add this. I ain't one for taking orders."

"So I've gathered."

"Or getting swatted for having an opinion. One day, I just up and decided I weren't going no more. Oh, I still left the house of a morning, but I'd go for a walk in the woods, or pitch rocks cross the pond. Watch the cars go by. Then I'd stroll on home like nothing happened. Well, two weeks later, the truant officer shows up, and he has himself a *long* talk with Mama. She sets alone in the parlor for a spell. Then she calls me in. Well, here I am thinking I'm done for, but all Mama says is 'Show me what they're teaching you at that there school.'

"So I write down some words, some numbers. World capitals and, I don't know, 1066 and 1776. She looks it all over, and she says, 'Well, hell, Melia, I can teach you this stuff. And I won't hit you with no birch rod, neither.'"

My finger made a slow sketch on my lips.

"So every morning, me and her, we took our lessons. I didn't have to write on a chalkboard or wear a dress. Best schoolhouse I ever had. Then every afternoon, we'd take apart some engine and put it back together. See, she figured me out, Hiram. She knew I was—I was made for the *real* world. Learning in the *doing*, that was our motto."

Hiram's long bony finger gave the back of his cig a whack. "That's how Earle learns. Show him how to build something, he gets it right off. I believe he'd make a fine woodworker or metalworker. Electrician, even."

"Ain't gonna be no trades for that boy, he's going to college."

Hiram's head drew back. "We're talking about the same boy?"

"Oh, I know, homework ties him up in knots, and his handwriting's a terror, but he's got a way of keeping at things. He'll make something of hisself."

"I don't doubt it, but it won't be from anything on a blackboard. Now if you're asking me who in this family *should* go to college . . ."

"Oh, yeah," I said. "Me and my fifth-grade diploma."

"I'm talking about Janey."

It was like the name come lobbing out of the sky.

"Janey?" I said.

"Who better?"

"Well . . . I know she's got a head for figures. . . ."

"She's got more than that. Who do you think's been balancing our books?"

"Uh . . ." My eyes squeezed down by half. "Guess I reckoned it was you."

"For a while it was. Then one night, about a month ago, Janey came over and asked me what I was doing. I showed her, and once she saw how *easy* it was—well, she asked if she could try her hand. I'm telling you, Amelia, those ledgers got balanced in about half the usual time. I checked all her numbers, too, five nights running. They always came out square."

"Hold on. You're telling me the bookkeeper for Brenda's Oasis is a nine-year-old girl?"

"And you're not even paying her. Know what amazes me the most? She does it all in her head. No scrap paper, no adding machine. Pure brain power."

"But . . ." My hands met right at the top of my skull. "When was somebody gonna get round to telling me this?"

"She didn't want you to know."

"How come?"

"She figured you had other plans for her."

"Well . . ." I dragged my hands back down my head. "Lord above, they ain't *my* plans, they was Mama's. Or *somebody's.* I mean, girls has gotta cook and sew and, you know, get themselves a husband."

"That's what they're supposed to do?"

"'Course."

"That's what you're doing?"

I set there a second. Too stunned to speak. "You oughtn't talk that way," I said at last.

"Why not?"

"'Cause I'm a bad example. I'm what you call the baddest example ever was."

"Why?"

"'*Cause.*"

I jerked my face away. Sat listening for a while to the cicadas.

"If you must know," I said, "I'm gonna die without a ring on my finger. And I ain't asking for nobody's pity, 'cause that's just how I'm made, and I'm okey with it—but that ain't what I want for Janey. That kind of life, Hiram, it's a lonesome valley."

"You know what?" He dropped what was left of his Lucky to the ground. "The most lonesome people I've ever met have been married."

I opened my mouth to protest. Then I closed it. 'Cause washing into my mind's view come Frances Bean. Setting all by herself at the end of that soda counter.

And then Crazy Ida in that godforsaken movie theater. Her face opening like the leaves on a plant 'cause somebody was talking to her.

And then, in a long sad line, the women at Mama's wake. Married, all of 'em, and 'cept for Mina and Mrs. Goolsby, not a one of 'em had a husband in tow. They was all walking the lonesomest valley I'd ever seen.

"Amelia," said Hiram, "society's already gone and washed their hands of us. Why don't we wash our hands of them? Do what we want, live how we want, love who we want. How does that sound to you?"

Well, it was just then the world sent another sound our way. A low rasping, like a gutter scraping against a tin roof. Didn't rightly know what it was till I saw Gus lift his head. *Dear Lord*, I thought. *That boy is growling.*

Then come three barks—short and high and sharp. In the next second, he was gone. Galloping like a quarter horse straight for the store. And the chain racing after him, whistling across the gravel and then, with something like a wheeze, snapping tight.

I heard the crash of glass and a man's cry, half-stifled. Then it was my own bare feet I was hearing, dashing cross the gravel.

Hiram was a couple seconds behind, only 'cause he was reaching for the Rayovac. The light exploded around us, dragging shapes out of the dark. A man. And, fastened to his flailing arm, a dog.

With a sad cry, the man flung Gus into the darkness. Grabbed his tore-up arm and hightailed it for the road.

I went after him, but before I'd got more than ten feet, a pair of headlights burst into view. Half-blinded, I swung an arm over my eyes. Heard a door slam, the scream of tires. In the next second, they was past me, churning up the road and screaming toward the mountains.

Sweat dripping off my chin, I turned and trudged back to the station.

The Rayovac was on the ground now, and in the angle of light it cast, I could see Hiram bent over something still and yellow.

Gus.

A second later, that dog was rolling his snout toward the sky and dragging himself up on his breadstick legs. He give his head a shake, and little drops of crimson scattered from his mouth.

"Jesus," I whispered. "He must've got clobbered."

Then I heard Hiram's dry chuckle. "It's not *his* blood."

Gus put his front paws atop my knees and scaled me like I was a mountain. Pushed his face right toward mine and showed me the red coating on each and every one of his teeth.

"You just got yourself a guard dog," said Hiram.

Chapter
TWENTY-TWO

It was but the one brick, but it sure made a nice crater in the store window. Cracked our Star Tobacco sign, too, and knocked over the coffee grinder and took a nice gash out of our rice bin and made a hash of the Del Monte display. By the time it come to rest by the cheese cutter, it'd made quite a career for itself.

We called up the glazier from Riverton. A shortsighted, hard-smoking cuss named Lewis Quint who'd given up drinking and was none too pleased about it. I'd say he swore a blue streak, only the words never made it out his throat.

"Mm firkin gum."

"What's that, Mr. Quint?"

"I said twenty bucks to replace it."

Hiram stared at the hole. "How much to make it plate glass?"

"Grrr. Mmmm. Forty."

Hiram frowned. "And how much to make the whole storefront plate glass?

"Mod sham, *hundred!*"

"That's right steep," I said.

"Plate glass makes us look professional," Hiram said. "You said so yourself."

"Gold plate'd make us look even more professional. We can't afford that, neither."

On and on we went till Lewis Quint flung down his hat and commenced to jumping up and down like Rumpelstiltskin.

"Eighty-*five!*"

"Done," said Hiram.

• • •

Well, what should show up that very afternoon but Harley Blevins's butternut Chevy Eagle? Strolling into the station like the lead car in an Armistice Day parade. Earle was already jogging toward it, but I put out my hand to stop him, and after peering inside to make sure there was no other passengers, I went straight to the driver's side. Drug Dudley out of his seat and flattened him against the car.

"Guess you're right proud of yourself," I said.

"For what?"

"The toilet weren't enough. The whitewalls and that nasty old tar. No, you was gonna break into the store and what? Steal all the Bit-O-Honeys?"

"Girl, you're talking crazy."

Well, here we come to the problem. There was a real, real, real small chance that I *was* crazy.

See, I'd never once caught Harley Blevins in the act of doing anything. He sure weren't the guy who heaved that brick through our window—he weren't tall enough—and whatever car that feller jumped in sure as shit wasn't a Chevy Eagle. If you was to dust the whole station for fingerprints, you probably wouldn't have found a single one belonged to Harley Blevins.

So there was a teeny tiny little speck of a chance that he was innocent. Only I didn't believe it.

'Course I didn't have no evidence to back me up. All I had was a feeling, and it's feelings that'll get you called crazy. Which there was a teeny tiny little speck of a chance I was.

Anyway, I grabbed Dudley Blevins's left arm and, with the calmness of the *truly* crazy, I unbuttoned his sleeve and rolled it up. A few seconds later, we was both staring down at the pale, veined skin of his forearm.

Not a mark on it.

"What the hell is going on?" he said.

"Feller tried to do a number on the store last night. Got his left arm chewed up by our *guard dog*."

"Left arm?"

"Yeah," I said. "Maybe you got another one somewhere."

I said it just to make him mad, but he got quiet instead. Rolled his sleeve down, then got back in the car and drove off without a word. The dust from his rear tires was just clearing when I turned and found Janey, looking cross.

"I could've told you it weren't him," she said.

I was all set to give her what for, but it looked like something already had.

"Girl," I said, "you been too long in the sun."

"Feels like it. . . ."

I give her a second look, then a third. The sunburn had gone and scalded her throat, left rows of bumps along her skin.

"You feeling hot?" I asked her, holding my fingers to her forehead.

"It's August, Melia."

"I mean inside."

"A little."

"You feeling itchy?"

"Something awful."

"How's your throat?"

"Pissed off."

"Show me your tongue," I said.

She did.

"Okay, put it back in," I said.

"What do I got? The streptococcus?"

"Something like that. Tell you what, Hiram's going into town to pick up some gaskets. Maybe he can have Doc Whitworth swing by."

"I'm a nurse," she said. "Don't nobody need to heal *me*."

But when we got her into bed, her temperature was 103. By the time Doc Whitworth showed up, the rash had spread all the way down her chest and her back. I probably should have stayed with her through the poking and prodding, but I had to go out on the front porch. 'Cause Elsie O'Donnell was waiting for me there.

Elsie had lived two doors down from us in Cumberland. She was part of a big Irish family, ten or eleven kids, the dad never around, the mama making vats of soap in the backyard. Elsie stood out 'cause she had red hair just like Janey's and was just as conceited about it. Then one day, Elsie took ill. Fever out of no place, crawling rash, throat of knives.

And a strawberry tongue. Just like Janey had.

Elsie hung on two months. They funeralized her in an open casket, and it looked like half her skin had peeled off.

Behind me, I could hear the screen door creaking open.

"It's scarlet fever," I said.

"Seems so," said Doc Whitworth.

He folded up his stethoscope and wormed it into a pouch in his carpetbag. "You'll need to bring her in for an injection," he said.

"Horse serum."

"It works, Melia."

Didn't work for Elsie O'Donnell.

"Now, she's going to have to stay off her feet for a while. Which means she'll need looking after."

"We're able."

"Just keep her comfortable. Make sure she's got enough liquids in her system and whatever food she can keep down."

"'Course."

"Oh, and keep Earle away. He's still young enough to catch it hisself."

"Yes, sir."

He hoisted up his bag and walked down the porch steps, pausing after each step, pausing longest at the bottom. "I'm sorry, Melia."

"What for?"

"Seems the Lord might've chosen not to pile on you folks like this."

"One more," I said, "I don't even know the difference."

• • •

Me and Hiram gave the nursing thing our best shot, but we didn't have Janey's knack, and we sure as hell didn't have the time. No sooner would I run inside with some cool water to splash on the child's face than Mr. Marcus Sutphin from Limeton would drive on by in his '27 Hudson, wanting to know why his fan belt keeps slipping. I couldn't tell him it was 'cause he had a 1927 Hudson, so I had to figure out if the bearing was dry or greasy or loose or just plain broken, and that'd take time, and just as Hiram was coming into the house to spell me, Mr. Marcus Sutphin's 1934 girlfriend would get a hankering for Hershey's chocolate almonds, and did Hiram have any of that Blue Moon pimento-and-American-cheese spread? And some Ritz crackers to go with?

Well, that would take the both of us out of the picture, and the only one who could step up with the nursing was Earle, only he weren't allowed nowhere near his sister, so he'd just stand there by the pumps, looking lost as an old kite, and the whole day'd pass like that, in fits and starts and gasps and me as tired by day's end as I'd ever been.

"We got to close up for a day," I told Hiram. "Or something."

But we both knew it would take more than a day to get that girl well. There she laid, shivering and dripping, not even enough strength in her to use a chamber pot. And pressing over every pore, the ghost of Elsie O'Donnell.

That night, we was getting washed up for supper when a knock come on the front door. Such a little mouse of a knock, I almost didn't hear it. Standing in the glow of our one lightbulb was Mina Gallagher. Near as surprised to find herself there as I was.

"Chester ain't here," I said.

"That's not why I've come."

We stood there.

"I understand you've got a sick child," she said.

"She'll be okay."

"Well, I'm . . ." She skittered her fingers up the side of her face. "I'm happy to sit with her awhile. If it's all right with you. You know, I—I nursed all four of my sister's children through scarlet fever. It takes a few weeks to run itself out and—and the thing is you all are so *busy* with your work, you can't possibly . . ." The weirdest smile climbed out of her mouth. "And my house is as clean as it's ever going to be."

I might've stood there the whole day in that doorway, trying to make sense of what I was hearing, but from behind me, I heard Hiram's low soft voice.

"We'd be most grateful, ma'am."

Chapter
TWENTY-THREE

That first afternoon, she stayed but a couple hours. Next morning, though, she was back bright and early with fresh bandages, sponges, compresses, towels, porcelain bowls. She stayed the whole day, spreading calamine lotion over Janey's rash, spooning water and orange sherbet and beef consommé into her mouth. Putting blankets on when she took a chill, taking them off again when she had the sweats. Cleaning her vomit, changing her sheets, plumping and replumping her pillow.

Speaking nary a word the whole time.

Oh, she'd consent to nibble on canned loganberries and Macfarlane Lang's savory crisplets, and for supper, Hiram coaxed her into having some warmed-over Franco-American spaghetti, but she ate all alone on the front porch, with nothing but a glass of lime-juice cordial to wash everything down. She left without even saying good-bye.

She was back the next morning, though, with an armful of books. *Hans Brinker, Little Women, Black Beauty.* Every so often, I'd pass by the room and hear Mina's flat, thin voice. *"The first place that I can well remember was a large pleasant meadow with a pond of clear water in it. Some shady trees leaned over it, and rushes and water-lilies grew at the deep end. . . ."*

Now, I figured she was reading to keep up Janey's spirits, but when I peeked in that afternoon, the girl was out like a light, and the words was still pouring out of Mina's mouth.

The third day, she brought a sponge and some Murphy Oil Soap and went to work on the floors. But every time Janey'd so much as move, Mina went running back to her.

We closed early that night 'cause Hiram and Earle wanted to have a couple hours' go at the tar. Me, I stuck around outside as long as I could, cleaning gunk out of the gas nozzles, but after a while, there weren't nothing for it but to go inside. Mina was just where I'd left her, in the husker chair by Janey's bed. In her lap was a pile of red yarn that was slowly getting knitted into . . . a hat? A glove? The breeze from the north window made her cotton print dress swirl, and at her feet lay Gus the guard dog, tail softly twitching.

"Is everything all right?" she asked.

"I was just checking."

Skin had started peeling off in thin, scabby flakes from Janey's face. In a little while, I knew, the skin would start to come off her hands, her fingers, her toes. . . .

"Fever must be going down," said Mina. "She's not hallucinating as much."

"She hallucinates?"

"Oh, sure. A little while back, she was going on about *dinosaur juice*. Isn't that funny?"

I tipped myself back till my head was resting against the wall. It seemed to me that my heart was cracking, just a little. "There's a history to that," I said.

"Is that so?"

"When Mama first bought this place, Janey didn't want no part of it. Couldn't stand the smell of gasoline, said it made her sick to her stomach. So Mama said, 'Well, think of how them poor dinosaurs feel. Turns out oil is just what's left of dinosaurs after they been dead a good long spell. Like, millions of years, right? So every time we pump gas, we're pumping dinosaur juice.' Well, Janey loved that. Next morning she was the first out of bed, jumping up and down on her pillow, shouting, 'Let's go pump us some dinosaur juice!'"

I half closed my eyes.

"So that's where that comes from," I said.

Mina said nothing.

"I guess I ought to thank you," I said.

"No need."

"I mean, it's right nice of you to do all this. Seeing how we ain't family or nothing."

"Well . . ."

I set on the edge of the bed. The sheets was new washed and crisp. Hospital corners.

"Listen, Mrs. Gallagher. Mama ain't round to defend herself so . . . I think folks might've given you some wrong notions about her."

"Melia."

222

"I swear to you, her and Chester never—"

"Melia, I know."

A wash of silence. Out of the corner of my eye, I saw her take up her knitting needles, then set them down again.

"You may not believe this," she said, "but I admired your mother. No, truly I did. I remember the first time I met her, I thought, *Well now, here's a woman grabbing life with both arms. Squeezing it dry.* It was—it was *warming* to be around her." She stared into a pocket of space. "I certainly can't blame a man like Chester for wanting to be . . . warmed." With her fingers, she brushed the underside of her chin. "Do you know the only person who ever made *me* feel that way?"

"Who?"

"Chester Gallagher. And I had to go and ruin it by marrying him."

She was silent awhile. Then she took up her knitting once more.

"When I was your age, Melia, I knew this married couple. The Renaults. I'd run into them maybe once or twice a week—they were friends of my parents—but I'd always find myself *staring* at them. Because they didn't make any sense, you see, they—they just seemed like two strangers sharing the same house. You couldn't imagine how they'd ever been thrown together in the first place. It was all just a terrible mistake.

"And then, just the other night, I was lying in bed next to my husband. We'd said scarcely ten words to each other all night, and that's when it struck me. We're that couple! The Renaults! And it doesn't make any more sense when you're in the middle of it. You go—*crawling* back through the years—like you're crawling through shag carpet, looking for an earring—trying to find that *point* where

223

everything started going wrong. But you can't, and then you wonder if maybe it was a *million* points—a million little—pulling aparts—and there's no use even mapping them all because you've become the Renaults, and there's no going back."

She give herself a little shake.

"Or so it sometimes appears," she said. "At three twenty-five in the morning."

The knitting needles fell into her lap just then, and her eyes went wide, like she was gazing through the ceiling and out to the night sky. Next second, she was laughing.

Laughing don't even cover it. Big honking gulps that she tried to stop with her hand and wouldn't be stopped. Who knew she had such a sound in her?

"What?" I said.

"Oh . . ." She fingered the wet out of her eyes. "I had a passing thought, that's all. I thought, *Mina Gallagher, if you're spilling out your soul to this girl who doesn't even like you, it's pretty obvious you need more friends.*"

She laughed some more then, only it weren't quite so fierce.

"Can't say I got much time for friends myself," I said.

"No," she said, softly. "I'd guess you wouldn't. What about that Blevins boy?"

I didn't say nothing.

"Well," she said. "Never mind. God knows there's no hurry."

A new breeze come rushing in from the north window, it made the candle flame shrink back. In the corner, by the porcelain bowls, a blue bottle fly was diving and dancing.

"You want a smoke?" I asked.

"No. Thank you."

We was silent again.

"It ain't that I don't like you," I said. "It's just—"

"You thought *I* didn't like *you*. And here we are."

She took up her knitting for real now. Her face, I noticed, had a clean hard line, and I could suddenly picture her in that very same chair ten, twenty years on—her skin looser, her eyes deader. Another lonely married woman to add to the list.

"Chester's devoted to you," I blurted.

"Oh," she said.

Another breeze come in, stronger than the last. We both cut our eyes toward the window, though there weren't much to see except a little alley of moonlight.

"I've been meaning to tell you," she said. "I like your sign."

Chapter
TWENTY-FOUR

I slept deep that night. Dreaming on what, I can't tell you. All I
recall is the shock of coming out of shadows and into edges.

It was a sound that did it. A short, sharp crack of thunder.

I jerked my head toward it, and then I heard Gus barking up a
fury and Hiram shouting in from the front porch.

"Get down!"

I'm already down, I thought, but my arms, without my telling them,
had gone and wrapped round Earle. We laid there, the two of us, in
that pure darkness, not even knowing what was on the other side.
Then come another crack of thunder. Even shorter and sharper than
the last.

From somewhere far off, I heard an engine gunning into the
night. And out of the near darkness, something now was stirring. I
could see shapes heaving out of the black—an elbow—a shoulder—
vanishing as soon as they showed themselves.

"Sweet Jesus," whispered Earle.

Then, just like that, come a fall of red hair.

It was Janey. A candle clutched in both hands . . . her bed-stiff legs tottering toward us and then stopping.

"Glass," she said.

I had some notion, I guess, of pulling her to safety, but when I lunged for her, something cruel drove itself into the sole of my foot. The word come back to me then. *Glass.*

Sure enough, in the candlelight, I found little winking jewels— one of them wedged good and hard in my foot.

Then I swung the candle toward the window. Ain't no brick had done that. No, sir, if you had to go and get your front window busted, you'd have wanted a hole just like this. Clean and small and round, with just a little web of cracks fanning out each way.

"That's just plain rude," whispered Janey.

The first shell never made it into the house. Passed through the drainpipe and lodged in a hunk of cinder block. The second had one hell of a ride before it was done. Went through the window, passed right over the bed where me and Earle was laying, banged off the coal stove, bounced off Mama's framed rotogravure of President Roosevelt (making another mess of glass), then dived through the braids of our kitchen rug and come to its final resting place about half an inch into our floorboards.

Hiram tweezed it out with a pair of pliers. "By gods," he said. "This one had *some*body's name on it."

His voice was dry and low, but when Sheriff Motherwell come creaking up the porch steps, Hiram was waiting at the door.

"These children could've been *killed*. You know that, don't you? You *know* that."

The sheriff looked a touch queasy. Every three or four words, he'd have to stop talking and put his hand on his belly, *appease* it like it was some jealous wife.

"We'll be glad to look into it," he said.

"Look *into* it?" said Hiram.

"Not sure what else you want me to do. Did y'all see the shooter?"

"It was pitch-black. . . ."

"Then how do y'all know it was Harley Blevins?"

There was a rush of quiet.

"I don't believe we said *who* it was," said Hiram. "I don't believe we once used Harley Blevins's name."

The sheriff put his hands back on his belly. A tiny belch come fluttering out.

"Melia," he said. "How 'bout you and me talk outside?"

I closed the door after us.

"Listen up," he said. "I'm gonna tender this suggestion but the once. Whoever's doing this . . ."

"Sheriff, you and me both—"

"Whoever's *doing* this, you need to go make your peace with him." He rested his beefy hands on the porch rail. "You're the only one can."

228

Chapter
TWENTY-FIVE

Next morning, I did everything like I always did. Ate breakfast. Drunk my two cups of joe. Put on my uniform. Helped Earle pump gas. Joked with Warner and Dutch and Elmer. Then, once I'd waved all the truckers down the road, I went and moseyed over to the truck.

"Where are you headed?" called Hiram.

I could see, just behind him, the slumbering form of Gus, one ear sticking up like a radio tower.

"Gotta go see Chester," I said. "Some paperwork or other. Be back in an hour."

Not a flicker on his bony face.

"An hour's about all we can spare you," he said.

"Oh, what? Like I'm gonna let you and Earle get near one of them engines? I got standards to uphold."

I shut the door. Put the key into the ignition and tried to turn.

I didn't have to do this.

I could get out of this truck right now. Tell Hiram I got the wrong date. Head back to the garage, forget all about it.

And wait to see what Harley Blevins does next?

As I drove off, Gus's black-rimmed eyes was following me the whole way.

When a feller gets too big for Walnut Ridge, what does he do? He sells his little A-frame on First Street and he heads north for the hills, where he can look down on what he used to be.

It weren't in Harley Blevins's makeup to buy some old plantation house. No, he had to go and build his own. Not so big as the real thing—just a couple stories—but it sure *acted* big with its veranda and its five columns. Marble fountain and pissing Cupids. The whole place as white as angels' wings, except for the shutters, which was ocher and cobalt blue. Standard Oil colors.

It wouldn't have surprised me none if some old darkie servant had answered the big brass knocker, but the woman who drug the door open was fair and freckled, well along in years, with arms that looked even plumper in their leg-of-mutton sleeves and curly bottle-blond hair that the August heat had done evil things to. Even now, she had her hand somewhere in its tangles, trying to sort things out.

"Morning, Mrs. Blevins. My name is—"

"I know who you are."

We looked at each other a good long time.

"Is Mr. Blevins around?"

"I believe he is."

"Would it be okay if I spoke to him?"

She cast her eyes down at her own feet. She was wearing red mules with ostrich feathers.

"Come in," she said helplessly.

The foyer had a chandelier so low, I had to duck to get under it.

"Bohemian crystal," said Mrs. Harley Blevins.

"That so?"

"The floorboards are Virginia pine." She started toward the back of the house, her mules dragging after her. "That tapestry is in the Aubusson style. You might also notice the china doorknobs. They're straight from Dresden. This here spiral staircase was custom designed by noted local architect Howard Baybury."

On and on she went, like the world's most bored-ass tour guide.

"The desk is made of red oak. It's called a secretary desk, and it's got itself a roll top, see? Now over here, be sure to notice the pocket doors. So called because they slide into the wall like they're sliding into somebody's pocket. . . ."

"Hey, Mrs. Blevins, I'm real sorry. I gotta get back to the station soon."

Her eyes swung back down to her shoes. Then she crooked her thumb toward the back of the house. "Past the kitchen and to your right," she said faintly.

"Thank you."

When I looked back, she was still there. Her thumb hovering in the air.

"Well, now," said Harley Blevins, rising up from his leather chair. "What a surprise. Lord, now, get yourself a seat. No, no, not that one, take the wing chair. More comfy on the old can, know what I mean?"

It weren't even a proper office, you must know. More like a sunroom, only with heavy drapes thrown up where all the light would've been and, instead of rattan and wicker, leather and chintz and a desk half the size of the room.

And on every wall, framed photos. Pretty much the same picture. Harley Blevins standing in front of some service station, shaking hands with some Standard Oil goon. The same smile, the same vulcanized-rubber bow tie, the same seersucker suit, the same straw boater, the same peppermint-stripe shirts. You could've cut and pasted him from one frame to the next, and no one'd have been the wiser.

And here he sat now, in the very same clothes, his hands joined at the back of his head, his patent-leather shoes (shiny as the day they was born) propped on the edge of his desk.

"How many windows you planning to shoot out before you're done?" I asked.

"I'm afraid I don't know what you're alludin' to. I was fast asleep all night, and I sleep sound, girl."

"One of your relations, then."

A smile played at the corner of his mouth. "Are you adverting to poor ol' Dudley? I got news for you, he ain't got the stomach for certain jobs."

I give a little nod.

"That thing you wrote 'bout Mama was low. Even for you."

"And once more, Melia, I must insist I was asleep when that—"

"Thing is, if Mama really *had* been a slut, you wouldn't be hating on her now. No, sir, if she'd have sat with you in the backseat of your Chevy Eagle—like you was always asking her to—I bet you'd be calling her a Christian woman."

232

He got out of his seat real slow. Walked round to the other side of his desk and laid one of his hands on my knee.

"Still got room in that backseat," he said.

If I hadn't seen his eyeballs flick, I'd of never known there was someone behind me. I swung my head round and found Mrs. Harley Blevins standing in the doorway with a tray. Two glasses and a pitcher of lemonade, with six lemon slices floating on top.

"Figured y'all might be parched," she said in a tight voice.

"You know what I'm parched for?" her husband said. "Some god-damned privacy. If it's all the same to you."

She stooped and set the tray on the floor.

"Hey!" Harley called after her. "Miss Elephant Ears? Why don't you shut that damn door after you? Let the grown-ups talk a little."

That door closed like a whisper. I peeled his fingers off my knee, one by one.

"Lemonade," he muttered. "Christ."

He walked to his liquor cabinet and pulled out a bottle of Bell's Royal Reserve. Poured about two inches into a cut-glass tumbler.

"You tell me this, Melia. If your mama weren't a little hot in the pants, how'd she convince Old Man Congreve to sell her that gas station in the first place?"

Very slowly, I poured myself a glass of lemonade.

"She listened," I said.

"Like hell."

I took a long swig, passed a palm over my mouth. "God's truth, Mama didn't have nary a design on that place. We was just driving on through—on the way to trout fishing—and coming down Route Fifty-Five, we see this sad ol' gas station. Sad ol' coot sitting in front, looking like he was serving forty years in Sing Sing. Our tank was three-quarters full, but Mama didn't care, she pulled right on over, asked him to fill it up. And being how she was, she couldn't help but talk the feller up. Turned out he had a daughter in Blacksburg, you know that?"

"Can't say as I did."

"His dearest wish was to spend his final years with that there daughter. Only problem was, he couldn't afford to move lest he sold the station, and the place was in such bad shape nobody wanted to buy it. 'Cept for . . . oh, how'd he put it? . . . some crawly old varmint."

Harley Blevins saluted me with his glass.

"Well," I said, "that's when the idea first come over Mama. The way she figured it, me and her was good at fixing cars. She had some money left over from her aunt Dot. No kinfolk to tie her down in Cumberland. So why the hell not?" I finished off the lemonade in three more gulps. "Deal was done in ten minutes, and all it took was listening to some lonesome old cuss by the side of the road."

Harley Blevins give his whiskey a twirl. "That is an inspiring tale, Miss Melia. You wanna know what I was doing at your age?"

"Something evil."

"You're right about that. I was three miles under God's earth. Digging coal for eighty cents a day in the Mill Creek seam."

"Just like Dudley's daddy."

"He tell you 'bout that, huh? Well, the difference between me and my brother was he couldn't see himself no place else and I could. Some days that was all I could see. *Else.* So, soon as I turned sixteen,

234

I hit the road. No prospects, not even two pennies to rub together. Just an itch to be gone.

"Oh, you can bet I took just about any job I could find. But the whole time I was—I was trying to see *through*, know what I mean? Which way was the world tending? Sometimes I'd just stop whatever it was I was doing and look *around*. Waiting for a sign.

"Well, one day I was hitching me a ride out of Harrisonburg when this old Pierce-Arrow come flying past me. Didn't stop, of course, the Pierce-Arrows never did, but I stood there thinking, *Harley, what does this world get more and more of each passing day?* Why, automobiles, that's what. And what's gonna make those beauties run to the end of time? Petroleum. Whoever can get ahold of that—front or back end—they's gonna have dollar bills coming out their assholes."

He set his glass on his leather desk pad.

"Well, I found me a station right off. It was this little ol' gas shanty over in Cedarville. Real shithole, just tar paper on some metal sheeting. Nozzles half coming off the pumps. It was a good location, though, right off Winchester Pike, and I *knew*, with a little fixing up, I could make the place fly. Trouble was I didn't have no damned capital. But there was a feller in town who did. Funeral director, if you can credit it, and he had himself a daughter. 'Course she weren't too pretty—nor bright—but she sure was sweet on me."

His hand curled round his glass, lifted it back to his lips.

"Now, I don't mind confessing it, Melia. In those days, I was a sinner. A heathenish wretch. But I got down on my knees and I said, *'Tell you what, Lord. You get this girl to marry me, you get her old man to lay out the bucks for this here station, you make all that happen for ol' Harley, and I'll pay you back, I swear.'*

235

"I was a man of my word, too. First year I turned a profit, I give back one-tenth to the church. Every time I bought another station, I put another chunk in the collection plate. And when the men in wool suits and neckties come from Standard Oil . . ." With a light smile, his eyes danced toward the photos on the wall. "Yes, ma'am, when they come a-calling, asking if I wanted me a wool suit and necktie of my own—why, that very next day, I put in another chunk. 'Cause the thing about God, Melia? He's a man of business. You honor your end, He honors His."

He cinched up his lips.

"And then you and your mama come along. Couldn't hardly believe my eyes when I first laid eyes on you. Little bitty things mixing it up with truck drivers. When y'all put up that grave marker for a sign, I swear I near bust a gut laughing. I said to myself, *Harley, you just hold out for a year, they'll be blowing out of here like cottonwood puffs.* But y'all hung on. Spite of everything.

"Oh, I know I should be the first to congratulate you, Melia— no, I *should*—but you just stick in my craw. You do. See, me and God had us a working relationship, and you got in the middle of it. You stole my customers. You made me look like a fool in my own town. You even turned my nephew against me."

"That's news to me," I said.

"And you wanna know the worst part?" He was smiling now, but just with his lips. "You even made me question my faith. 'Cause when the Lord ain't living up to His end of the deal no more, a church-going man starts to wonder. He does."

"Maybe God weren't never on your side in the first place," I said. "Maybe he ain't on nobody's."

"Now that is a sinful thing to say, Melia Hoyle. It is sinful, and it is mistaken, 'cause what I concluded? All *this*," he said, sketching a circle round me, "this is just the Lord's way of testing me. He knew things was coming too easy for me. I was getting a little . . . ha!" He grabbed some flesh round his belt. "A little prosperous, yeah! A little *soft*, needed me some hardening up. That's why the Lord brung you into my life."

He brought his glass to his lips, realized there was nothing left in it, set it back down.

"I'll give you ten thousand dollars," he said. "For the station and the store and that thing you call a house. That's more than anyone else in God's creation'd give you."

I closed my eyes.

"Think what you could do with that money, Melia. You could quit busting your ass eighteen hours a day. Send Earle to college. Put Janey in some pretty dresses." A light pause. "As for that so-called daddy of yours, you could set him up with all the hooch he can handle. Buy him his own distillery, why don't you?"

"He don't drink."

"My error."

I unshut my eyes. Harley Blevins was staring straight at me.

"You hold on to that there station, Melia, it'll bury you. You let go, you walk away the richest girl in the Blue Ridge. What's it gonna be?"

I stared at the glass in my hand. Then I set it on Harley Blevins's mahogany desk. Watched the ring of sweat well up from underneath.

"It's no," I said. "It's even *more* no than the last time you asked."

He set there a long time. "How come you always do just what I expect you to?" he said.

237

He opened his desk drawer and pulled out a brown kraft envelope. Unwound the string and tossed it to me.

Inside was a stack of pictures, maybe ten or twelve. Nothing like the ones on Harley Blevins's wall. No, sir, each picture had but the one man in it, and he didn't look pleased to get his picture took. Nobody was shaking his hand. He was all alone, looking frontward, then sideward, with dull, heavy, lost eyes.

And in every picture, one of those eyes was skewing out of its orbit.

Name	WATTS Hiram John				
Aliases	None				
Born	1889	Trade	Laborer	Comp	Fresh
Marks	Lazy left eye				

"I gotta admit," said Harley Blevins, "that boy made it too easy on me. Never once gave 'em a phony name."

My head weren't clear, 'cause all I could think in that moment was somebody must've liked Hiram a whole bunch to snap so many shots of him.

Only it wasn't just the photos. It was the words at the bottom.

MO, etc.	Larceny

On it went, page after page.

Larceny, House, Public House-breaking
Larceny, Shop and Warehousebreaking

Shop and Club Housebreaking
_____

Officebreaking
_____

Burglary
_____

Larceny, Shop, Officebreaking
_____

And sometimes, tucked at the bottom of each sheet, an extra detail or two.

Begs in residential areas and breaks into houses he finds
_____
unoccupied.
_____

Gains access by means of bodily pressure.
_____

Forces lock.
_____

Breaks window in rear of premises.
_____

Breaks public houses in afternoon.
_____

Uses various methods of entry.
_____

The words got fuzzier the more I looked at 'em . . . 'cept for the two words that appeared at the end of near every page. They stood out just fine.

Works alone.
_____

And two more words, on the very last page.

Often inebriated.
_____

Now, I'd seen a million mug shots in my day. On post-office walls or train-station corkboards. Hung up outside taverns, glued to telephone poles. I'd pass 'em by without another look. This was the first time they ever looked back at me.

I restacked the sheets, set them in my lap. Sat there waiting— for what I couldn't tell you.

"Don't mind saying, Melia, it took me a coon's age to gather all these. Had to call in a passel of favors, grease a whole mess of county clerks' palms. And this here's just the Atlantic seaboard. Give me another month or two, I bet I find a trail all the way to California." Harley Blevins's finger stroked the rim of his Scotch glass. "Lordy, it makes a body shiver. To think Walnut Ridge has had such a vicious and hardened criminal living in its midst all this time. It's a wonder we all didn't get ourselves kilt."

From a ways off come a packet of sounds. A lawn mower. A mourning dove. Some fool cricket rubbing its legs together.

Harley Blevins took the pictures off my lap, stuck them back in their kraft envelope. "If I recall," he said, fishing a watch out of his coat pocket, "the Warren County Courthouse is just a twenty-minute drive from here. I am a hundred percent sure that Miss Wand over there at the juvenile court would be most interested in this here dossier. Her boss, too. Did I ever tell you Judge Barnswell's an old buddy of mine? Me and him play poker near once a week. He ain't got much knack for the game, but to keep things friendly, I forgive him his debts from time to time. For which he is most grateful."

Once more he leaned back in his chair, laced his hands behind his head. Looked out through those damask drapes.

"I reckon you gotta decide," he said. "What's more important to you? That make-believe family of yours or that good-for-nothing gas station. Reckon you can't save both."

Chapter
TWENTY-SIX

Hiram was in the middle of his afternoon nap when I got back. His head against the wall, his feet on the counter. Hanging there in that perfect suspension. All these weeks, I'd never once seen him fall. His eyes quivered open. With a light rasp, he rocked himself into a sitting position.

"Everything okay with Chester?"

"Sure."

"Did he say he wants his wife back?"

"Why would he say that?"

"'Cause she's been here all morning."

My head made a little swing round the store.

"In the house," he explained. "With your sister."

"Oh, yeah."

"I was making a joke, Amelia."

"'Course."

He squinted at me. Then he set to wiping the counter. "If you're hungry, there's some soft-shell pecans in the back aisle. Only about four weeks old."

"I ain't hungry."

Stuck for something to do, I picked up a broom and started sweeping by the door.

"You don't have to do that," he said.

But I liked it, honestly, the whisper of the straw on the oak floors.

"I reckon it's time we took a little vacation," I said.

He stopped wiping the hardware cabinet and looked at me.

"Well, you know," I said, "we got but the one week before Janey and Earle gotta go back to school. I reckon we could, you know, close up shop and—I don't know, drive round. Hell, look at the ocean, I ain't never been to the ocean. It can't hurt a body to get out now and again."

"And then come back," he said.

"Well, sure. Of course come back."

He give his rag a couple of shakes.

"I mean, ain't you ready for a breather?" I said. "Setting behind that counter day after day?"

"Can't say I am. This is the best job I ever had."

"Oh, come on," I said, jabbing at him with the broom. "Better than playing in *Julius Caesar*? Or writing for the pictures? Selling ladies' hats?"

"Thousand times better."

"Aw, you could do a damn sight better than this old dump. We all could."

I wasn't looking at him, but he was sure looking at me.

"Dear God," he said. "That bastard is breaking you down, isn't he?"

"No, he ain't."

I leaned the broom against the wall. Real careful, like it might break.

"We keep saying no," I said, "there's no telling where it'll end."

"And where's it gonna end if we say yes? You think he'll quit with us? No, ma'am, he'll pull the same stunt a few months down the road. Some other family, and they'll say yes, too, and before long, he'll have his boot on every neck for a hundred miles around." Scowling, he jammed the rag back into his apron pocket. "Probably end up in Congress by the time he's done. You want to know what that Blevins fella is? He's an animal. Thinks all he has to do is piss on something to make it his. Well, he can piss on us all he likes, but this place isn't his. *We* aren't his."

Oh, I thought, *but we are.*

Once more, my head flooded with the *other* Hiram—that slack, rubbery, dead-eyed face. . . .

"Now, if all you want is a few days off," he was saying, "we could drive on out to Canaan Valley. But we've got to be back for Labor Day weekend 'cause that's prime business time. And, oh boy, do we need to start laying in for the leaf change. Do you know tourist numbers peak in the first two weeks of October? Think of all the cameras we could sell. Road maps, trail guides, compasses. I bet we'd even find takers for lederhosen. . . ."

I didn't feel unkind slipping out the door. He weren't talking to me no more.

For a little while, I stood out front, watching the cars pass by.

Then I went into the house. Janey was asleep, and Mina Gallagher was in her usual chair, the bag of yarn by her feet. Only the knitting needles was nowhere to be seen, and in her lap was one of the cheesiest, trashiest movie magazines it has ever been Hiram Watts's pleasure to sell. I could even see the headlines over her shoulder.

Claudette Colbert's Mother Speaks Out. . . . Robert Donat's Most Private Sorrow. . . . How Loretta Young Guards Her Beauty Complexion. . . .

Mina's own complexion got a little rouge-y when she saw me. "I was just on my way home," she said, jumping to her feet.

She was about a yard from the door when I thought to call after her. "Mrs. Gallagher?"

She spun her head round real slow.

"I just wanted to thank you," I said.

"Oh."

Silence.

"I heated up some oxtail soup," she said. "For when she wakes up."

"Okay."

"Also, it occurs to me you might start calling me Mina."

"Okay."

Then she was gone.

Her chair was still warm, though. I set there for a good stretch. The old skin had mostly peeled itself off Janey's face, and the new skin was thin and veined and papery.

"Is it Sunday?" she said, out of the blue.

"Naw, it's Thursday."

"Thursday night?"

"Afternoon."

"How come you ain't working?"

"Don't much feel like it."

"Oh."

"There's some soup if you want."

She yawned. "Ain't hungry."

We set for a while.

"Listen," I said. "I got a math problem."

"Shoot," she said, pushing herself up on her elbows.

"It's a minusing problem. Like, say we was to minus this one thing. Do we end up with less than if we minused this other thing? That kind of problem."

"I suppose it depends what you're minusing."

"Well, just for example, say we let go the station but we . . . get to keep Daddy Hiram. What would that leave us with?"

"Compared to what?"

"Well . . . keeping the station and . . . letting Daddy Hiram go."

"Where's he going?"

"Damn it, girl, nowhere. It's just a what-if."

She set all the way up now, stretched her legs in front of her.

"Let's see," she said. "We let go the station, it's kinda like losing the last piece of Mama. On the other hand, Mama was always saying blood's the most important thing in the world. So if she was here right now, she'd be telling us to hold on to Daddy Hiram. 'Cause think about it. Mama's the reason he come in the first place."

I nodded. Frowned down at the floor.

"Listen, Janey. I gotta tell you something."

It felt like I had scarlet fever myself, that's how hot my face was.

"Mama ain't the reason that Daddy Hiram's here, okay? I mean, Daddy Hiram ain't—he ain't even really—"

245

"Melia, shut up."

I looked up at her. "Sorry?"

"You must be dumb as dirt if you think you're telling me something I don't already know."

Next thing I knew, I was sitting on the edge of the bed. Couldn't even remember how I got there.

"But you was just talking about Hiram being blood," I said.

"Well, heck, I didn't think you'd get so hung up on a *word*. If you want to know, he's better than blood, he's *sent*."

I stared at her. "And just who do you think sent him?"

"I got to spell out everything for you, don't I? Mama, that's who."

Well, I searched her face, looking for patches of fever.

"Like from heaven or something?"

"Oh, for—Melia, she had a *plan*—a plan we didn't know about. And the plan was Daddy Hiram."

I knew then the child was off her nut.

Hiram weren't nobody's plan, he was a chain of accidents. A coal truck happened to catch some gravel as it turned right onto Totten. It happened to spit Hiram out its back. His body happened to block our pump. He happened to mention Shakespeare. If any one of those things *hadn't* happened, then none of it would've happened, and Hiram wouldn't be setting in that store right now, wondering how he was gonna scrounge up lederhosen.

"Sometimes," said Janey, "I theorize she wrote him a letter. Or sent him a Western Union. Or maybe it all come from praying."

"Mama praying . . ."

"Oh, I know it ain't like her. All I can think is she done it when we wasn't looking."

Your daddy. He's . . .

He's what?

And just like that, my head filled in the sentence. *He's coming.*

This whole while, I'd been thinking she was gonna give me a name. It never once crossed my mind that all she really wanted to say was he's on his way. Melia, he'll be here. Any day now.

Oh, maybe if she'd had more words, she'd have told me how unpromising he'd look right off and maybe there'd have been a little warning about the criminal history; that would've been useful. Then again, maybe Mama didn't know herself. Maybe all she was riding in those last few seconds was a feeling.

Well, there I was, setting next to Janey, and nothing had changed and everything had. I don't know that I'm much closer now to pinning down the feeling of it. But imagine the coldest day of the year and you're out in it, shivering in the sleet and snow, wind knifing down from the mountains. You couldn't be a grain colder and still be drawing breath. And that's when it hits you. You ain't cold at all. Ol' Man January, he can do his damnedest and it don't matter, 'cause you're wrapped against him and always have been. And never knew.

I stood up from the bed, real slow.

"If Hiram asks, tell him I had to go back into town."

I weren't about to go through Harley Blevins's front door again. No, this time I went all the way round to the back. By now, it was raining, and the rain was dripping like syrup from the sleeves of my uniform as I watched Harley Blevins's office window blink through the fog.

A single light was blazing, and the outline of the great man himself was stamped on the drapes. I knocked on the glass—three times, hard and short. Listened to the scrape of the chair. Saw a pair of hands flatten like frogs against the pane. A second later, the window was open.

"First thing you should know," I said. "We ain't no good-for-nothing gas station. We're kicking your ass every day of the year. And we ain't no make-believe family, neither. We're the real deal, and ain't no Miss Wand nor Judge Barnswell nor Harley *Blevins* gonna change that."

I could feel a single tear burning the bottom of one eye.

"So do your worst. Do your *worst*, you devil. You ain't getting our family, and you sure ain't getting our station. 'Cause that ain't in the plan."

He closed the window and turned away.

Chapter
TWENTY-SEVEN

Next morning, a little after eleven, a man come walking down the road. Tall and lean in a flannel shirt and dungarees, with what looked like a rucksack thrown over his shoulder. I was getting ready to throw a couple pennies at him when I noticed something familiar in the slant of his shoulders.

Dudley.

"Lost your ride?" I called.

He didn't answer, just grabbed me by the hand. Before I knew it, we was circling round to the back of the store. He didn't have no loving in view this time, 'cause once we was out of sight of the road, he flung down his rucksack. That's when I realized it were a shotgun case. With two double-barrels poking out.

"What the hell," I said.

"Shut up," he said, "and listen. That feller who threw the brick through your window? The one got his arm chewed up?"

"'Course."

"That was Tom Goggins."

"Who is?"

"A handyman, does odd jobs for my uncle. The other day, I seen he had these bandages all up and down his arm, and I asked him what happened, he said he got bit by a skunk." Dudley looked at me. "That weren't no skunk, Melia. Now, old Tom, he ain't a bad sort, but he's down on his luck, like a lot of folks, and he ain't too particular about the work he takes on." Dudley paused. "It was him put the bullets in your house, Melia. He didn't have no choice, he said my uncle had him over some kinda barrel, only he wouldn't say what."

In my head, I saw a whole new stack of mug shots. Biding their time in some other compartment of Harley Blevins's office.

"So I went to my uncle," said Dudley. "Asked him straight up if he was at the back of this."

"What'd he say?"

"'If I was you, I'd recollect who puts this roof over your damn head.'" Dudley give his head a shake. "So I said, 'Tell you what. You can keep your roof.' And I walked out."

His voice was hushed as he told it. Like he was watching it happen to some other wretch. And now he leaned a little closer.

"Tom Goggins left town today. He told me he couldn't do that dirty work no more, said it was eating him inside. Said next time something happened here, it was gonna be more 'n just a couple rounds."

"The sheriff," I muttered.

"He ain't gonna do nothing," said Dudley. That's when he reached down and pulled one of the shotguns out of its case. "Take it," he said.

"Oh, hell, I don't even know how to use the damn things. I sure as shit don't want 'em round Janey and Earle."

"You don't got no choice now."

"The young man has a point," said Hiram, pushing his head round the corner of the building.

Smiling softly at us, he drew the other shotgun from Dudley's bag and cradled it like a length of wood. "Over-under double-barrel. Used to know my way pretty well around these." He pulled the butt into his shoulder, pressed his cheek to the stock, and rotated the barrel toward the house's roofline. "Hope you got something a little better than buckshot."

"Three-inch shells," said Dudley.

Hiram lowered the barrel till it was pointing at the ground. "Where you hanging your hat these days, son?"

"Nowhere, kinda."

"Well, it just so happens we've got a room over the store."

Dudley looked at me, and I looked at him.

"Oh," said Hiram, "I'm not gonna sugar it for you. Room's hotter than damnation in the summer. Colder than an Eskimo's ass in the winter. Tolerable nice in spring, but you can't keep the window open too long or you'll get all fumey from the gas."

Such a dazzlement, hearing my own words circle back to me.

"So what do you say?" said Hiram.

"It's right decent of you, Mr. Watts. . . ."

"No, it's not. It's not even my property. Amelia's the one that's got to sign off."

My face got a grain warmer.

"Hearing no objections," said Hiram, "I will consider the deal closed. Now, then, son, why don't I show you to your new digs?" His right hand rested lightly on Dudley's shoulder as he walked him back round the store. "You've come at just the right time. Earle's heading back to school in a week, and we're going to need a fella to man the pumps. Seems to me you'd be perfect for the job. Think on it, will you? Say now, have you ever eaten chop suey? No? Well, strap on the feed bag, brother. . . ."

Dudley went to sleep an hour before nightfall. Stumbled back down the next morning in some old clothes of Hiram's and drunk three cups of joe, one after the other. "Put me to it," he said.

So for the rest of the day, he mopped the service bay, cleaned gutters, charged batteries, stacked fan belts and lamp bulbs and radiator seals, changed tires, cleaned oil. He might've gone straight through to nightfall, but Earle was mad to practice his shooting, so off they went into the hills behind the house, Gus following hard on. Don't know how far they traveled, but from time to time, you could hear a little crack echoing back down on the hills.

"Lord," said Janey, flopped in her bed. "You're jumpy as a cat."

"I ain't no such thing."

"Then why'd you just draw the bolt on the door? We don't never draw the bolt."

"Wind's kicking. You want the door blowing in on us?"

She squared her jaw and glared at me. "What if it does?"

"Well, then. All the dust and unmentionables from the road."

"Unmentionables," she said.

"Shut up and go to sleep."

To my vast surprise she did, a little after eight. Dudley and Earle come back not long after, carrying their rifles over their shoulders and dragging the last threads of daylight with them. Me, I made a real stab at sleeping, but I knew it weren't no use, and after what felt like ever and a day, I got up and threw an old raglan sweater over my shift and tiptoed outside.

Hiram was snoring on the porch swing, and Gus, he was lying in a bundle of old tarps. His head cut toward mine, and one of his bristly ears ratcheted up.

"Good boy," I said.

It'd been a long time since I'd climbed the steps to the room over the store. They was steeper than I recollected. Also, the knob turned slower. But turn it did, all the same, and I gazed into the bluing shadows and found the outline of him in the bed. For a while I listened to his breathing. Then I eased myself onto the mattress and pressed myself, light as I could, against his back. He stirred and started to rise.

"Don't," I said.

So we laid there like that, neither of us making a move. If his head so much as twitched my way, I'd give it a swat. "Hsst." Then I'd nudge my chin into the back of his neck. He hadn't had a bath since Christ knows when, but I didn't mind. The sweat and the dirt—the smell of fermenting apples in his hair—it was *him*.

After some time, I hooked my arm round him.

"Okay if I talk?" he said.

"I guess."

But he held off for a spell.

"I wanted you to know I'm sorry," he said.

"You didn't do nothing."

"All those times you said my uncle was doing evil on you, and I never believed."

"Well, he's your kin," I said. "You're supposed to take his side."

"Point is I'm sorry."

Even in the dark, I could see how the little hairs on the back of his neck stirred when I breathed on them.

"Reckon I'm sorry, too," I said.

"For what?"

"Just felt like saying it." I slid my free hand into the tangle of his hair. "Thing is, I really did want to go walking with you, Dudley. That time in the woods."

"Tomorrow's Sunday," he said.

"So it is."

"We could go and lie on our rock."

I drew out a strand of his hair. "It's *our* rock now?"

"Ain't nobody else claimed it. Possession's, like, nine-tenths of the law."

"Who told you that?"

"I read it."

We went quiet again. The space between his breaths got longer and the breaths deeper, and it suddenly washed over me. He was sleeping! Can't explain why it was so amazing, so fearful, a body falling asleep in my arms.

I dozed off, too, but never for long. Sometime toward morning,

Dudley's breathing changed into a high, choked hiss. *Brakes*, I remember thinking. *Castor oil*. I believe I actually tapped him on his chest like he was an engine that needed to be sounded. Then he jerked up in bed.

"Smoke," he whispered. "Smoke."

Chapter
TWENTY-EIGHT

Stooping to grab his shotgun off the floor, Dudley raced for the door and galloped down the stairs—then stopped. On every side of him, smoke had piled up.

"Damn," he whispered.

In the next second, a sharp fire crack come ringing in our ears. Putting a finger to his lips, he crept to the front door and peered out the window. Then he closed his fingers round the door handle and, after one last glance at me, pushed the door open.

I watched the door swing after him, saw the smoke surge round. Then I heard the sound of something hard meeting bone.

Swallowing down the poison air, I stole to the back of the store. The windows there was double-hung, and it weren't no trouble to open one now and squeeze through. And there I stood, on the other side, blinking in my bare feet.

Dawn was still an hour or two off, but smoke was gushing toward the sky and mattressing against the front porch of the house. My eyes hurt so bad, I had to smear 'em with my forearm just to keep 'em open. I pressed myself to the wall and inched round to the front of the store. And now the heat, deep and furious, tore the smoke open to reveal two towers of fire, right where our gas pumps used to be. Each tower as high as a man.

And I could see fire snaking round the columns of the porte cochere, chewing on its shingles, stripping off its paint.

For I can't say how long, I wandered at queer angles, like an old witty, pulling back from the blaze one moment and then lunging at whatever caught my eye. There was Harley Blevins's butternut Chevy Eagle . . . there was the hose hanging out Harley Blevins' gas tank . . . there was the gas trickling out the hose . . . there was the channel of fire heading straight for the store. . . .

Through our new-bought plate-glass windows, I could see purple-brown haze. I could smell the ripe scent of roasting food. Pork and beans and ketchup and granulated sugar. Cream corn and soft-shell pecans.

So many things rushing in on my senses, but I never once got a load of Gus. Not till I tripped over him.

He was still tied to his chain, and his legs was splayed on both sides, and there was a seam of black round his closed eyes. Next to him lay the remains of a steak, and all I could think was *I didn't know Gus liked steak.* I leaned over him, put an ear to his chest. Somewhere down there a heart was fighting.

From the nearby darkness, I heard a low, clotted groan. Crawled toward it on my hands and knees. And there was Hiram! Lying in the gravel with a good chunk of his left side missing and nothing to stanch the wound but his own quivering hand.

The smell of gasoline rose from him like swamp mist. Gasoline in his shirt and trousers, his hair and skin. All he needed was one spark to go up like a bonfire.

A great roar then as the porte cochere's last column toppled and the roof come down with a hoarse cough and the fire rolled toward us like a creek. Numbly, I grabbed Hiram under his arms and started to drag him away. But the gravel was an agony on him, and the harder I pulled, the deader his weight.

"We can't," I huffed. "We can't. . . ."

His lips was moving. I lowered my ear and heard . . .

"Janey . . . Earle . . ."

The house was nothing more than a shape now—a notion—shrouded in sulfur smoke. I took a step toward it, trying to part the haze with my hands . . . and then heard the voice I'd been waiting for all along.

"They're just fine."

Harley Blevins, standing between me and the house.

It took me a second to recognize him in his overalls. His face was hollow with shadow under a duck-hunting cap. A sawed-off shotgun was slung over his shoulder.

"I bet you're full of regret, ain't you, young lady?"

Now here's the part you won't strictly credit. It hadn't crossed my mind till now that I was responsible for any of this. It all seemed like something happening to some other girl—some other family—in some other world.

Harley Blevins give his temple a scratch with the stock of his shotgun. "Now here's what you need to understand, Miss Melia. This is all 'bout the bottom line. See, if word ever got out that Ol' Harley got bested by some little girl in his own backyard— that'd be bad for business, wouldn't it? On the other hand, if that same little girl got hauled through courts and torn from her grieving family, well, that might make it into one of them bleeding-heart newspapers, and that'd be bad for business, too. So what's a businessman to do?"

He paused now, for savor.

"An accident, that's what. Kinda thing happens all the time."

At the edge of sight, that creek of fire was rolling, ever so hungry, in Hiram's direction.

Talk, Melia. Buy space.

"I don't see how bullet holes would go down as no accident. . . ."

"You know, I got a feeling nobody's gonna be looking overmuch for holes."

The heat was like nails, driving into my skin.

"So you just gonna shoot us outright?" I whispered. "Like a bunch of old mares?"

"It'd afford me no pleasure. I tell you what, girl, there's times I think if you'd have been my bride, I'd be governor by now, and you'd be first lady."

"First lady in . . ." The smoke caught me. "In hell, maybe."

A flicker of light from his eyes. "See now? You *are* a believer, Melia Hoyle. That is gonna delight the soul of Our Lord."

He was walking at me.

"We can make a deal," I said. "Can't we?"

Still walking.

"I just gotta get Hiram to a doctor . . . I'll do whatever you want. . . ."

Still walking.

"What do you *want*?" I cried.

"What you got?" He took his shotgun off his shoulder and swiveled it at me. "You prepared to *beg*, Melia?" He cocked his head back toward the Chevy Eagle. "You prepared to get in that there backseat and make a man happy?"

"I'll . . . which one do you . . ."

Then he raised his gun and put me square in his sights. And it was Mama's words come sailing back. *Smile, Melia. Smile 'em all to hell.*

That's what I was doing when the blast come.

It sounded like Judgment itself. Only it entered my body like a feather.

I still had legs to stand on, eyes to see, a heart pounding for all it was worth. Death, that old cheat, he was just like life, only more so.

The only one who looked truly *changed* was Harley Blevins. His head swayed like wheat, and the skin sagged off his jaw. His knees went. Then his hips. Then the rest of him, puddling on the ground.

From the great daze of fire and shadow stepped Earle Hoyle, eleven years of age, holding the shotgun he'd just learned to use the day before.

He dropped it to the ground now. Turned his face to mine, and in the sulfur light that bathed us, he looked wiped clean.

We held each other hard.

"Let's get our daddy," I said.

The blood was curdling out of Hiram as we carried him to the garage. I looked up then and saw Janey floating toward us like some apparition. Her bed quilt was wrapped round her, and in her arms was a mess of bandages—her whole supply, best I could tell. She knelt by Hiram and wrapped his midsection till the blood had slowed to a leak.

"Hush," she said. "All is well, brave soldier."

"We got to get him to a doctor," said Earle.

But I didn't want to move him again, not if we could help it, and our only telephone had gone up with the store. I took Earle very gentle by the shoulders, stared right into him.

"I need you to drive into town."

"No. . . ."

"The keys is on the post just inside the front door. You head *east*, okay? Anywhere you see a light, you start banging. Someone opens the door, you tell 'em there's a fire and a man's been shot."

"What if I don't find nobody?"

"You keep going. Worse come to worse, you drive yourself to Front Royal. You remember where the fire station is?"

"Corner of North Royal and Peyton."

"That's my boy. You keep going till you get help, and then you come right back, you hear?"

"Why can't you come with?"

"'Cause I gotta save the house."

His eyes clouded as he stared into that glacier of smoke.

"We ain't got time for this, Earle. When it's all done, I'll set and weep with you, but right now, I need you to park yourself in that there truck, can you do that for me?" I dabbed his face dry, cupped my hand under his chin. "You're my big man."

In a matter of seconds, his taillights was swallowed by smoke—but not before they called out the still form of Harley Blevins.

And in that instant, I saw Earle disappearing into a different kind of smoke. A police interrogation room with no windows, just sheriffs and deputies. Blinding him, kicking and punching and jabbing him. *Was it you shot the gentleman in question? Was it you?*

Next second, I was taking hold of Harley Blevins by the arms and dragging him straight to the blaze.

Telling myself the whole way that I was just dragging out an old carpet or a bag of kindling. The heat was monstrous on my face and back, but I kept going till I was within reach of it. Then I planted one foot on Harley Blevins's hip and pushed till he was rolling into the fire's arms. His overalls went black, then bright orange. Steam rose off him, and his flesh crackled like something on a spit. His own words come rocketing back.

Nobody's gonna be looking overmuch for holes. . . .

The rest is just heat lightning. Flashes in the dark.

I've got my ear to Dudley's mouth. Making sure of the breath that's coming out. Staring down at his hard, soft face. Dragging him . . . where? . . .

I'm watching martins and jays and mockingbirds, bursting from their homes in the eaves and screeching into the night. Thinking of all the *life* that's been over our heads all this while. A whole other world pressed on top of ours . . .

I'm watching the roof of the store peel back like a sardine tin.

Watching a gale of flame boil toward the sky, spit out plume after plume . . .

I'm watching the first sparks land on the front porch of the house. . . .

I'm stumbling toward the well. Sending down the pail and drawing it back up. Running to the house and flinging the water and running back to the well. With each pass, the air in my lungs shrinks down. A thimble . . . half a thimble . . .

Couldn't tell you how many times I traveled from the well to the house and back again. Might've been ten, might've been a million.

I do recall that somewhere in the midst of the scurrying, the queerest notion entered my head. It was almost like the smoke was swaddling me. Hugging me so tight that when at last I went crashing to earth, it bore me up a little so I wouldn't land too hard.

Then it pulled away of a sudden so I could see all the things that'd been shut from sight. There was Dudley sleeping off the knot in his head. There was Earle driving down Strasburg Pike. Mama! In her best gingham dress, waving from the far side of the road. Clear as sun in her Joan Crawford slippers.

And alighting right in front of my face—out of nowhere and out of nothing—that old redbird. Peering into me with eyes so large and dark, it weren't no trouble to swim right through.

Chapter
TWENTY-NINE

A sound. Lonesome as the moon. Rising, falling, rising again.

Dudley's face, pale and beady. Earle's face swimming around it.

A man I don't know, bending over me. Hat says VOLUNTEER FIRE. *That's funny—he don't look like a fire.*

The dark folding over me. Like a blanket draped over a birdcage.

Chapter
THIRTY

"*Mama . . .*"

M   I woke to air. Running through me like current. My eyes blinked open, gazed round.

Light was streaming over me. *Sun*light, sawed into diamonds, sprawling cross a woolen blanket.

Atop that blanket lay an arm.

My arm.

I commanded it to rise. It did.

There was another arm did the same thing.

Piece by piece, I put the world back together. I was laying in something that looked very like a bed. I was wearing a light cotton gown with a paisley pattern. To my right was another bed, empty. Between me and the bed was a small nightstand, with a vase of marigolds on it.

(I hate marigolds.)

Straight ahead of me was a window. Directly above me, a sky-light. To my left, a wooden bench . . . and in the bench, a shape. Gathering feature the longer I looked at it. Rising and speaking.

"Mornin'."

Dudley.

"Don't talk," he said.

Well, if you've learned one thing about me by now, it's that I don't like taking orders. But here's the funny part. I *couldn't* talk. My fingers went dancing up my throat, aiming to pry the words loose, but all they found was plastic.

"They put a tube in," explained Dudley.

A tube.

I leaned over and saw a squat metal tank below the bed.

"It's oxygen," said Dudley. "You took in a lot of smoke, Melia. The tube's to help you breathe till you can do it on your own."

Oh, the strangeness of it. Not able to call your air your own.

"It's only for another day or two," said Dudley.

I laid there, stunned, all the same. Then Dudley handed me a legal pad and a pencil and said, "Write down whatever you want to know."

I set the pad in my lap. My fingers curled round the pencil, then jerked across the paper.

What day?

"Monday."

Which meant the day before was Sunday. Which meant the day before was . . . what?

I glanced up at Dudley.

Your head?

266

"Aw." He give it a shy rub. "It's all right. I still get blurry, but they say it's gonna pass, so . . ."

I stared at the pad. I watched the pencil form the names.

Janey

Earle

"They're fine. Staying with the Gallaghers. Janey's setting up and being bossy."

I scrawled another name and was surprised to see whose it was.

Gus

"Giving Mrs. Gallagher plenty to clean up after."

I paused. Then I wrote . . .

House

He drew in a breath.

"Your front porch is a goner, but the rest of it's still standing. There's a lot of smoke damage and stuff, but y'all should be able to move back in before too long."

But what if we don't want to?

"Anything else?" asked Dudley.

I swallowed. Tried to get the pencil to write, but it wouldn't.

"Hiram," he guessed.

I nodded.

"He's hanging on, Melia. They sewed him up right pert, but there's some healing still to do."

See him?

"He ain't woken up yet," said Dudley. "Soon as he does, I'll come find you, okay?"

Without even thinking, I scrawled . . .

Thanks

267

"Well, if that don't beat all. I just got me a thank-you from Melia Hoyle. Tell you what, I'm gonna take that goddamn paper home and frame it."

Shut your yap

"Now that's more like it," he said.

I think I must've dozed off not long after. Slept on and off through the afternoon, then woke to voices in the hallway. I could hear Dudley saying, "She ain't ready!" And some other voice, quieter and deeper, till at last it rose into hearing.

"Son, I'm gonna say this one more time. Step aside."

Next thing I knew, Sheriff Claude Motherwell was standing in the doorway with his white-blond hair and his raw face and his dyspeptic belly.

"How are you, Miss Melia?"

I made a circle with my pointer finger and thumb. *A-okay.*

The sheriff dragged the chair over to the side of the bed and dropped himself in it.

"I wanted you to know how sorry I was to hear about your latest losses. God is my witness, I believe y'all have took more punishment than Job."

There was a stretch of silence. Then the sheriff give his fat thighs a slap.

"Hey, now, got something needs clearing up, you don't mind." He picked up the legal pad from the floor. "Seeing as you're able to *write.*" He tossed the pad in my lap. "What do you know, here's a pencil, too. Makes things easier, don't it?"

He was smiling everywhere.

"Now, Melia, we in the Warren County Police Department pride ourselves on being *thorough*, know'm sayin'? So when Mr. Blevins's remains come in, we didn't just shove 'em in some drawer somewhere, no, we called in a medical examiner, and we got a post-*mortem* done. You know what a postmortem is?"

I nodded.

"Well, it's a peculiar thing, Melia, seems there was a—a *bullet* hole in Mr. Blevins. Passing all the way through. You still with me?"

I nodded.

"Now I know, what with everything going on, you had a lot to trouble your mind that night, but . . . I was just wondering if you could tell us who fired that bullet? You can write it down if you don't mind."

I had to stop now and then to keep the pencil from flying ahead of me. When I was done, I angled the pad toward the sheriff.

Mustve been same varmints
shot Hiram

The sheriff frowned.

"You get a good look at them varmints?"

I shook my head.

"License plate? Uh, body type? Coloring?"

I shook my head. Then I wrote . . .

Dark

"Well, here's where I'm having trouble," the sheriff said. "I can't rightly figure what Mr. Blevins was even *doing* there. Seeing as you and him wasn't on the best of terms. I mean, why would he even be hanging round Brenda's Oasis at such an ungodly hour?"

I stared out the window. Purple shadows was bleeding down from the mountains. A monarch butterfly was dozing on the ledge.

"Melia?"

Tryin g to

put out f ire

"You're . . ." The sheriff's eyes squeezed down to lumps. "You're telling me Harley Blevins was trying to put *out* the fire?"

And when I nodded, he set back in his chair.

"How would he've known there was a fire to put out?"

I shrugged.

"Melia, I'm gonna need more than that."

So I wrote the words for him. Neat and slow and even.

Mustve been driving by

The sheriff give a soft chuckle. "Just driving by, huh?"

I nodded, kept writing.

Miracle

"Well, yeah," said the sheriff. "That *would've* been a miracle."

Very slow, taking care with each letter, I wrote . . .

Harley Blevins = hero

Saved us

Tell the world

The sheriff read the words to himself. Read them a few times more.

"So that's your story?" he said quietly. "You're abiding by it?"

He leaned in and give me the searchingest look a body ever give another. Didn't make a whit of difference, though, 'cause there weren't an X-ray in the universe was gonna see through me.

Abiding

His head dropped a little. Then he set back up and, with delicate fingers, pulled the sheet off the pad. Folded it in three and tucked it in his shirt pocket.

"I assume Mr. Watts will confirm your account when he comes to."

I nodded.

"Reckon I'll be on my way, then."

He was near to the door when he turned round one last time.

"Ol' Harley sure underestimated you, didn't he?"

I went without the oxygen tube for an hour that afternoon. Two hours next morning. Morning after that, I was walking. Dragging the tank for the first two laps round the floor, then going without.

What I hadn't done yet was speak. But when Dudley come round Thursday morning, he made a point of asking me how I was, and not having any legal pad nearby, I went ahead and answered.

"Fair to middling."

I could see him wince, but I believe my shock was greater. That desperate creak of a voice. Like something that'd been living in a cave all its life.

"Don't you stew," said Dudley. "Voice is the last thing to come round, that's what the doc says. Here's the thing, though—I hear Hiram's ready for visitors."

"Give me an hour."

I went back in my room and practiced speaking in that new voice of mine till it stopped scaring me. By the time Dudley come back, I was very near to resigned.

Hiram's ward was at the end of the hallway. There was ten beds in it, but only two was filled, one by a TB patient, who lay with his face to the wall, coughing up what was left of his lungs. Three beds down lay Hiram, in a gown very like mine.

All I saw at first was a gray head and a pair of long, lank, veiny legs. The rest of him was blocked by the woman who set alongside his bed and rested her chin on his arm. Such a *private* pose that I flushed and started back, but Hiram's good eye cut our way, and he raised his head a fraction, and the woman jumped to her feet and swung round.

It was Ida. Her hair wrapped like ermine round her neck, her hand already reaching for Hiram's.

"I should be going," she said.

She give us each a nod as she passed, then vanished into the hallway without a look back.

Which left the three of us stuck in place, awaiting orders from on high. Then Dudley said, "How 'bout I leave you two be?" and ducked out of the room, and it was just us two.

"Don't know as I ever seen your legs before," I said, circling round the foot of his bed. "Bare nekkid."

"Ain't they pretty?" he said.

I angled my face a little to the right of him so I wouldn't have to look at him head-on.

"You sound just like Greta Garbo," he said.

"Like hell I do."

"Without the accent."

"You're a liar," I said. (Though, for a second, he had me wondering.)

"Everything okay with Ida?" I asked, trying to keep my croak light.

He sheathed his hands cross his forehead. "Ida," he said, "has got other fish to fry. I believe we've seen the last of her."

I nodded. Looked down at my hands.

"Listen," I said. "If the sheriff ever comes and asks you who was—"

"I'm to say it was too dark to see anything."

"Yeah."

Lord, it was quiet. Just for company, I found myself staring at the feller three beds down. Who wasn't even bestirring himself now 'cept to cough.

"You'll have to forgive me," said Hiram.

"What the hell for?"

"I didn't play it smart, Amelia. I saw the fire go up and I went *running* at it. Without a thought. Fish in a barrel."

I come round the side of his bed, took his dry hand in mine. "Point is we survived."

"Brenda's Oasis didn't."

"Aw," I said. "Who needs that dump anyway? Always more trouble than it was worth."

"I miss my counter." He drew in a long breath, like he was sucking on one of his Luckys. "The one thing we always scrimped on was insurance."

"Premiums was too high."

"So we always said."

I set on the edge of his bed. Brought my other hand on top of his. "We had us a good run, Hiram."

"Yes, ma'am."

"Mama would've been proud."

"I suspect you're right."

He put his other hand on top of mine, and we set there a good while. At some point, the other feller ceased his coughing, and a silence settled over us like snow. Then, from somewhere far off, come the sound of running feet.

Very particular feet, I knew 'em soon as I heard 'em. Sure enough, when I angled my head to the doorway, there was Earle, bounding into view.

"You gotta come with me!" he cried.

"What for?"

"Just the once, could you shut up and do like you're told?"

Chapter
THIRTY-ONE

Well, it didn't take me but ten minutes to collect my bill and be on my way. Doc Brown give me an extra tank of oxygen, and the nurses popped a couple of oranges in my hands and opened the front door for me, and before my eyes had even got used to the sun, Chester Gallagher was pulling up in his Buick sedan.

"Hop in," he said.

Earle was in the front, Dudley was in the back, and nothing seemed right.

"What the hell's going on?" I said.

Not a word.

"Chester, you're my damn lawyer. You gotta tell me."

"I'm gonna have to plead the Fifth."

Nothing to do but drag myself inside and pull the door after.

Oh, but I had the sinkingest feeling as we headed north out of town, and when we took a left on Strasburg Pike, my stomach swerved in clear the other direction.

"No," I said. "I can't."

But the car bore on.

"I said I *can't*. I can't go back."

"Shh," said Dudley, giving my forearm a squeeze.

How strange and terrible the road looked to me now. Like I'd last traveled it a million years ago. I tried to close my eyes, but they was still wide open when we hit that last turn and the sign come soaring out of the noon haze.

BRENDA'S OASIS.

"See?" cried Earle. "It never come down, Melia. Barely even got smudged."

He was right. The desert and the water and the camels, they was near as fresh as the night they went up. And that was the cruelest blow of all somehow. To have that sign looking down on all the waste and wreckage. Like a queen gazing on a dead kingdom.

"Stop," I whispered. "Please stop."

And when that failed, I shouted, best I could.

"Will you stop the goddamn car!"

That's when Hiram's porte cochere swum into view.

I rolled down the window and leaned my head out, stared until I couldn't stare no more. 'Cause, of course, I'd seen that porte cochere swallowed by fire. Seen it crumble and fall. The only way it could be standing now was if I was dreaming it.

But there was the four columns, braced and firm and true. Just like I remembered. The only thing that didn't fit was the man who lay sprawled atop the roof, raising a John Henry hammer to the clouds.

Warner. Warner the trucker.

"How you?" he growled down.

"Uh. Okay." I stared at him some more. "How you?"

"Tolerable."

"What you *doing* there, Warner?"

"What the hell's it look like? Laying down shingles. Hey, watch your head there."

I spun round, and there was Joe Bob, carrying a length of ceiling vault. And there was Dutch, bending a gutter, and just beyond him was Elmer, and, to the left of Elmer, Merle.

"How'd you fellers even . . ."

"Word travels fast in the hills," said Warner.

Then I heard someone calling my name. It was Frances Bean, in rolled-up sleeves. Her hands was stained with paint.

"Hot enough for you?" she was saying.

Directly behind her was a wall. A free-standing, load-bearing wall. Exactly where the front wall of the store used to be.

And not far off, two *other* walls. Waiting to make corners with the wall that was standing. And, a few yards past, *another* wall, ready to make a fourth.

And alongside each of these walls, a human being. Hard at work.

It was like some veil was being peeled away, piece by piece, from my eyes. Suddenly I could see dozens and dozens of people—people I knew by sight—swarming across what was left of Brenda's Oasis. Pouring concrete. Sanding floorboards. Carving molding. Laying down nests of wire.

Basil Buckner was taking an adze to a ceiling beam. Farmer Stokes was pouring fresh gravel out of the back of his truck. Frances Bean's husband was cutting sections of drywall. Maggie McGuilkin was screwing a knob onto a door, and Mrs. Hicks and Mrs. Buckner was carting away barrows of sawdust and wood chips.

Ladders was rising to the sky, and hammers was ringing and saws grunting. Body after body was bent in the heat, bearing down and dragging up, and in that fog of sweat and toil, under the ministrations of a thousand hands, Brenda's Oasis was rising from its ashes.

Over there, by the garage, lay the remains of our old icebox, waiting to be hauled to the junkyard. But *here*, just a few feet from where I was standing, a carpenter was fashioning a new one, the *same* one, right down to the mirrored doors. On the far side of the road lay our old pickle barrel, a blackened stump of its former self. Here on this side, a cooper had made one even bigger than the last, and a blacksmith was girding it round with iron hoops.

Lewis Quint, the glazier, was fitting a new plate-glass window, and a crew led by Mr. Hicks was buffing down a slab of wood that, less my eyes deceived me, was going to be Hiram's new counter.

Why, you might've thought the whole population of Walnut Ridge had turned out for this very occasion. There was Minnie-Cora Harper and her newest beau. There was Lizabeth Shafer and Gwendolyn Davenport. There was Mrs. Goolsby, carrying a pitcher of sweet tea from worker to worker. *Pastor* Goolsby, using a hammer claw to pull nails out of charred wood.

And there, on her hands and knees, was Mina Gallagher, scrubbing the last bits of soot from the store's stone foundation.

I was gazing out on truckers whose names I hadn't even got

down yet. On townsfolk I hadn't seen since they got their palms read by Madame Ouspenskaya. On children who'd never done nothing more than climb into our tire swings. Here they all was, with their wrenches and pliers and planes and screwdrivers. I believe it was the closest thing I'd seen—will ever see—to a miracle. And so frail did it seem to me in that moment, I almost didn't want to breathe on it.

But then—one by one—the workers stopped what they was doing, set down whatever tool they had in their hands, wiped their brows, and looked at me.

Someone—I think it was Chester—set down an old milk crate, then helped me stand on it. I must've spent a good minute or two just clearing my throat till I remembered that was how my voice sounded now.

"Hey, y'all. . . ."

Next second, I heard someone yell, "Speak up!"

"She can't!" shouted someone else.

"Listen now," I said. "My voice ain't much—I mean, it never—I never was much of a public speaker. . . ."

"Neither was Moses!" called Pastor Goolsby.

There was some laughter at that.

"What I mean," I said, "is there *ain't* no words. Not really. For what y'all have done. I mean, I can't believe you'd—I never thought you . . ."

I never thought you give a rat's ass about us.

And still they stood watching. Quiet as Quakers. Waiting for something I couldn't dredge up. I think I might be standing on that crate this very minute if Warner hadn't bellowed down.

"*Quit your yapping, girl, and get to work!*"

And so I did.

I confess, being just out of hospital, there weren't too much I could do. Anything too strenuous, my windpipe'd squeeze down on me, and I'd have to go trotting over to Chester's car for a whiff of oxygen.

So I kept it small. Cleaning brushes. Carrying paint buckets. Pouring water and sweeping up mess and sending up pulley buckets of nails and screws. Sometimes, I'd just set and watch. Astonished that all this was going on round me without no plan nor blueprint, no supervisor nor foreman. Bubbling up like a spring.

Oh, I knew a brand-new gas station didn't come for free. Someone'd have to pay for all this hardware and lumber and labor. But as the afternoon wore down and the air got prickly with the thought of rain, it begun to come home to me that there would be neither bill nor reckoning. The citizens of Walnut Ridge had done the one thing I never would've expected in a million Sundays. They had gathered round their Gas Station Pagans and raised them up.

Round about four thirty, a car come rolling in. A car that, from a distance, looked very like Harley Blevins's butternut Chevy Eagle. In fact, it was. It shuddered to a stop three yards shy of me, set there for a spell in the heat. Then, inch by squeaking inch, the driver's window rolled down, and a man leaned toward me. A man I never seen before, with a scrub of mustache and a trail of scab and scar winding down his forearm.

"Afternoon," he drawled.

"Hey, sorry, mister. We don't have no gas today, but if you—"

"I'm Tom Goggins. I suspicion my name is known to you."

We was quiet a spell.

"It is," I said.

"Well," he said, "that's a grief to me." His hands clenched the steering wheel, then unclenched. "Miss Melia, I would like you to know I didn't have nothing to do with this last business."

"I know that, Mr. Goggins."

He nodded. Breathed in and breathed out. "I've also been asked to hand something over to you."

He reached toward the passenger seat and brought up a brown kraft envelope. Next thing I knew, it was resting in my hands.

"You may want to check," he said, "just to be on the safe side."

Sure enough, every last mug shot of Hiram Watts was there. In a neat stack, fastened with a paper clip.

"They're yours," I heard Tom Goggins say. "Courtesy of Mrs. Blevins. To do with as you will."

I started to speak, but something stuck in my throat. So I took a breather and tried again.

"You be sure to thank Mrs. Blevins for me, will you?"

"I will."

"Tell her to stop by anytime she likes."

"She said the same 'bout you. She happened to notice you enjoyed her lemonade."

"That I did," I said.

He reached into his pocket and pulled out a Zippo lighter. Set it in my palm and closed my fingers round it. "I reckon there needs to be another fire," he said.

"You may be right."

"I won't never call us even."

"We're even."

I give him half of a wave, he give me the other half. The car pulled away, slow as a milk wagon.

In the end, the only hard part was finding someplace I wouldn't be seen. I had to cross the road and then head east for a spell. I set the envelope on the gravel, and then I lit each corner. The day was humid, but the envelope caught straight off. In less than minute, it was a pile of ash. I give a kick, and the ash scattered in soggy clumps.

We never saw the sun set—the clouds had it too wrapped up. Bit by bit, though, the heat lifted off, and the hammers rang quieter, and a hum rose as people set down their tools and made their homeward plans. Minnie-Cora's new beau (who turned out to be her old beau) picked up his guitar and began to strum. From out in the dusk, a voice picked up the tune, and some other voice joined in, and before long, there was a ragged choir.

> *Show me the way to go home*
> *I'm tired and I want to go to bed*
> *I had a little drink about an hour ago*
> *And it's gone right to my head*

Even with a normal voice, I ain't never been the singing kind, but I set down on a pallet of two-by-fours and listened. After a couple choruses, I felt a knee nudging mine. It was Chester.

"Move over," he said.

So we set there, the both of us, the voices ribboning round us.

Wherever I may roam
On land or sea or foam
You can always hear me singing this song
Show me the way to go home

And as the voices started dying out and folks gathered up their belongings, Chester said, "Not such a bad day's work."

Through the thickening air, I saw four freestanding walls, webbed together by joists. Three new barrels, a new icebox. A stack of oak floorboards. A stack of cherrywood shelves. And a white-washed porte cochere, looking like it was new sprung from Hiram Watts's mind.

"Not half bad," I allowed.

"They'll be back tomorrow."

"I don't doubt it."

Chester stretched out his legs. "It's too damn bad about the pumps," he said. "I mean, your underground tanks are intact, but without anything to pump the gas *out* . . ."

"Everything in due time."

Chester nodded.

"Oh, hey," he said. "I went home and picked up my mail and . . . cripes, my eyes aren't what they used to be. Can you read this for me?"

He brought something letter-sized out of his pocket. Soft and cream-colored.

"You getting a better class of client, Chester?"

"This one isn't a client."

Even in the dying light, I could make out the Standard Oil watermark.

Dear Mr. Gallagher,

In response to the unfortunate incident at Brenda's Oasis in Walnut Ridge, Virginia, we at Standard Oil of New Jersey have been authorized to donate two (2) mint-condition calculating pumps—free of charge—for use by the station's past and current owner.

We hope that, despite recent unfortunate calamities, Brenda's Oasis and Standard Oil will continue to enjoy a long and mutually fruitful business relationship.

Please contact us soonest in order to discuss delivery of aforementioned pumps.

Yours most sincerely,
Ralph Blore
Vice President, Affiliate Operations

I read it three times through.

"This your doing?" I asked.

"Word travels fast in the hills, Melia."

Greatly to my surprise, I commenced to laugh.

"Explain yourself," he said.

"Oh, it's just . . . Harley Blevins was always saying we had substandard pumps."

Chester had himself a laugh, too.

"Well, then," he said. "It was decent of him to get you some new ones."

"Nothing decent about it. Standard Oil's just covering its ass. They know what he was up to."

"Be that as it *may*"—Chester wiggled the letter out of my hand—"there's a saying somewhere about gift horses. And their mouths." He refolded the letter, stuck it back in his jacket. "Now, I already phoned Mr. Blore. Pumps should be here by Monday. I also called your suppliers, and they're ready to kick back in starting tomorrow. If everything comes together, Brenda's Oasis could be back in business by middle of next week." He eyed me. "Guess I thought that would make you happy, Melia."

My gaze drifted from west to east.

"Kinda hard to think on the future," I said.

"It'll be here before you know it," he said. "And hey, now, while we're on that subject, I've got something else needs discussing. I have taken inventory of that house of yours, and it'll be two or three weeks before it's fit for humans."

"Where you going with this, Chester?"

"Well, now." He stood up, squared his shoulders. "You may not know it, but the Maison Gallagher, as I now prefer to call it, is a hell of a lot bigger than it looks. Why, at this very moment, it is hosting an aspiring nine-year-old nurse, an eleven-year-old hoarder of trash—I'm sorry, *treasure*—and an emaciated mutt of highly dubious ancestry. Who will never eat steak again. But here's the wonder! There's room for one more."

And lo and behold, here was Mina Gallagher. Sidling up to us like she was answering a signal from on high.

"What Chester *means* to say, Melia, is would you do us both the kindness of staying in our home? Till you get back on your feet."

As she spoke, I couldn't help but see her hand curve itself round Chester's elbow. They stood there, the two of them, making one front.

"It's just for now," I said.

"'Course," said Chester. "You think we could stand you for longer than that?"

Chapter
THIRTY-TWO

There was but one person that didn't have no intention of staying at the Gallagher house, and that was Hiram. Oh, he didn't have nothing against Mina and Chester, but soon as he knew he was leaving the hospital, he told anybody who'd listen that he wanted to go *home*.

"It's a mess," I told him. "Reeks of smoke half a mile away. The floors and beds are soaked through. There's scum on the walls and nothing in the larder."

"As long as it's got a roof," he'd say.

Well, it turned out the mattress to his old bed weren't too badly off—at least it didn't squish when you laid on it. I dug a ratty quilt out of the closet, and Mina brought over a pillow and a fitted sheet, and Earle, he brought Gus, who was longing so bad for the old homestead he come near to tearing down what was left of the front door.

Hiram was walking with a cane now, but he took the last few steps to bed by himself, and Gus jumped in.

"Looks like we're good to go," he said, thumbing down his lids.

When I pulled up next morning, he was already standing in front of the store. Staring at it with God-fearing eyes.

"What you waiting for?" I asked.

"Guess I lost my key."

He shuffled from aisle to aisle, taking in every improvement. The oak floors, still smelling of Murphy Oil Soap. The track ladders and the new hardware cabinet—eight-sided and revolving—and the icebox. The pickle barrel, even stouter than the last, with its handsome iron hoops. The pea, rice, and bean bins, each with their own glass front.

He saved the best for last. The cherrywood store counter, planed down to the smoothness of new skin, shiny with mineral oil and beeswax. And sitting atop it a spanking new National cash register, courtesy of Venable's Drug.

"I'll be," he said softly. Using his cane for balance, he propped himself on his brand-new stool. "Don't know that I deserve all this."

"You'll get used to it," I said.

We hadn't put out word on when Hiram was coming back, so every customer who walked in the store that morning give a little shout of surprise at seeing him there. From outside, listening to all the greetings and pleasantries, you'd have figured the old times had marched right back into town without missing a step.

But your eyes would've told you different.

Like you'd hear Joe Bob call out, "Hiram, what you got in this here blend? It's your best joe yet." Then you'd watch him pause in the doorway on his way out and give his head a hard shake. Minnie-Cora Harper, she brought in her new (old) beau, chatted up a storm, then left with an ugly crease on her forehead. Dutch went in noisy as an osprey, then staggered out with a face grave as winter. Mrs. Goolsby run back to her car like Old Scratch was on her tail.

And here's the thing, not a one of 'em would look me in the eye as they left. Even Warner! It made me wonder what all them folks was seeing that I couldn't. So I went in the store myself, but all I found was Hiram fast asleep.

An hour before his usual nap time. And instead of being tipped back in his stool, he'd just gone and laid his head on the counter. When I come back half an hour later, he was just sputtering back to life. When closing time come, he shuffled out toward the pumps, beckoned Dudley over, and leaned into his ear.

Now, I couldn't hear what was being said, but when I got to the station next morning, Dudley was getting the lay of the store. Item by item, Hiram walked him through the inventory. Told him which shelf placements worked best. How to keep the coffee from turning bitter. Little tricks to make the ice last longer in the icebox. Where to order pickles from, where not to. When to go with the Heinz supplier over the Campbell's supplier.

"Now listen, Dudley, some lady tourist comes in looking for a Nestlé bar, what do you do?"

"Sell it to her?"

"Then what?"

"Don't know."

"You say, 'How 'bout some film for that Beau Brownie camera of yours? Say now, is your husband a fisherman? Well, now, there's a lure that drives Shenandoah trout wild with desire, and it's right over here. . . .'"

"I don't think I can do all that, Hiram."

"There's no trick to it. You're just showing them all the things they'd be buying if they only knew. . . ."

Again, if you was just to *listen* to him, you'd have thought he was back in business. Only he fell asleep even earlier than usual and slept for longer, and when two o'clock rolled round, he tapped Dudley on the shoulder and said, "Packing it in, my friend."

He slept the rest of the day. Woke a little after seven in a fever, his breath coming in quick hard gasps, his heart pecking like a bird. He was able to swallow down some aspirin, though, and when I left him at nine, he was fast asleep with Gus curled up at his feet.

Next morning, he was still asleep, but all the sheets and linens and quilts had been thrown off, and Gus was running round the bed, barking up something fierce and giving a specially nasty look at Hiram's feet, which had swollen to near half again their size.

I put in a call to Doc Whitworth, who was there inside an hour, clutching the same bag he'd brought to see Janey. This time I didn't have no front porch to wait him out, so I hung over by the garage, finding new ways to arrange socket wrenches. Can't rightly say if the time passed quick or slow. All I know is I looked up at some point and Doc Whitworth was there, the bag still in his hand.

"Want to go for a walk?" he said.

"Can't you just—"

"Let's walk," he said.

We didn't go far, maybe fifty yards west, before his head lowered a grain.

"It's not looking good, Melia."

"They got the bullet out," I said.

"I know."

"They got it *out*. They sewed him *up*."

"The infection's spreading all the same, and there's nothing we can do to stop it. His organs are shutting down."

I don't know why, but I thought of the organs they used to have in movie theaters—before the talkies come. Shutting down and nothing left but pictures flickering on a screen.

"How long we looking at?" I said.

His hands circled by his side. "Maybe a couple days. Maybe a week."

"And there ain't nothing else you can give him?"

"We can set him up with some morphine. To ease the pain."

"Pain." I snorted, half turned away. "We got Emmett Tolliver's moonshine for that."

"I could find you a nurse, too, if you like."

"You're looking at her."

"Melia . . ."

"Oh, *what?*" I said, turning on him. "You think it's too big a job for a little girl? You think I don't got enough *experience* in this line of work?"

"I'd say you've altogether too much." With sad eyes, he watched a produce truck trundle down the road. "Do me the one favor," he said.

"What?"

"If you're going to stay with him, at least don't sleep here. Give yourself that much. Spend your nights with the Gallaghers."

"How can I do that?"

"You won't do him any good if you're dead on your feet, Melia. Sleep in a real bed and come back the next morning. Will you promise me that?"

I started walking back toward the station. Long, twitchy strides. Then I stopped and waited for him to catch up.

"Only if Hiram's okay with it," I said.

He nodded. Swung his bag to his other hand. "Wife's holding supper."

"'Course."

"I'll check in tomorrow, shall I?"

"Sure."

"Can't tell you how sorry."

I closed early that evening. Looked in on Hiram to make sure he was sleeping. Then sent Dudley home with a message for Chester and Mina. Ate a dinner of Kraft Caramels and Sugar Daddies.

The night come on slow, and in the space of time just before the sun snuffed itself out, I found myself staring at the branches of the crape myrtles. Wondering how it was they could carve themselves out of the sky like that.

"Jesus, what time is it?" Hiram stood wobbling in the front doorway.

"You shouldn't be up," I said.

"I can't just lie around all day. I'm not a fungus." He give his head a long scratch. "Any chance you can rassle up a cig for an old man?"

I got him a pack of Lucky Strikes from the store. Lit one for him and one for me.

"Where the hell's the porch?" he said.

"It went away in the fire."

"Huh." He stared at the ramp beneath his bare feet. "Where are we going to sit, I wonder?"

So I fetched a couple of saggy-ass cane-bottom chairs from the house. It took him a few seconds of writhing before he could get anywhere close to comfort. We was quiet awhile. Then, from nowhere, he said, "I'll miss this place."

"Hell," I said. "It's not like you got anyplace else to be."

"I have many places to be. I only said no one was—"

"—expecting you at any of them. Yeah, I remember."

Five and a half months ago.

"What I mean," he said, "is this is probably the most beautiful place I've ever been."

"Go on."

"No, I mean it."

"What about Hong Kong?"

"Bah."

"New York. San Francisco. What about Hollywood?"

"Just a big ashtray with palm trees stuck in the middle. It doesn't have *this*," he said.

By now, there weren't no hard edges left anywhere. Just a soft hump of purple that I knew to be mountains.

"You gotta understand, Hiram. To me, all this was just what was keeping me from going anyplace else."

"And where was it you wanted to go?"

"Anyplace else." I smiled, dug my heel into the gravel. "Don't know as I had a special place in mind. Pittsburgh, maybe."

"Well, now," he said with a wriggle. "I've got news for you, Amelia Hoyle. There's nothing keeping you here but *you*."

"Spoken like a rolling stone."

He chuckled. "Not anymore, ma'am. I'm head to toe *moss*."

"Thought it was fungus."

We was quiet, smoking our cigs. Though I noticed, after a while, Hiram weren't even smoking his, just bringing it in the direction of his mouth and letting it drop again.

"Know what?" he said. "I hope you do some rolling of your own, Amelia. But don't be surprised if you end up where you started. You're the deep-rooting kind of plant." The cigarette—just one long pillar of ash now—fell to the ground. "You should be getting on back."

I stood up. Give him the once-over.

"You sure?"

"Of course I'm sure. Gus and I have some serious hay to hit."

"And you don't need nothing?"

He shook his head.

"There's some cans of Franco-American if you get hungry."

He nodded.

"I'll come by early tomorrow," I said. "Just to be on the safe side."

He shrugged. But as I was walking back to the truck, he called after me.

"Amelia."

"Yeah?"

"It's an honor being your dad."

"'Course it is," I said.

Well, true to my word, I was back by five thirty the next

294

morning. I give a little knock, for politeness' sake, then pushed the door open.

It was quiet, which I figured to be a good sign. He was still sleeping, wasn't he? I turned the corner and pulled open the curtain, and there was Gus doing his little worry dance about the bed. And there in the middle of the bed lay Hiram. Who weren't worrying about nothing no more.

His brogans was fresh polished, his shirt and trousers ironed, his hair washed and combed. At the foot of his bed sat a row of six empty bottles, all with the same label. OPIUM CAMPHORATED, FOR U.S.P. TINCTURE: LIQUID NO. 338.

Lord only knows how he put his hand on that much laudanum. I can't imagine Doc Whitworth would've gone to such a risk, so either Hiram smuggled it out of the hospital himself or he bribed somebody to do it for him. The only thing I can say for true is how he forced that bitter liquid down. Beneath his outstretched right arm sat a half-empty bottle of Dr Pepper.

The same soda-pop chaser I'd used with Mama in her final hours. Which Hiram Watts knew full well, just as he knew this was the bed where she'd given up her last breath. What better place, he must have thought, to make his own peace?

I set myself down next to him. I wrapped my fingers round his cold, cold hands. I said, "The honor was all mine."

Chapter
THIRTY-THREE

Hiram Watts left this life in the early morning hours of September the eighth.

His death was noted in the *Warren County Register* and was mourned by the regular customers of Brenda's Oasis. Warner the trucker was heard to say that Hiram was plenty all right.

Mr. Watts was buried on a hill overlooking Jenkins Orchard next to a woman he'd never met. The funeral ceremony was private, attended only by Mr. Watts's three children and by Mr. and Mrs. Chester Gallagher.

No speeches was made nor prayers said, though Janey Hoyle did, upon request, sing "Amazing Grace." In addition, she supplied the wildflower arrangement, and Earle Hoyle fashioned a cross from sticks that was judged even finer than his last effort.

It was decent weather for a funeral. Very nearly cool in the shade of the locust tree.

The mourners departed for home a little past eleven.

•   •   •

That's how it all seems even now, like it was happening to some other idiot.

The next time I recognize *me* in the picture—well, that ain't till the next day. I remember standing in front of the store, trying to figure out what to do with all the flowers folks had brung. Lilies and snapdragons and zinnias and I don't know what else, piled to God's shoulders. Wouldn't have been too much trouble to make 'em look pretty, but I didn't have it in me. So I just stood there.

As for the flowers, they set the whole week, wilting and rotting, till Mina come and swept them all away.

Not too long after, a parcel arrived for Janey. Small and flat, bound in butcher's paper.

"Ain't my birthday till next month," she said.

"Well, who cares?" I said.

She peered at the return address. "Where's Los Angeles?"

"Open it!"

Two seconds later, we was staring down at a framed photograph of Clark Gable.

Wearing the same surgeon's shirt he wore in *Men in White*. His face turned maybe a quarter away from the camera and the light playing just right. In the clean blank space just across his heart was written the words . . .

To Janey, with all my deepest respect

297

I touched the picture, saw the words, heard the little rush of air from Janey. But my senses kept snagging on something that weren't part of the picture. A monogrammed note card tucked into the frame's lower right-hand corner. I pulled it out and read,

Hiram, you old cuss!
When are we going to take the boat out to Catalina again?

The same hand as had signed the photo. And right beneath it, the letters *CG*.

I looked at Janey. "It's not . . ." I looked back down. "I mean, it can't . . ."

"It is," she said.

My hands was trembling so hard now, I didn't know where to put 'em.

"Melia, you okay?"

"Yeah," I said. "No. It's just . . ."

Clark Gable was real. Clark Gable happened.

And if Clark Gable happened, Hong Kong happened. And ladies' hats in San Francisco happened, and writing ads in New York City happened, and playing Casca in Chicago happened . . . and what in God's name *hadn't* happened?

"I know," said Janey. "You thought he was full of hooey. Well, *I* knew better. Daddy Hiram never said an untrue thing in his life."

Only he did, I thought. At my specific request.

And in that moment, the only excuse I could come up with was that whatever Hiram had lied about had turned out true after all.

Soon as we moved back into the house, the Gable photograph

went on the wall next to Janey's bed. Which made Earle no end of jealous, owing to that he didn't have a movie star of his own. So I cut out a picture of Myrna Loy from *Photoplay* and got a frame for it and got Mina to write, *To Earle, A fine young gentleman and a most promising individual.* Earle give it one look and tossed the picture on the bed.

"She ain't so much," he muttered.

But that very afternoon, Myrna Loy's likeness went on his wall. Hasn't come down since.

• • •

Christmas was quiet, I won't lie. But Earle took it on himself to cut down a blue spruce, and we set it by the front window and decorated it with strands of old popcorn and Kellogg's Rice Bubbles. The Gallaghers bought Janey some tortoiseshell combs, and Earle got a black-lacquer box for his treasures. Me, I got a knife-pleated chiffon dress in pale rose with pleated cuffs and something called a fichu collar. It was a young woman's dress—that much was clear from the moment I lifted it out of the box. I glanced at Mina, and she put up her hands and said, "No hurry." But red bars was crawling cross her cheeks, and Dudley was looking away.

• • •

Somewhere in February, Janey's teacher, Miss Fensterman, come to see me. We stood outside on the new front porch, and she went on about how Janey weren't performing to her usual standards. Weren't raising her hand or writing on the blackboard or eating her lunch or even cleaning the erasers.

"There's no fathoming the girl," said Miss Fensterman. "She acts so *sad* all the time."

I could feel my nostrils flaring.

"What the hell makes you think she's acting?"

She stopped blinking for a couple seconds. "I was—I didn't—"

"Tell you what. *You* go and lose all the things my baby sister has lost in life and see how sad *you* feel."

Didn't trust myself to leave it there, so I walked back into the house and slammed the door after me.

Later that night, I made a point of asking Janey to help me balance our accounts. Truth is, the books had fallen way behind since Hiram left, so the two of us set for a good long time in the light of an old kerosene lamp, and I watched her running her fingers down each column—doing the sums in her head, just like Hiram said, and making little clucks every time she caught me out on something.

"You can't add for beans, Melia."

"Did I ever say I could?"

"You need someone full-time on this."

"Part-time, maybe."

She frowned, bent her head closer to the page. "Might as well be me. I ain't got no use for school no more."

I studied the back of her head in the greasy brown light.

"Well, now," I said. "School might've been a waste for *me*, but . . . Daddy Hiram said you was some kind of mathematical genius. Said you was smart enough to go to college. So I don't know, maybe we should give this thing another shot. See what happens."

"Another shot," she said.

"For his sake."

She raised her head, pushed the ledger away.

"How's he even gonna know, Melia? He's dead."

"Oh, hold on there, missy. You don't think he's got a say-so in all this? You don't think he's looking down right now? I'm telling you, if you don't go and make something of yourself, he's gonna haunt you all your days."

"He already does."

Well, I had no reply for that. So we set there for some time, staring down at those fool numbers. Finally, after I don't know how long, Janey said, "I'll tell Miss Fensterman I was just restin' my eyes."

• • •

Earle was doing his level best to hang on in school, but he kept saying as soon as he turned sixteen, he was gonna sign on with the Civilian Conservation Corps. Learn something *worth* learning.

No question, with Hiram gone, he'd become a broodier cuss. Quiet at breakfast, quiet at supper. Quick to disappear. Every Sunday, him and Gus'd spend hours in the woods, no matter the weather, and not come back till the sun had near dropped off the mountains. His Great Heap o' Treasure got smaller and smaller. Sometimes I'd glance through the front curtains and find him setting in one of the tire swings. Too big now even to make it move and not caring if it did.

Round about March, he started having nightmares. The come-running kind. It was hard to know what to do—he didn't want to be held no more, but he was okay with me setting by his bed. Most of the time, he never went back to sleep, just laid there with tearless eyes, waiting for the first sign of light.

"You want to tell me about it?" I asked him finally.

But he didn't say nothing.

"Is it the same dream?" I asked. "Each time?"

Still nothing. But I figured there was but one event that could keep calling him back again and again. It had to be the night of the fire.

Hell, hadn't I spent a lot of time there myself? Only I'd never had to point a gun at a man and take his life from him.

"You didn't do nothing wrong," I said. "You know that."

He stared up at the ceiling.

"Listen now," I said. "We just gotta find us a new way to look on this. I mean, we was in a by-God battle, Earle. Just like the World War. There was this country, and its name was—its name was Harleyana, and it was evil, and it was trying to invade the good country of—I don't know . . ."

"Brendaland," he offered.

"You're getting it now. And all it come down to in the end was one lone soldier, brave and true. And if he hadn't have been there, why, there'd be no Brendaland left, and the world'd be a sorrier place. I tell you what, if I had something shiny to hand, I'd pin a medal on that soldier right now. Maybe you got some tinfoil hidden away somewhere?"

"In the lean-to . . ."

"Well, okay, I'll make you a medal tomorrow. But here's the thing about being a soldier. There comes a time to stop fighting. So next time you—you go *back* to that night—see if you can't just set your gun down. I mean it! Drop it on the ground and walk away."

"Just like that?"

"Why, sure. 'Cause once you start walking, you *know* you'll end up right back here. And we'll be waiting on you, same as always."

I don't know if any of that took, but the sleep got easier after a time. One thing never changed, though, and that was Earle's feeling toward guns. Wouldn't go near 'em, not even on a bet. Shotguns, cap guns, air rifles—it didn't matter. Whenever his friends asked him to go squirreling, Earle'd shake his head just the once and tell them to come back when they wanted to catch trout.

• • •

Business kept strong through the winter. Dudley worked the store, when he weren't dreaming up next week's special or running the newest ad to the *Warren County Register*. Me, I did my best to keep the gas flowing and the engines lubricated, but the rush got so fierce sometimes I'd catch myself doing something I'd never done before—wishing for another mechanic. I even went and talked to a couple of Harley Blevins's old employees. Oh, they was decent enough fellers, knew their way round an engine, but when it come down to it, I couldn't find no one I trusted like I trust myself.

Guess that's something I'm still working on.

So here we was living on the cheap, making our bank payments, paying down our debts. Making the goddamn thing *work*. And the whole time I felt like we was in some rickety old Model T with four bald tires. All it'd take was one blowout to send us swerving off the road.

See, in the eyes of the law, me and Janey and Earle was still orphans. And orphans wasn't supposed to be running their own business, living in their own house. Orphans was supposed to be wards of the state. So what was gonna happen when the state decided to come for us?

By now I was pretty sure nobody in Walnut Ridge would rat us out—not so long as we kept their cars humming. As for Judge Barnswell of juvenile court . . . well, Chester kept him stocked up with Cream of Kentucky bourbon and took care to lose to him once or twice a week in seven-card stud.

When I thought on it, there was but one soul in the world who could kill the whole deal for us. And that just happened to be the same person who come bicycling past the station every Sunday, just a little after the Happy Creek United Methodist Church let out. Her hat was pinned to her head like a dead butterfly, but there weren't nothing could keep the frizzy locks of Miss Wand tied down for long. Strand after strand went whipping into the breeze, and what with the sleeves and the skirt of her dress flapping away, too, she looked like a parade's worth of flags.

But whenever she got to Brenda's Oasis, she slowed to a halt, and everything about her went quiet—her head quietest of all—and she stayed there for near a minute staring up at our sign.

And me staring at her the whole time, like she was a Model T tire about to give way. Sometimes I'd think I should just have it out with her, see which way she was tending. But looking back, I don't think she knew herself. That's why she come by every week, waiting for a sign. And the only sign she could find was ours.

So winter barreled into spring, and spring slipped away without a thought, and then June come round.

You'll get to know early June. Those first knuckles of heat come bowling up from the south and meet those cool soft bellies of mountain air, and the heat gives a punch, and the mountains punch back, and every barometer inside of ten miles gets drunk-dizzy, and the haze, before your eyes, turns from blue to gray to white and then back again. It's like the world's trying on summers in a store mirror.

Well, that's what it was like *that* morning. The morning a Studebaker Dictator, deep green, come driving down Strasburg Pike.

Moving as quiet as a car can move, I believe, and still be moving. I thought for sure it was lost, but once it turned into the station, it seemed to know where it was heading.

Earle was still at school, so I was working the pumps, and Dudley was painting his sixteen-year-old charms onto some old biddy'd come in for a candy bar. Even from thirty feet off, I could hear him. "You telling me you don't have the newest Rand McNally? Lordy, roads change round here near every day. You can get lost inside an *hour* without an up-to-the-minute map. Hey, now, is that husband of yours a fisherman? He *is*? . . ."

So there I was, waiting for that Studebaker to come my way, but it hung back.

By now, the glancingest of rains had started to fall. I went up to the car real slow, and I doffed my cap and peered through the tinted windows, and I said, "Can I help you, mister?"

The door opened, and a woman got out.

She was dressed right smart for Walnut Ridge. Silk-and-linen summer dress with a wide-brimmed straw hat and ivory heels. White gloves dangling from pink arms.

"Hello, Amelia."

"We met?" I said.

She tilted her face toward the rain. "I think it's my hair," she said. "It's not so long as it was."

I stood there, utterly still.

Looking back, it weren't *just* the hair, it was her whole being. The only sign of the old Ida was the trace of nerves that clung to her as she kept cutting her eyes back to the car.

"Well, now," I said. "I figured we'd seen the last of you."

"I guess I did, too," she said, soft as mist.

It come back to me in a beat. The sight of her flying through those hospital doors.

"It weren't right what you did," I said. "Running off and leaving him like that."

"I know," she said. She give me a sheepish smile, then palmed some of the rain off her face. "If it makes you feel any less sore, it was his idea."

"That so?"

She cut another glance back at the car. "Hiram always used to tell me I was—I was a *bird*. A wild bird that had never got around to using its wings. He'd say, 'Ida, you've been in this nest too long. It's time you took flight.'"

"Then what you doing back here? You get tired of flying?"

"Oh, no," she said.

And in that very moment, she looked clear gone. Like to the far side of Mongolia. Only something must've called her back because she said, "There's this one matter."

She opened the passenger door of that car, and she reached in and brought out a wicker basket, lined in powder-blue cloth. In this basket was a baby. Fast asleep.

My hand went to my throat as I took a half step forward.

"Yours?" I whispered.

Ida hesitated, like she weren't even sure herself. Then she nodded.

"Yours and . . ." I started to say.

But I didn't need to finish the sentence.

"It's why I went away in the first place," she said, smiling mournful. "I couldn't possibly have the baby in Walnut Ridge, not with all those wagging tongues. So I went and stayed with my cousin in Newport News." She looked down at the basket. "And out she came."

What a surprise to see Dudley ambling over to us. Wiping his hands on Hiram's old apron and flashing that professional smile. Soon as he saw that baby, though, the smile dropped right off his face.

"I can go," he said.

"No," I said. "Don't. I was just gonna ask Miss Ida what she thought she was doing here. With that there baby. Which she didn't want nobody to see till now."

Her face fogged over. "Hiram . . ."

"Hiram ain't here. Hiram's gone."

"But he always told me . . . if I got in a bind, there'd be a place here."

"A place?" I said. "Here?"

I stared at Dudley. He stared back.

"Well, listen, Miss Ida," he said. "There ain't much room here to spare. I mean, I sleep at the Gallaghers' most nights, and all that's left is the . . ." A glint of panic as he switched his eyes my way. "The bedroom over the store and that's—that's where . . ."

Where Hiram used to sleep.

Hotter than damnation in the summer. Colder than an Eskimo's ass in the winter. Tolerable nice in the spring, but you can't keep the window open too long or you'll get all fumey from the gas. . . .

Only it'd gotten a sight nicer since it was rebuilt. Had a real mattress now. Better ventilation. But I still couldn't bear for nobody to live up there.

"That might do nicely," said Ida.

Then she did the most extraordinary thing. She took that baby out of its basket—still wrapped in its linen blankets—and set it in my arms. And my arms, without my knowing, folded themselves into a basket. So the baby never knew no difference.

Ida looked at the baby, then at me.

"She's been well cared for, Amelia. I promise you that. And she's very easy. Already weaned, drinks right out of the bottle. Sleeps till five in the morning—longer, if you hold her. She won't give us any trouble, I promise."

Us . . .

"Now, it so happens," she said, "my father isn't speaking to me anymore, so we—we can't look for much help in that direction. But I'm here to tell you I've got a little money left over from my aunt Adela. I don't know how much, exactly, but it's bound to be a help, isn't it? Oh, and this car!" With a cry of triumph, she swung back to the Studebaker. "Great Caesar, we could sell it. Sell it tomorrow. And get . . . oh . . ."

"Somewhere between nine hundred and nine fifty," I said, numbly.

"Well, then! That's something." Her eyes was mad with purpose now, ranging the whole circuit of Brenda's Oasis. "And in the meantime, there must be something I could do. To help pay our way . . ."

She stood for some while in the lightly falling rain, like she'd forgotten where she was. And me, I kept waiting for Dudley to say something. Something like *Just 'cause your hair's all normal don't mean you ain't as loco as ever.* Something like *We can't afford two more mouths to feed . . . even with the Studebaker and Aunt Adela's money. . . .*

Not five minutes before, I'd been pumping diesel into a bunch of eastward-bound trucks—wondering somewhere in the back of my head where I could get my hands on lederhosen. Cars was whistling past. The air was silvery with summer.

Now I had this warm bundle pressed against me and Ida's pale stricken face before me, and all I could think to do was look at the baby she'd left in my arms.

• • •

That's when I gazed on *you.*

• • •

Your eyelids had just fluttered open, and they was still a-tremble, trying to decide if they wanted to close again. Maybe it was the rain that woke you for good.

I saw one blue eye staring at me. Another blue eye skedaddling away. I knew for true that you were his.

Well, here's the thing. If a body has bottled up every last one of its tears for five or six years . . . when those tears finally burst loose, it can be a scarifying thing. Looking back, I'm astounded I didn't drown you.

Funny part is the harder I cried, the happier you got. I reckon you thought I was playing some kind of game with you. So, even with my tears outrunning the rain, I was smiling, too. And when Dudley's hand landed on my shoulder, that felt like a smile, too.

"She got a name?" I heard him ask.

Ida hesitated. "Elizabeth. But if you don't—"

"Elizabeth," I said.

It come out so easy. Sweet and clean, like I'd been saving it up my whole life.

"Now, listen here," I said, running my free arm across my face. "Ain't nobody gonna shorten this girl's name by one letter. Ain't gonna be Lizzie. Nor Liza nor Beth. *Elizabeth*, you hear?"

They was too scared to answer.

"And another thing," I said. "If you're gonna stay here, Ida, it's on one condition. You gotta adopt us."

I believe her face lost a gallon of blood.

"There ain't nothing to be feared of," I said. "All you gotta do is sign your name to a piece of paper, and it's done. I ain't gonna look to you for nothing, and Earle and Janey pretty much take care of themselves. And then, soon as I'm of age, I'll take 'em back from you, I promise. You won't even notice."

I couldn't look at Ida, so I watched the rain, dripping like sweat, from the Brenda's Oasis sign. Then I heard her say, "If you don't mind adopting me, too."

• • •

Which is just how it come to be seen by the folks of Walnut Ridge. Every time they looked at Ida, they saw a gal with barely enough sense to—well, come in out of the rain. But thanks to Mina, she's gotten mighty quick with the broom, and she always has a fresh pitcher of tea for the customers. She can't cook like Hiram, but soon as we showed her how to do chop suey, she took to it right off, and it was chop suey for breakfast, lunch, and supper till we had to beg her to stop.

She cuts her own hair, once a month, using the rearview mirror of our truck.

And every morning, when you wake up, hers is the first face you see. You may have noticed she don't lay on the hands like the rest of us do, but I think that's 'cause she still don't trust herself. She never knew her own mama, and her daddy weren't but half a daddy, so she's feeling her way there.

It weren't so long ago, her and me had just got you down for your afternoon nap, and your hands was doing that little clutching motion they do when you fall asleep. Like they're squeezing an india rubber ball. Then they went still, and we could hear your easeful breathing. Ida stared out the window and, in a soft wondering voice, said, "I should've gotten adopted a long time ago."

• • •

Miss Wand no longer bicycles past Brenda's Oasis. But every Sunday, Dudley and me go to our rock, regular as church folk. We lay there, side by side, for as long as the weather allows. Holding hands, mostly, but now and then he'll hook one of his legs over mine or curl his hand real soft round my neck, and some part of me'll turn to water and the other part to ice, and there ain't no way to make the two sides meet.

"Sorry," I say. "It ain't like I don't want to."

Well, here's what I got to tell you about Dudley Blevins. He's got the patience of a Christian martyr.

"There ain't no hurry, Melia. We got acres of time."

Only how much time we got, really? I look back on Mama and Hiram, it's like they was gone in the flap of a wing. We knoweth not the hour. So one night in June, Dudley and me was setting out on the porch swing, listening to the cicadas rattle. Next thing I knew, I was straddling him and giving him the best kiss I could think of.

And that's when I said, "I ain't gonna be no Frances Bean."

His head pulled back an inch. "What you talking about?"

"One of them lonely married ladies. Laying awake at nights and setting alone at soda counters. You marry me, it means you're all in."

That's when he pointed out he hadn't asked me to marry him yet.

"Well, so what?" I said. "You in or not?"

That's when he said he was.

• • •

And if you're wondering if that's how I always dreamed of being proposed to, the answer is no.

• • •

I can't say when it was I got the notion. Maybe it was seeing you passed around amongst all the Gallaghers and Hoyles and Blevinses on the occasion of your first birthday. Coos and kisses showering down on you, and how much of it would you ever recollect or know or feel?

312

Well, that got me thinking on how much of my own life was lost to me. All those curves in the road, the switchbacks and hair-pin turns that led to the one surprising destination of me. Mama took that map with her before I could think to ask for a copy, and not even Rand McNally can draw me one now. So I thought the best gift I could give you was a map of your own. For when you're ready. Maybe you won't even need to look at it till you're an all-grown woman. I look forward to that day, though I expect I'll always miss the quiet little baby that rested in my arms that soft-raining June morning. I hope you know it was love that brought her here. And keeps her here till the last sun sets.

Yours very truly,

Amelia

ACKNOWLEDGMENTS

Walnut Ridge isn't a real place, but Warren County, Virginia, is, and I owe a debt to Jim Heflin of the Laura Virginia Hale Archives for his research assistance. Special thanks also go to Abby Yochelson, Wally Mlyniec, Margaret Wood, Laura Godwin, Christopher Schelling, and Dan Conaway. Throw Don into the mix, too.